Untaken, Too: 12 Days Following the Rapture

End Times, Volume 2

C.O. Wyler

Published by C.O. Wyler, 2024.

UNTAKEN, TOO: 12 DAYS FOLLOWING THE RAPTURE

First edition. March 28, 2024.

Copyright © 2024 C.O. Wyler.

ISBN: 979-8224532629

Written by C.O. Wyler.

To Michael ~ Thank you for being a loving Christian husband and friend ~ *"to God be the glory."*

~ Numen ~

She's coming around. She's going to make it. Since her ratings have sky-rocketed and viewers are increasing, let's allow her into our inner circle and tell her who we are. It's not as we'd planned, but that way we can improve our program and control her at the same time. Our viewers won't know, and we won't tell her.

~ **Day 1** ~

B ang. Bang. Bang-bang.

Stop. What's that incessant noise? Stop it!

"Sarah! Sarah, answer me!"

Go away! Stop banging already.

I'm awake, but I must've been dreaming—what a terrible, horrific dream! Something about being in Hell, as if I were completely alone, helpless, and not in control.

So not me.

Yikes, what a nightmare! I've never had a dream like that. It was one of those where I felt paralyzed. I couldn't move a muscle in my body. Hate that kind. No control. And I'm all about control.

Where am I?

I try to open my eyes, but only the right one obeys my command. I try to lift my left arm to rub the gunk from both eyes, but it refuses my directions.

"Sarah! Can you hear me?"

Who's calling me? What do they want?

Slowly, I lift my right hand.

Where am I, and how did I get here?

I feel my face. One side is swollen, but the other is intact. A faint trickle of drool runs out of one side of my mouth.

I lightly pat the eye that seems swollen shut, willing and prompting it to open. It dismisses me. My fingers move to my working eye. As I push away what appear to be dried tears and mucous, I see through blurry vision and realize I'm sprawled out on the dark wood flooring of our Southern California condo, somehow lying at the base of the stairs to our upstairs bedrooms and bathrooms.

Why? Why am I lying here like this in my own home? What happened to me?

Where's Dennis? Shouldn't my husband be at my side, helping me get up?

I hear our front door handle jiggle. The banging and pounding start again. I hope it's only disturbing me, not our next-door neighbors.

Who knows what time it is, or what day it is? If I had to guess, I'd say it is morning based on the room's lighting.

Once again, I question how I ended up on the floor in this strange position.

"Sarah! It's Zoey. Come open your door. After the way I left last night, I wanted to come over and touch base."

Grogginess and confusion conspire, causing me to ignore my dear friend—my only true friend besides my husband and maybe Jeremy.

I take time to consider the rest of my limbs. Let's see. I feel like I've been frozen in the same position for years, if not decades. My one eye gravitates to the bottom of my left foot. How awkward. I've never seen this angle of it; it's not natural.

And why am I wearing those silly, colorful, pain-to-put-on toe socks that Silvia gave me? Oh yeah. They were a joke as a Christmas gift one year from my older sister, but they turned into my go-to socks when I'm cold or sick. Hmm.

"I'm concerned, Sarah. I called several times this morning and got no answer. And with everything that's happened lately, I thought I'd stop by, but your door's dead-bolted, so I can't use my spare key to check on you."

Still concentrating on my poor body, I try to flex my toes, but pain shoots up the calf of my left leg. I can't see my other leg or foot, but I tell my brain to acknowledge them. I get a tingling sensation on the extremity, like it's been asleep for ages and is finally waking up, but it doesn't want to move.

"Sarah, now I'm standing on your patio over by your great room bay window, right by your orchids. I can see the back of your head on the floor by the staircase. You must be hurt! Can you move? Can you get up? Speak to me, please!"

I want to respond, but all I can produce is a guttural moan. I rub my dry lips together but get nowhere.

"Don't worry. I'll come in through the garage. I'll have to guess your password to open the overhead door. Probably your house number; everyone uses that these days. Hope that's okay. Hold on a sec!"

"Denny?" I ask, only to myself. It would take too much energy to say his name aloud—if I could get a word out.

Next, I hear the squeaky garage door opening.

Seconds pass.

"Sar, I'm almost there. Hold on, girlfriend!"

Our inner garage door unlocks and opens as my friend's voice echoes through the condo, "That was the strangest thing! I tried your house address and birth date. I guessed

Denny's birthday was the code, but it didn't work. Then, out of sheer frustration, I typed 2, 4, 6, 8, and, lo and behold, it opened! That was a cool sequence that I never would have considered. Glad it worked."

Hmm. I question her remark. That's not our door's access code.

There's a shuffle of feet in the laundry room and hall as she passes the downstairs bathroom.

Before I know it, Zoey's long black hair is tickling my skin, teasing me to react as she leans over my body. With my right hand, I try to push her away but fail, my arm collapsing on my chest.

"Oh! Sarah! What happened? Did you fall down the stairs? Can you move? Can you talk?"

I moan and blink my right eye.

My friend carefully, slowly, glides her hand over my face. Another tear squeaks out, and she softly brushes it away.

"Alexa. Call 911. Call 911 now," she demands in her controlling business-like voice. Having a top position at one of America's largest banks, she knows how to get things done. Pronto. There's no pussyfooting around with this determined woman.

The electronic device offers no reply.

"Right, you told me the one in the great room broke." Zoey jumps up and runs into our kitchen, presses the Alexa button on the refrigerator, and repeats her directive.

This time the device acknowledges her instructions. "Holy Cross Hospital has been informed of the situation. We have your physical address on file. Please stand by."

Returning quickly to my side, Zoey rants, "I hate LA. I hate the San Fernando Valley. I hate Granada Hills and everywhere else right now! It's like we've been nuked or something. Yesterday just won't go away. It's ridiculous and unacceptable."

She gently touches my left hand. My one good eye opens wide with the horror of pain, and she rapidly retreats and offers a quick apology. She takes my right hand and holds it tenderly in hers, and I blink; a tear runs out of my eye that's swollen shut.

Unashamed of my appearance, I'm thankful she's dutifully inspecting my body. Hesitantly, she moves to my breasts, constantly watching my facial movements. When my good eye doesn't counter in angst, she travels to my hip and legs, lightly pressing and patting, looking for any reaction. I try to follow her hand with mine, but I give up.

With each shallow breath, I wince. Yes, I hurt.

She doesn't make contact with my oddly angled foot. She's silent and focused, not engaging with me as she probes every part of my being.

"Alexa, what's the ETA on an ambulance?" she asks loudly.

I wonder if it'll answer with her being far away from it.

Unbelievably, it does: "We're sorry to inform you, but there's no estimated time of arrival for an ambulance. Reason unknown. Would you like me to contact the police? There may be delays."

"No, don't call the cops, Alexa. Like they have time to come. The city's gone berserk, and it's no use right now."

Meanwhile, she moves my right leg into a straighter position and glances at my response.

I only glare into her dark brown eyes.

"Is there anyone else you'd like me to contact?" Alexa asks politely and casually, as if another bottle of wine and a box of chocolates need to be requested.

Wanting to help, I moan.

Immediately my cautious caregiver gives a loud command: "Call Bruce and Barbara." She corrects herself, "Call Dad and Mom."

"Calling Daddy and Mom in Oregon," replies Alexa.

After three rings, my mom answers, "Sarah, good to hear from you. Did Denny finally show up? Is everything okay?"

Zoey, true to form, interrupts her with a booming, take-charge voice, "Barbara, this is Zoey. You know, Sarah's friend who lives in her complex?"

"Yes, good to hear from you. Is something wrong?"

"Yes," answers my decisive neighbor. "Sarah's had an accident, and it appears that she's fallen down the stairs at the condo; I found her on the floor in front of them. She seems to be semi-conscious, but I think she may have some broken bones. There's no pool of blood, but she may have hit her face on something as one side of it is mashed up and badly swollen."

"Oh my! Did you call an ambulance, Zoey?"

"Yes, but after what happened yesterday, I bet Holy Cross doesn't have any available. Do you think I can—or should—move her? I don't know what to do!"

Is that a touch of panic in her voice? If so, I'm surprised by her noted concern as she's one of the most steadfast, independent women I've ever met; I've never seen her this emotional—this wired.

"Let me ask Bruce. Hold on."

Zoey turns to me. "Sar, how ya doing? Are you in any pain? Can you blink once for yes or twice for no? Or maybe moan if yes and blink if no? Yeah, that sounds easier. Make a noise if you're in pain, okay?"

I can't say I'm writhing in immense pain; I hurt and am stiff and uncomfortable. I bet there'll be pain if I move, which I don't dare do.

"No response? That must mean you're not in terrible agony. Good. Blink if you're okay, okay?" commands Zoey.

My one eye blinks.

"Good. Great!"

Mom interrupts, "I have Sarah's dad on the line now, and he's been updated."

"Zoey, this is Bruce. Can Sarah talk or respond?"

"She moans here and there, and she responded with a blink when I asked her if she was okay. But what should I do next? Should I move her? I don't want to cause any further damage. Like what if her back's broken, and I move her, accidentally crippling her for life?"

I hear my dad explain: "Well, she mustn't be in severe pain, but she could be in shock. Things to watch out for are cold and sweaty skin, rapid breathing, or a weak pulse."

Zoey's holding my good hand again, carefully checking its palm for any moisture; there doesn't appear to be any. Yet.

Daddy continues, "You're right. It could be hours before an ambulance will be there, so I think you should try to get her to the hospital. She can't lie on the floor forever. Is

Denny around? Did he show up? If not, can you get ahold of a neighbor or maybe John—no, he's a cop; he's got his hands more than full right now. How about her co-worker, Jeremy? Think he could help you move her?"

"No, Denny's a no-show. It appears he was taken," she answers strangely, without any emotion.

With my mind still in a jumble, I listen to her talking but have no clue what she's saying. Why isn't Denny here, and what does she mean that he was taken? By whom? And why?

"That's a great idea. I'll call Jeremy and her next-door neighbor...do you remember his name?"

"I think it's Alex or something that begins with an A." Mom adds, "Adam, like Adam and Eve! Yes, and his father, who's elderly—maybe in his nineties. His name might be Jacob. I've met them, but I've forgotten the important details."

"Great. Okay, let me get off the phone and get ahold of Jeremy and Adam. I'll somehow drive her down to the hospital, maybe in Denny's SUV. I'll keep you posted as soon as possible. Oh, and can one of you call Denny's Aunt Amy? Do you have her phone number? Maybe you can let her know about her nephew and what's happened to Sarah, please?"

"Sure, we'll call Amy. Thanks, Zoey, and thanks for calling. Please let us know if there's anything we can do. And please tell her we didn't have much structural damage from the earthquakes or aftershocks. So many have. All right, we'll be hoping for the best. Thank you so much for being there for our girl."

Alexa announces the call has ended.

Zoey gets in my face—eyes locking on eyes, well, eyes to one eye. "Where's your phone? I need it. I want it for when we take you to the hospital."

Of course, I have trouble responding. My lips part a fraction of an inch, but no words form. Instead of looking at her, I glance upward, up the stairs to our bedroom. Then I raise my right hand and point with my first finger. At least, I have control of some parts of my body.

"Right. I got it! It would be charging by your bed. Everyone does that at night!"

Excitedly, she runs upstairs, past Denny's office and extra bedroom, and into our bedroom. Within seconds, she clatters down the stairs and is once again next to me.

"Got it. Good. Now, since I don't have your password, I'm going to face-ID you with your phone, so it recognizes you. But man, one side of your face is pretty swollen, so I hope this works. What did you hit your face on? A stair or the wall or what?"

She seems to be rambling—probably pestering me to keep me awake and engaged. Zoey's like that—she's always the person you want on your side during a calamity.

"Scrolling. Scrolling. Found him! I'm calling Jeremy. Hold tight, don't go away, or pass out on me, okay?"

She's no longer in my limited view, but I hear her fiddle with the phone.

Seconds later: "Jeremy? Is this Jeremy who knows Sarah Colton?"

There's a pause. I only hear one side of the conversation.

"Great. Jeremy, it's Zoey Agar; I'm friends with Sarah. We may have met before. Anyway, I have a favor to ask you."

Silence. He must be replying.

"Sarah's been injured, and I need someone to help me move her and get her to the hospital."

Another pause.

"No, I called for an ambulance, but none are available."

Pause.

"You can come?"

Longer pause.

"How soon?"

Pause.

"Great. Do you know where she lives?"

Driving instructions are quickly relayed. Zoey ends the call and turns her attention back to me. "I didn't know he lives so close to us. Right off Chatsworth Drive, that's like on the other side of the 405 Freeway in Mission Hills. He's practically down the street from the hospital."

She pats my working hand and announces, "I don't know how long you've been lying here, but I bet you're dehydrated. Hold on, let me get you some water."

Zoey leaves my side again. A cupboard door opens; the sink faucet turns on and off, and it sounds like a paper towel is ripped off its holder.

In less than a minute, my friend is kneeling next to me again, dipping the paper in the water and dripping the liquid onto my parched lips.

What a vigorous feeling. My tongue feels alive again, unstuck to the bottom of my mouth. My one eye sparkles, begging for more nourishment, and my friend quickly obliges.

"Good girl. Okay, I'll be right back. I've got to get ahold of your neighbor, Alan—no Adam—and his dad. Hold on a minute."

I hear her unlock the front door's deadbolt and open the door. Next, through the thin condominium walls, Zoey's familiar pounding presents itself on our neighbors' door.

It is amazing what a drop of water can do for the body and soul. I already feel better, more alive than mere minutes ago. I flex my fingers a little on my good hand.

Zoey said Denny is gone. He left yesterday—"taken," as Zoey put it. Taken by what or whom? Did he get arrested or something? What went wrong? Where did he go and why? Did he leave a note? I can't figure it out; my mind isn't working right.

However, the only thing that's vaguely familiar is that I drank too much and fell down the stairs trying to go to bed. It was the stupid pinky toe on the colorful sock that caught on the top step and made me tumble. But why can't I recall anything before that?

Redirecting my thoughts to the present, Zoey and Adam are having a conversation, but most of it is muffled so I can't understand much. His father is mentioned several times, their voices growing louder as they approach me. Both are now in my view, one on each side of my body. Adam has squatted down and is inspecting my face.

"Quite a shiner you got there, Sarah," he says, presumably to humor me.

Zoey answers, "I think she tumbled down the stairs."

"No doubt, no doubt at all. And I bet that backflip hurt." He turns toward Zoey and says boastfully, "Since I am a pharmacy tech, here's what I suggest. I've got some of my dad's Vicodin, and, as I already explained, he disappeared right in front of me while we were watching television. Man, I still can't believe it. Yesterday was such a bizarre day. So, assuming Sarah isn't allergic to the meds, we'll give her some."

I wonder what he's talking about—his dad disappearing? What happened?

Zoey counters, "Um. I don't know her allergies. What if she has a negative response to it? Can you think of something milder instead?"

"Yeah, you're probably right. How about Motrin? That's less potent stuff. Do you think she can tolerate that?" Adam's talking as if I'm not in the room, about me, not to me. I wave my right hand to get his attention, but I'm ignored by both.

Zoey says, "Yes, I've seen her take that before. Let's give her a couple of those. Is that okay with you, Sarah?"

Finally, I'm included in the conversation.

"Hmm-hmm," I barely but audibly reply.

"Oh, wonderful, Sar! You can almost talk! This is great, girl!" My friend is ecstatic.

"Good." Adam goes back into his medical mode. "Here's what I'll do: I'll get my dad's wheelchair-accessible van out of our garage and swing it in front of Sarah's, so we can easily get her into it. We'll use Dad's oversized wheelchair for transporting her. The vehicle will offer a smooth, safe ride, and that way she won't be moved more than necessary."

He stands up and crosses his arms. "Zoey, why don't you find some Ibuprofen? There's probably some upstairs in one of their bathroom cabinets. You'll need to mash two or three pills to a powder and mix it with some water to give it to her."

"Got it," Zoey replies.

Adam mentions he'll be right back and goes off on his mission, mumbling something about Poppa and why he's gone.

Once again, I'm splayed across the floor, afraid to move and unable to help or fend for myself. I'm usually the one in control like Zoey and even Adam, but this time I'm not. It's as if I'm an invalid, relying on others. I don't like it either. I hate not being in control.

My mind reflects on yesterday. I try to concentrate on anything in the recent past, but I only bring up a memory of Denny and me being in some sort of fight, all because of his Aunt Amy mouthing off about something she said that I disagreed with, and he didn't. Probably about her incessant preaching and pious religion. Well, that couldn't have been a worse scenario than my dream about being in Hell when I fell down the stairs.

After what seems like hours, not minutes, Zoey is back by my side. This time, she has a shot glass with a cloudy-looking solution in it and a spoon in her hand. She reviews my injuries as she explains how she wants to administer the watered-down painkiller.

But as abruptly as she starts to spoon the liquid into my mouth, she puts the utensil and small glass down on the floor. "I have an idea. This may be easier."

She leaves my side and returns seconds later with two throw pillows that were taken from the great room's couch.

"I'm going to lift your head and put the pillow under it. I want you to make a noise or scream as loud as you can if you feel even a smidgen of pain, okay? Look at me. Don't turn away from my eyes, and tell me immediately if there's any discomfort."

"K," is my only letter spoken. I'm so proud of my re-found communication skills, and I know she is, too, by the gleam in her eyes.

The pillow gets into position above my head as Zoey lifts my disheveled long blonde hair and carefully holds my skull as if it's a top-of-the-line Tiffany glass. I feel no pain whatsoever and visually give her the approval to continue.

When the task is completed, my head's higher, and I'm resting more comfortably.

With a smile, Zoey appears to be giddy with glee. "Okay, we're going to try the same thing with your good leg, but I'll put the pillow only under your right knee to give your leg relief. We'll keep the top half of your body angled more than the bottom half. Moan or scream if there's any pain at all. One. Two. Three."

Since I'm mostly on my side, only my knee is softly lifted, and the pillow is inserted. Much better. I don't flinch during it. It's my left wrist and wacky foot that are starting to hurt.

"Great! You're doing great, girl!"

As she stirs the medicinal concoction again and carefully dribbles it into my mouth, she says, "This is only six hundred milligrams of Motrin, so it won't knock you out. I used to take it for menstrual cramps, and it helps. I know you've popped two at a time with those headaches you get, so I think three is acceptable. Headaches can be so tiresome. I think sometimes that they're allergy-related, don't you? But Motrin's probably safer than Tylenol. That's what one of my online dates, who was a doctor, said. I personally would've taken Vicodin or Oxycodone myself, as I know it works better, but I'm glad we didn't go that route, not knowing your background. I think we did the best thing. Good, one more spoonful and you're good to go."

While we finish the task, the garage's inner door opens and closes. Adam must be back. I hear wheels rolling on the wood flooring.

"I got her to take three Motrins. Do you think that'll help?" Zoey asks my neighbor.

"Couldn't hurt. Maybe it'll help a little. Oh, I see you moved her. Did she have much pain doing it?"

"N—o," I triumphantly announce, my stretched-open fingers reacting to my excitement.

"Perfect! She speaks! Good news."

I doubt he's as thrilled as I am. I force myself to smile out of one side of my face.

"The van's parked in the back, but it'll be hard to maneuver Dad's wheelchair around the cars, so we need to move one of them. Do you know where the BMW or VW keys are, Zoey?"

"Check by the front door, on the half-moon table. That's where they dump everything. And while you're there, can you find her purse or wallet?"

"Sure...found both."

He returns to my side and places my wallet on the floor next to my head. "I'll be back. I think if we move Sarah's VW, we'll have better access since it's closer to the house door. Getting down the one step will be tricky, though."

"Okay," I proudly reply. Once again, Zoey flashes her bright whites at me.

My phone rings, and my friend fishes it out of her pants pocket. She swipes the front of it with her thumb, and then she realizes she needs my mug shot for access.

When the phone accidentally clanks to the ground, she drops the used spoon and now empty glass, and lets out a mild profanity. Picking up the phone, she hurriedly holds it up to my face for verification. When its screen turns on, she quickly answers hello.

"Yes, good. Okay. In five minutes. Best to park on the access road. You'll see a mobility van in front of their opened garage. That's her place. Come in through the garage."

Pause.

"Yes, she's doing better than when I first got here."

Pause.

"Okay. Bye."

"Good news, Jeremy's almost here. I'm sure the three of us can get you in the van and down to the hospital."

Using several towels from the downstairs bathroom to lay under me, my gracious caregivers lift my broken body into the wheelchair, making sure my hand and foot are amply protected. There's a lot of huffing and puffing plus a few cuss words by all of us.

Yes, the move is painful. Yes, I grunt, swear, and cry more than a few times.

By guarding my every movement, not only do they make sure I avoid excruciating pain—except when anyone touches my left wrist and left foot—but they also get me into Adam's dad's van, which has an automatic side door lift. Without incident, the team works like pros in unison.

I don't know the words to thank them; only tears show my gratitude.

To further amaze me, Zoey, always thinking about appearances, grabs the soft, all-white throw from our great room couch to hide the ugly "I love Israel" sweatshirt, hot pink sweatpants, and funky toe socks I'm wearing. And I'm not a bit embarrassed about my apparel, only thankful to my rescuers.

While Adam drives the van, Zoey sits shotgun, incessantly asking me how I'm doing. Jeremy follows us in his Suburban.

Zoey looks over the front passenger seat and says she wants to update my parents, so she needs my phone's passcode. I slowly speak the six digits, imitating each number with finger motions on my good hand. But when I come to the number eight, I must repeat it vocally several times while flashing five and three fingers. After several tries, we work together so she can access the device.

When she calls my parents, the conversation is brief, only stating that we're en route.

Meanwhile, during the short two-mile drive, Adam emits expletives more than once due to the abundance of abandoned vehicles left roadside. When we're on Rinaldi Street under the 405 Freeway overpass, our driver blows his top because we must maneuver around a gang of a dozen older teenagers standing on both sides of the street. It appears they've been taunting the homeless camps based along the freeway pylons as they're pushing a few individuals around. I can see through the blackened side windows that they're dressed in all black with strapped-on semi-automatics—yes, guns! As we zigzag by, two of them bang their fists against the van and scream, "Death to America" and "Death to Israel."

Thankfully, no shots are fired at either of our vehicles, although Adam tells us he noticed through the rearview mirror that Jeremy may have had a rock or brick thrown at the front window of his SUV, as there's now a rather noticeable crack in the glass.

"Like the Bible says, 'there's nothing new under the sun.' Is there?" Zoey asks rhetorically. "A tragedy happens, and everyone goes insane by hurting and stealing from others because they don't know what else to do."

I'm shocked at her comment, not only because I've heard that verse so often from Denny and Aunt Amy, but that she said it. She's like me, not one to be religious. I, also, am befuddled seeing how people are acting and reacting.

Why? And why now? Why do we suddenly live in an anarchy of fear and confusion?

It appears that no one is in control.

Surprisingly, we make it through every green light without stopping once for a red one.

When we arrive in front of the emergency room doors, only a few people are loitering outside. Adam jumps out of the van, promptly goes around it, and opens the sliding door.

Zoey climbs into the cargo area, unlocks the
wheelchair's brakes, smooths out the white throw that
modestly covers my body, and assists me through the
hospital's front doors.

Inside, people are mulling around with a few sobbing in
groups of two or three.

I feel bad they're dealing with loved ones being injured,
sick, or dying as I know it's emotionally draining.

When we approach the desk, a woman in her late sixties,
who looks frazzled and doesn't visually acknowledge us,
states she'll be with us in a while due to the staffing shortage.

Finally able to say a full sentence on my own, I audibly
sigh and, politely as possible, ask between labored breaths,
"How long a wait?"

"I don't know. Probably a minimum of three hours," the
employee responds without looking up. "I've never worked
at this station before, so I suggest you enter as much info
online as possible over there at the kiosk. I know that may
speed up the process. If you can figure it out."

Due to Zoey's job, she is a whiz with computers and any
database program. She walks over to the computer screen
and flexes her fingers over the keyboard. Then, after fetching
my phone out of her pocket and retrieving my health
insurance card out of my wallet, she rapidly fills in the
required information.

Still stranded by the greeting desk with the unengaging
woman who repeats the wait time to the next person in line,
I sit motionless until Jeremy and Adam arrive.

When they enter the building, Adam heads over to
Zoey, and Jeremy approaches me.

Immediately, I apologize and beg him to go home. All three of them have done enough for me.

Jeremy scoots down to eye-level as he pushes his brown hair out of his face and rests his hand on my good arm. "Sarah, babe, I'd never leave you here. As I told you on the phone last night, I'm here for you, and I always will be."

I have no idea what he's talking about, but I act like I do by nodding.

"Unlike Denny and my parents." He chokes on his words as he rubs his thumb too hard on my good wrist without realizing it. "I can't—I can't. Um, we both have no one."

I want to stop him, to have him explain everything and these weird words I keep hearing, but I don't have enough gumption to talk or care. I know he's upset; it's obvious, but I can't deal with someone else's problems right now. I can only deal with mine.

"And now that I have a few minutes alone to talk to you, I want you to know I'll wait if you want me to. I don't mind, really. I'm here for you, and only you."

Oh, great. He's never been this emotional or forward with me. What am I involved with here? I know Jeremy has a thing for me and has for a while, but he's always been like the brother I've never had. We work closely together at *Valley News* where I'm a journalist, and he's one of the best video technicians in the state.

Granted we've spent years working together, but I'm happily married and not seeking an extra-marital relationship. Sigh. What happened yesterday?

I divert the awkward conversation by mentioning his SUV window being hit by a brick or rock. He shrugs and says it's no big deal, that his insurance will cover it.

With the strained silence between us, I'm thankful when Adam walks over. "Okay, I've done my job, so I'll be on my way. I'm glad I helped with the use of Dad's wheelchair and van. I think I'll stop in at work and check to see if I can help any other damsels in distress. It's not like I have anything else to do."

He adds, "All I can say is to be careful out there going home. It's a warzone. I'm going to start packing some heat, and so should you. I'll touch base later. I talked to Zoey; I didn't know she lives in the next building over, by our complex's pool. She must have a nice view. Anyway, glad you'll be taken care of now, and let me know if there's anything else I can do for ya. Bring back the wheelchair whenever you no longer need it. Oh, and nice to meet you, Jeremy."

I thank him and provide a small wave goodbye. I'm so thankful he helped us. Interesting guy. I don't think he's ever been married or has a girlfriend, and I'm guessing he's in his mid-fifties. If he says that his father is gone, I wonder if he'll get out more and maybe date or if he'll stay a hermit like I've always assumed he was.

Jeremy wheels me over to where Zoey is still clacking away at the kiosk's keyboard, smiling at her obvious accomplishments.

"I got you, girl! This was easier than I expected, and hopefully, it'll speed up our wait time," she says. "And get this: Remember that doc I dated a few months ago? He took me to a classical pianist concert at the Hollywood Bowl. Nice guy, and I thought we had some chemistry, but he had to rush to Israel to see his ailing mom. As you may recall, he never called back.

"Well, Amir Syrak, doctor of internal medicine, is listed as one of your doctors. I don't think he's your primary because his photo was posted farther down on the screen, so you must have had a prior appointment with him. I sent him an online message about the situation via your portal so it looks like it came from you, and, of course, mentioned me—yours truly. Waiting for his response."

She stops and looks at me, "Oh, and I forgot—you're only twenty-eight? I thought you were closer to my age. If you're still in your twenties, you're still a youngin."

Jeremy laughs, most likely at my friend's dating antics; it's nice to find some humor in the situation.

Then he asks, "Hey, are either of you two ladies hungry? Maybe I'll wander over to the café and get us some food."

"I'm good," I reply. How nice of him to think about nutrition during a time like this.

"Zoey, how about you?"

"I'll take anything—I'm easy when it comes to men and food. Thanks."

He chuckles and lifts his eyebrows toward me. "All right. I'll be back in a few." As Jeremy leaves, my stomach growls. I wish he hadn't mentioned the topic.

Then I realize that I need to use the restroom, and I hate to ask Zoey to assist me with one more thing. I wait patiently until she's finished with the computer. I also notice my hand and foot are starting to throb in sync with my heart's pumping.

I try not to move. Oh, how I want to be in control of my bodily functions again.

Once Zoey completes her task, she scans the room, turns to me, and asks where I want to sit and wait. I motion her closer and meekly request to go to the bathroom.

"Oh, duh! I bet you have to go. Here you were lying on the floor for most of the night. Of course, you need to pee. Let's find a bathroom and get you some relief."

When we enter the women's restroom, Zoey immediately takes me to the accessible stall.

"Well, I doubt you're going to be able to do this all by yourself, so let me help. Guess you and I are up for another challenge. This'll be a first for me."

She backs the wheelchair into the wide area, lining it up with the toilet, and then moves around the side of it to get in front of me. She stops and shakes her head, trying to figure out the best way to get me from the chair to the commode without causing me more pain. She faces me with her arms under both of my armpits and starts to lift me off the chair. We're so close that I'm self-conscious of my breath—it must be bad because it's been so long since I've brushed my teeth. I must stink.

But as I look at her obvious love for me by agreeing to such a personal task, suddenly, I pass out.

~ **Day 2** ~

I've been floating in and out of consciousness for hours.

All I can figure out is that I'm in a bed of some type. Realizing there's something cool covering one of my eyes, I open the other one. A shiny bedrail to my right jets out of white sheets where most of my body is snugly tucked. My left foot sticks out and is elevated, held hostage by some sort of apparatus hooked up to the ceiling. My left hand is wrapped and resting across my chest. My hand and foot are protected by thick padding.

I vaguely recall a hospital employee telling me they were doing x-rays and to be as still as possible. I remember something about my hand and foot being in immense pain and then minutes later the agony dissipated. I assume I've been well-medicated based on the stupor I'm in.

"Sarah, Sarah Colton, can you hear me? Are you awake?"

I acknowledge the question with a whimper.

"Good. How are you feeling?"

"Okay." I try to speak clearly, but the words come out jumbled.

I hear a machine in the background shushing and beeping. There's an intravenous line going into the back of my good hand.

"My name's Carol, your attending nurse. We had to give you Morphine to relax you for x-rays, and, for now, the worst is over. The doctor will be in shortly."

An overweight woman with no smile, who I'm guessing to be in her late forties, approaches the side of my bed. Her voice is monotone as she places her warm, plump hand on my good arm.

"You were extremely dehydrated, which is probably why you passed out. We have you on saline through an IV to help."

For some weird reason, she starts to cry, right in front of me. I don't know what to say, especially when she wipes her tears away and immediately apologizes for her breakdown.

"I'm sorry, I know I'm not being professional, but I can't believe it; I just can't believe they're missing. It makes no sense. None at all."

Bewildered, I try to be compassionate, which is not one of my strong points. I don't know what to say.

"Sarah, it's Zoey." My friend breaks the solemn mood from somewhere in the room as she comes closer to me. "I heard you woke up—here I leave the room for a minute and miss the action. Well, passing out is one way to get a room. And you did it on the floor in the can while I was trying to hold you up! I'll have to remember that one—ah, such drama. How are you feeling? I've been here keeping watch all night. And I let your parents know what's going on. All's good. You're going to be okay; I know it."

The nurse composes herself and adds, "Yes, your dear friend has been an angel. With the shortages of RNs, LPNs, and staff right now, having her in the room was helpful throughout the night. Few would go to the lengths this one would. She's a keeper."

"There's nothing else to do. My job has pretty much shut down since the world fell apart, so this works out well," Zoey replies. "I've been sitting here watching the news most of the night. You wouldn't believe all the stuff that's happened out there. I turned it off and tried to get some shut-eye a couple of hours ago. No such luck."

She's holding a lidded container, no doubt a cup of strong coffee.

"Thanks." I struggle to get the word out. I feel like I am regaining my strength, but I'm hoping the drugs stop making me so loopy.

"Morning, ladies!" Dressed in a white lab coat, sky-blue polo shirt, and dark blue jeans, a good-looking doctor enters the room. "Sarah, I don't know if you remember me; I'm Dr. Syrak. About a year ago, I stood in for your primary care physician and treated you for the flu. My, you know how to get our attention. Also, I heard you fell down a staircase and passed out."

He pauses, then turns around to face my friend. "And Zoey, great to see you again!" He gives her a too-long handshake. "We must catch up after I go over Sarah's chart with her, okay?"

"Definitely, Amir. Oh, sorry, I mean, Doctor Syrak," Zoey teases.

They both seem pleased to have met again.

He returns to my bedside and lightly touches my good arm. "So, Sarah, do you want me to go over things with Zoey here in the room or alone? Either way, I need your approval."

I went through so much with my dear friend yesterday; I insist that she stay.

The doctor silently agrees and sits down on a rolling stool, wheeling himself over to a computer screen. He logs in and makes a few notes, most likely on my chart.

He multitasks by talking and typing in broken segments.

"We took several images." He types for a moment, stops, and looks up at me. "And it looks like you have broken your wrist in two places." Another pause and more typing. "Which can probably be fixed with metal inserts." He types some more. "I've contacted our on-call orthopedic surgeon, requesting to get your operation scheduled for later this afternoon or evening. Your foot is a mess." Typing. "Three small broken bones, so the surgeon will address that at the same time. I'm confident you'll be able to walk again, over time. You've bruised a couple of ribs." More typing. "Perhaps when you hit the stairwell's walls or spindles. And your face, well, luckily you didn't break your jaw," he adds, "but your eye will most likely swell more, and it'll be colorful looking." More typing. "But there's no noticeable damage to your vision. We have a cold compress on the area to lessen the puffiness." He finally stops typing. "I've currently got you on Morphine to keep you comfortable before we do the surgery."

He gets up, takes a long breath, and moves closer to my bed to inspect my bodily damage.

"Also, I'm not sure you're aware, but a quick qualitative blood test showed that your hCG indicated you were pregnant, but based on the amount of recent blood loss—" He stops talking and looks kindly into my eyes, "I'm sorry to say, but you may have miscarried or aborted in the last twenty-four hours."

When he says the words, the memory comes crashing back. Yes, I used that stupid at-home pregnancy stick and found out I was going to have a baby—a baby I didn't want. Dennis's baby. And then something happened where I was in pain and must have miscarried. The experience is starting to come back. Yes, it makes more sense now.

"Since we can verify you lost a bit of blood vaginally while in the restroom, we want to make sure you have no unusual internal bleeding. There may be complications due to your low red blood count, which is called anemia, or an infection in the uterus or some retained placental tissue. Because your hemoglobin dropped under seven, we went ahead and gave you a unit of packed red blood cells."

Zoey audibly gasps from across as the doctor continues. "The plan is to get you into surgery ASAP, and then monitor your bleeding to make sure you didn't have a partial miscarriage, as that's something else to consider."

He adds, "Although the hospital is dealing with some issues right now, I recommend you spend another day or two here after your procedure to make sure you do not pass out again and lose more blood."

After returning to the computer keyboard to type something, he resumes his medical advice. "Although it looks like you had a rough day yesterday and got banged up, I would say your chances of fully recuperating look promising."

Meanwhile, Nurse Carol takes my blood pressure and pulse, adjusts the saline drip, and checks the monitor, repeating numbers to the doctor to enter on my electronic chart.

Dr. Syrak asks, "Do you have any questions or concerns that I should know about?"

I only shrug since I have nothing to say, except that I'm elated I'm not paralyzed for life. Instead, I'm more thankful that I didn't get seriously hurt. Guess I'm in better shape than I thought.

"Okay. So, I'll let your nurse know when the doctor can get that surgery scheduled, hopefully today."

He gives me a reassuring smile, then speaks to my friend, "Oh, and, um, Zoey, would you care to meet me out in the hall for a sec?"

My dear friend winks at me and walks out of the room behind the handsome doc.

In less than a minute, she returns, beaming. "Oh, I must look like a train wreck, but that was impressive. Amir and I are going to give it another try. Right off the bat, he apologized for not touching base with me. He said his mom passed away, so he had to stay longer in Israel and only returned to the States two weeks ago. He's playing catch-up at work so doesn't have much time off—especially after what happened recently—but he wants to meet for dinner in the cafeteria tonight! Strange date, but whatever, this is going to be interesting." She's bubbling with excitement.

"Great," I reply, "I'm happy for you, Zoey." My voice is gaining strength now that I'm talking in complete, coherent sentences.

"Ok, but let's talk about you. What can I get you? What do you need?"

"Did you get ahold of Amy?"

Zoey wags her head. "No, when I talked to your mom this morning, she said she left a voice message with her, so I used your phone and tried—I, also, got no answer. Do you want me to keep trying?"

"No, let's wait. I'm still confused. I remember you stopping by my condo and me falling down the stairs. Oh, and the baby thing. But that's about it."

"Right, we drank. We talked. We drank. That's why you fell down the stairs. Too much alcohol. And those silly socks are the culprit! Blame them, dear!"

I look down at my raised leg, but it's all wrapped up.

"Yeah, those crazy socks! I bet they had to individually cut off each knitted toe. They're beyond ugly!" She spouts as she shakes her head.

"What else happened? Tell me!"

"Do you remember much about people missing—those who were 'taken' as I call them?"

"I'm unsure," I reply.

"There was a super strange, hopefully once-in-a-lifetime occurrence, where there was this crazy sound, and then people instantly evaporated—left, gone, disappeared. It was bizarre!"

"Really?" I question the ramifications of people no longer here.

"Denny, your Denny was one of them! You found him missing in his office upstairs—left his clothes and all. You rescued his wedding ring under a chair. That happened before I stopped by. Surely you remember that, don't you?"

"Maybe." I toy with the idea; the memory of finding his contact lens and tooth filling flitters through my brain.

Zoey asks, "Do you remember your parents having to go through not one but two earthquakes in Oregon? Does that ring a bell?"

"Sorta. Yeah, it might be coming back to me a little."

There seems to be too much to process. With my good hand, I rub my working eye, wondering if it's a good thing for the memories to come back fully and completely. I question if maybe I'd be better off not recalling them.

"Oh, there were car, boat, train, and plane accidents everywhere—poof, just like that, people gone." She snaps her fingers. "Last night every news channel mentioned it could be an airborne virus of some sort, or even aliens taking them away! Yeah, aliens!" She lets out a huge, dramatic sigh.

"Now don't freak out, but the news is reporting that all children, like elementary school age and younger, are missing—gone—as are most of the disabled and a higher percentage of the elderly. And your sister Silvia and her husband Tom in Florida? Well, their little ones can't be found. They disappeared in their cribs. It's surreal."

"Oh, that's horrible." My mind clicks. Jack and Jasmine are so young; they were adopted less than a year ago. Silvia and Tom must be undone.

Another thought absorbs my brain: I had just learned I was pregnant; I didn't want to tell Denny about it as we'd been in a fight, and he had stormed upstairs into his office. After considering all my options, I decided to have an abortion.

I was washing a dirty lasagna pan and saw two little girls on the swings outside our kitchen window. I reached down to get a scrub brush in the cupboard and heard an odd tri-sound, one that I'd never heard before. When I looked out the window again, the girls were nowhere to be found. I went to tell Denny, but I got a sharp pain and went into the downstairs bathroom, where I assumed I miscarried based on how much blood there was.

Yes, it's starting to come back!

Zoey centers me back to my current life, stuck in a medical bed. "Yes, horrible, but we're here, safe and sound in a hospital, somehow having survived it all. They say these people were taken, but as I mentioned to you the other night, I think we should consider the other side of the coin: We are the ones who were untaken."

"Oh," is my only reaction because I don't know what to think.

"Yes, and that's why everyone is walking around crying, wild teenagers are acting like Rambo mercenaries, and hospitals and everywhere else are short-staffed."

She explains in detail some of the tragedies that happened around the world, apparently in every city and town, and at the same time. The disappearances affected every human being in some way, whether they were missing or having to deal with the missing.

And my Denny's missing, too. My dear husband who had been acting strangely the last few days.

All the people disappearing explain the heartbroken nurse, the frazzled lady at the desk, Adam's dad being gone, Zoey's over-talking, and Jeremy acting weird. They're all processing the loss of their loved ones.

Oh my. I don't like this, no, not one bit. I resent this disruption in life, in my life.

My phone, which is sitting on a nearby retractable table, rings, and Zoey jumps up to answer it.

"Hello. Oh, perfect timing, Bruce! Sarah's awake and speaking! Hold on a sec."

"Daddy? Mom?" I squeak out, mainly out of raw emotions from the last day and a half.

"Oh, Cupcake," my dad quietly answers. "Yes, we're here. We're so glad Zoey has kept us in the loop and that you're awake. Have you seen the doctor yet? Any prognosis?"

"I'm okay. Trying to get surgery today." It's a strain to say so many words.

"Well, listen. As you know, we were planning to fly down next week, but the way things are going, even at the airports, we decided we'll drive down instead. If we leave by tonight, we should be there in about two days. You know Mom can't sit in a car too long, so we'll have to stay at a hotel tomorrow night in Sacramento. By then, your surgery should be over, and you should be home, so we can help take care of you. How does that sound, dear?"

"Great. I like it. I love you both." A tear escapes my good eye; I wipe it away.

"Perfect. So don't you worry—we'll keep in touch with Zoey on our ETA."

Static fills the phone. A pause occurs.

"Sarah, it's Mom. How's the pain?"

"I'm fair; I'm on Morphine. Pain's there, but not intense."

"Good. Stay on top of it, and don't let it get out of control. And get some rest before the surgery."

I exhale and say, "Okay, Mom."

We three say our goodbyes.

I hand Zoey back the phone, but, before she has a chance to put it down, it rings again. This time, it's my sister Silvia calling from Florida. I wave Zoey off from handing me back the phone since I've been talking too much and fighting exhaustion. After my sister says the hurricane passed them but did quite a bit of damage to Disney World, she is given an updated version of my status, including that our parents will be driving down.

When the back-and-forth conversation ends, Zoey returns the phone to its spot while I reflect on how pleased I am that I heard from my sister. I'm glad my parents will be here in a few days; it'll be comforting to have them take care of me.

As Zoey again asks if I need anything, Jeremy walks in with a bouquet of white daises with baby's breath in one arm and a legal-sized manilla envelope in the other.

It's nice to see cheer within the gloom.

"Afternoon, Gorgeous! These should brighten your day." He approaches my bed in high spirits and sets the glass vase on the table, right next to my phone. "How did you sleep? Great to see you got a room. Are you in much pain?"

Not knowing how much he knows, I thank him for the flowers, commenting that they're beautiful. In short, concise sentences, I briefly tell him I need surgery on my wrist and foot, and that I'll live another day.

"Well, actually, the flowers are from Carl. I stopped by the office earlier, and our boss insisted he buy you something special when I told him about what happened. He went on and on about how the flowers are his wife's favorites. Mentioned he had the same arrangement duplicated for her when he ordered yours."

"So sweet," Zoey chirps in, not to be ignored. "How's the paper handling all the news, Jeremy?"

"It's crazy at *Valley News*. We can't keep up with it. I heard that even the Source, our mainframe that dumps data all day long from around the world, is having issues. Had to have a tech clear its cache at one point. It's a mess. But Sarah, I—well, Carl and I have something amazing to show you."

He grasps the manilla envelope and unclasps the shiny tab at its opening, slowly pulling out three identical sheets of glossy eight-by-ten-inch cardstock.

"You did it, Sarah! You did it, again! Congratulations!" He has a genuine look of joy on his face. "Your pic went viral—it's been picked up by syndicate, and everyone in the universe can see it. You are, once again, the talk of the town. No, talk of the world!"

He dramatically places the three identical photographs on my lap: it's a boy's hand, looking like it wants to wave, taken from under the seat of an airplane.

Zoey says, "No way! You told me about this the other day." She grabs one of the copies and reviews it. "It's from the plane crash in the field behind our complex. Remember, Sarah? You and some muscle-builder guy rescued the only survivor, a fifteen-year-old kid who had manners. Oh, that's so cool!"

I did it! My memory is as clear as ever: I was standing in front of a torn fuselage with my cherished Nikon camera taking the photo of the boy—his name was James—and we got him out of the plane to safety. Later, he came to my townhouse to clean up and wait for his mom to get him. Said he met some guy named Eddie on the plane, who I want to do a follow-up story about. Yes, I remember. James was such a nice kid.

The photo is perfect. I proudly scrutinize every part of it. I couldn't have done it any differently or better.

Jeremy picks up the third copy and praises me for its angle, lighting, and composition.

I did it. Again!

The other time I had a photo get picked up by syndicate was a few years ago when the governor's son was shot in a convenience store, and I happened to be at the end of the chip aisle with my camera bag. When I clicked the button at the perfect moment of the bullet flying into the boy's head, the tell-all picture gave the police all the verification they needed to arrest the two jerks. And I survived the ordeal after weeks of therapy.

I used that same therapy to get me through the plane crash and deal with the death that surrounded me. I can get through this physical accident—I can heal and take back control of myself after the surgery. I know I can! I can overcome this, too.

"This is phenomenal," Jeremy says with admiration. "Your last pic was good but tragic because the gov's son died. This one's also devastating, but it shows hope and reassurance that someone not only lived through a horrific plane crash but also that he survived the worst day in history."

He pats my shoulder and gives me a stiff hug as if he's afraid to hurt my body.

Regardless of everything that's happened, I'm now crying over something as simple as a photograph. But the tears are mainly from accomplishing a lifelong goal of making a difference as a journalist. This is me; I acknowledge as I shake the paper. This is me, whose mantra is, "I'm in control. Sarah Colton, you're in control."

And without any of us speaking, Zoey and Jeremy have glassy eyes, too.

"Great job," Zoey finally says. "Wait until your parents hear about this. It'll make their day."

Carol reenters the room, asking, "Sarah, do you recall when you last ate? The surgeon wants to know." She fluffs up my pillow and notes the saline IV bag is almost empty.

"Um, I don't know." I give Zoey a quizzical look.

Jeremy interrupts, "Well, you never got to drink your smoothie that I bought from the cafeteria. Apparently, you were out cold on a bathroom floor."

Zoey says, "I doubt you had anything to eat in the last two nights. We did have those chocolates with our wine before I left your house. You must've had that lasagna for dinner with Denny."

I nod in agreement, and the nurse assents that it's been around thirty-six hours since I last ate or drank anything. No wonder I feel so weak and tired, then add to the mix the pain meds.

Zoey scratches her head. "Oh, wait. I did give her a shot glass or two of water with Motrin when we found her yesterday morning. Was that okay to do?"

"Yes, that's good, Zoey. You did fine," Carol says. "That means we can get her surgery scheduled right away. Let me check with the surgeon and get back to you." As she exits the room, the three of us shrug, not wanting to discuss what's coming next.

We go back to talking about the photo, and Jeremy tells us how delighted Carl was when he saw it went viral. With all that has been going on, it was something positive and refreshing to see.

Minutes later, my nurse returns with a hurried tone in her voice. "All right, it looks like Sarah has an appointment with Dr. Tsai for surgery, so we have about an hour to get her ready." She excuses herself as she physically nudges Zoey away from one side of my bed to change out the saline bag and update my chart. "That means the visitors need to go."

"This is good, Sar," says Zoey as she gathers her purse. "You just have to get through today, and things will start getting better."

She turns to Jeremy. "I have a favor to ask. Since our dear patient will be out of it for several hours, and I've no way to get home, is there a chance you could drop me off at my house? I know it's a little out of your way, but would you mind?"

"Sure thing, Zoey. I have to drop off Adam's wheelchair, so now is a good time to do it."

"Thanks, that really helps." She looks at me and explains, "Now I can go home, take a shower, and clean up so I can come back for dinner with Dr. Syrak, and then I'll be here for you when you wake up from surgery. I'll bring you some more comfortable clothes and your toothbrush. If it's okay with you, I'll spend the night again. Does that make sense?"

Of course, I'm sure she had the plan in her head once her date with the doctor was made. That is how Zoey and I think; we try to always stay ahead of the game, and we succeed most of the time.

My friends say their goodbyes, with Jeremy lingering seconds longer like he wants to say something, but he doesn't.

When the two leave, Carol explains the need to get ready to be wheeled down to pre-op for surgery.

In a quick call to my parents, I inform them about the upcoming procedure. They tell me their car is almost packed, so they'll start driving down. I ask them again to call Amy and update my sister.

After all the excitement of being awake for a few hours, my eyes—well, mainly one eye—get heavy. As I try to readjust in the bed, my uncomfortable body twinges—especially my left side, which took most of the trauma.

I desperately want to go to sleep and have all this disappear when I wake up.

Right when I drift off, Dr. Tsai arrives what seems like minutes later, introduces herself, and reviews my x-rays with me.

We discuss how my wrist has a distal radius fracture with two breaks, so I will need a plate inserted; the bones will be held in place with screws. My foot has several fractures, so it might need plates, pins, and screws. Afterward, the wrist will be braced, but the foot will have to be in a foot cast.

My surgeon goes over my online chart, checking for allergies to medicines and other bone issues. Either she's friendly and easygoing or I'm beyond thinking about arguing with whatever she dictates.

The second she leaves, a tall man enters the room and states he's my anesthesiologist. He also reviews ad nauseam my medical chart, asking again about drugs I am allergic to and if I've had any food or drink recently. I try ardently to answer all the questions, but I'm exhausted and spent.

While he asks his barrage of questions, Carol returns and has me take a pill, which the doctor explains is a cephalosporin—an antibiotic—as if, at this point in my life, I care what goes into my body.

Let this be over soon!

As I try to stop dozing off, he finally concludes, "Okay, Sarah, I think it's best to administer general anesthesia for you, mainly based on your current injuries and condition. This way you won't remember any of the surgery, and hopefully, you'll have less pain throughout the procedures and while recovering. Is that acceptable?"

I let out a snort and move my head up and down. I'm so done with this gig.

"Great. We'll see you soon." He finishes his charting as I wish for peace and quiet.

Later, I sense I'm in an elevator and two people are hovering over me. Then I notice the lights in the ceiling as someone asks my name. Dr. Tsai appears, as do more staff. I hear talking, but I don't bother to try to understand what's said. The rhythmic beeping of a nearby monitor is soothing and comforting. The other doctor, the tall anesthesiologist whose name I can't recall, greets me and explains something. My good hand with the IV is secured somehow and what feels like a cool liquid enters my veins.

All my discomfort vanishes. I am at peace at last. At least for now.

"Sarah? Sarah Colton?"

"You're in post-op. You did well, and your surgeries are over. How are you feeling?"

I'm groggy. I'm tired.

"Sarah?"

"Sarah?" questions a second voice.

Ah, I love being in this blissful sleep. Relaxed. Comfortable. I want to roll over, but somehow I can't. I want them to stop asking me questions.

"Time to wake up, sweetie," the first voice speaks again.

I know I need to pay attention, but I'm so relaxed at this second.

Yet out of the fog, I remember I have to wake up. I must move on. I have to be in the real world, not a world of non-existence.

"I have a little juice for you to sip. Doesn't that sound good?" The other woman coaxes me.

A cold drink sounds marvelous. I separate my lips, and a straw is inserted. I suck, and the liquid travels to the back of my throat. It's like diving into a cool pool on a hot day. Wonderful.

"That's good." She keeps talking, maybe to someone else nearby. "Yes, she's awake, doctor. She should be more coherent soon. And yes, the patient in Bed 8 needs to be checked, please. His BP has dropped again."

There's an interesting chasm between being conscious and unconscious. In one, you're somewhat in control—you can leave or sometimes change the situation. But when you're not conscious, you have no liberty to change anything, no control. Most of the time, you're only an observer of what's around you, whether in a dream state or not. Yet you can't control it or yourself. While being conscious frustrates and challenges you, the other is accepting without understanding. Right this minute, I don't know which one I prefer.

As the past two days tease my brain, I acknowledge that I can't be stuck in unconsciousness, but must welcome reality heartily so I can somewhat control it, and control is how I thrive.

After separating confusion from reasoning, my intellect wins, and I return to the real world.

Finally, back in my room, I fall soundly asleep for what seems like a few hours. A new nurse enters, rouses me, and provides a lukewarm smoothie, roughly telling me to drink it for my nourishment. With my good hand, I sip the chalky substance, which reminds me of the Ensure drinks they advertise on TV. It doesn't taste great, but it tastes good enough to satisfy my grumbling stomach.

I look down at the left side of my body. My foot is, once again, strapped to the hanging strap, but now it's in a hard cast, covering my entire foot and lower leg. My arm and hand are wrapped in tight padding, held above my heart with another strap. My left eye is uncovered.

After finishing my required dosage of healthy-living, packed-with-nutritional-supplements shake and discarding it on my bed table, I use my good hand to touch my bad eye. Gently patting the swollen lid, I coax it to open. It does. As the slit widens, I can blearily see the room and my overly protected body. I'm so thankful that I'm not blind. It's also nice to be alone.

An hour later, Zoey enters, and you can tell she's frustrated by her clipped actions, by the way she enters the room with intent. "Didn't I tell you this would happen? I'm so glad we moved all that money the other night—do you remember? Of course, with the world falling apart, everyone and their mother are on a run for their money but can't touch it."

My friend is dressed to the nines with a cobalt blue short skirt, scooped-neck black sleeveless shell, and black sandals with simple silver jewelry accessories. Her hair is pulled back, and her makeup looks great.

She carries another bouquet for me; this time they're white tulips, as she knows they're my favorite. She quickly puts them next to Carl's on the side table and continues her monologue.

"Yeah, it's an I-told-you-so moment, and your awesome friend Zoey pegged it. We did the right thing, but get this—I go to get gas and stop at the florist and food store, and sure enough, no one accepts cash. Everything must be credit or debit now. Period. So how are the six percent of American adults who have no bank account going to survive? Will they walk into Walmart with their employment check and walk out with a Walmart debit card? And to make matters worse, I may be high up at the bank and think I am in the know, but, well, all banks across the globe are shut down, as I told you they would be while they refigure and reset things. Yet everyone at my moderately high level is told not to go to work."

Zoey continues, "Something's off. We're told 'we're not needed,' yet all the banks continue making money, forcing everyone to use their credit cards while they charge exorbitant interest rates, even during a worldwide crisis. Drives me crazy how everything's always about money. And it's only going to get worse before it gets better!"

She stops her tirade, peers at me, and finally asks how things went in surgery. I can tell she's distracted, as she makes a smart comment about my uncovered black eye looking like beautiful hues of purple with a tinge of blue that nicely matches her outfit.

In an oversized tote, she shows me she brought one of my favorite sleeping shirts—light pink with tiny black and white llamas printed on them—a pair of loose black drawstring sweatpants that'll need to be chopped up to fit over my foot, clean underwear, and a few toiletries. She sets the bag on a side chair.

Realizing my tiredness, my friend doesn't stay long—she says she must meet Amir downstairs in five minutes, but she'll be back in a couple of hours, hopefully, to find me sound asleep and catching up on my needed Zs.

Later, the tall anesthesiologist and my nurse approach my bed. The RN checks my vitals on the machine—while the physician wheels the stool over and says, "Dr. Tall. Remember me?"

I almost laugh aloud when he says his name. Go figure. I'm surprised I couldn't remember it. It's rather fitting. "Yes. Thanks, Doc."

"The meds are wearing off nicely, and you did well during the surgery, although your blood pressure fluctuated a bit, so we had to give you some Ephedrine. Dr. Tsai took you off Morphine and switched you to Vicodin for the pain. It'll work better, but don't depend on it."

"Okay." The last thing I want to be is a drug addict hooked on prescription meds.

"Code Blue Room 408," is announced over the hospital intercom. The nurse looks at the doctor, and he nods. She sighs and leaves the room as quickly as she came.

"But I do have a question for you," he quietly says.

"Yes?" I wonder what he's concerned about now.

"When I was at the head of the operating table, I noticed you have some sort of implant inserted behind your right ear. I couldn't find anything in your medical chart about it. Is it a new type of hearing aid or what?"

I blink. I remember. I have a surgical implant—a device that a company inserted a few weeks ago. It was a start-up company that Denny got involved in through his work as a consumer electronics representative. Since I keep telling my husband we need the extra money, I talked him into having it implanted in me as I find its concept a bit interesting. The small unit is in its beginning stages; it allows someone to read my mind. See what I see. Hear what I hear. They're paying me good money to be their guinea pig, and I feel it gives me a sense of control. It was turned on the other day, I think.

I start to reply, "Yes, I..."

Sarah—Sarah Colton. Do not answer the question.

I'm confused. What was that? Who was that? What's going on?

I stare at the doctor; he stares back, looking like he's waiting for my answer.

Sarah, we'll explain later. Say it's an implant. Say only that.

Beyond stunned at the male voice echoing inside my head—a voice only I can hear based on the nonchalant look on my doctor's face—the only words I speak are "Yes, an implant."

Dr. Tall shrugs it off and takes his leave.

I've no clue what to think, and truthfully, I don't want to deal with whatever it is. That was strange, very strange. But right now, the only goal I have is to sleep. Right. Now.

~ **Day 3** ~

As if in a dream, I feel like I'm at the bottom of a deep lake. I can look up and see the way to sunlight through the murky, dirty water. But I've no interest in rising, in going up to breathe air, in filling my lungs. I'm in no pain or discomfort. I simply exist. It's as if I've resigned myself to staying here, at the lake bottom among the gently swaying grasses and thick mud. Alone.

A hand appears above, reaching down, wanting to pull me up. But I've no energy to reach up, to hold onto my redemption; I have no desire to save myself.

Sarah, you're okay. You're alive. Don't be afraid.

That same odd voice I heard yesterday is back in my head. I open my eyes and peer around the darkened room. The hospital walls look familiar. My leg continues to be strapped in place. My arm still can't move.

"Zoey?" I call out, hoping my friend is nearby.

Sarah, she's not here. She didn't stay the night but left once she heard you were sleeping comfortably. You've nothing to fear now.

The voice is a man's and sounds calm and convincing, but I'm unsure what's happening around me.

Sarah, we know you're worried. That makes sense and is normal. It'll all be explained. You go back to sleep. You need your rest. You did well, given the circumstances. We're proud of you. Rest now.

My good hand flails around in the dark, hitting the table off to the side of my bed.

Before I know it, a nurse is by my side, asking if I'm okay and if I'm in any pain.

"No, I don't think so. What time is it?"

She replies in the dim lighting flowing into the room from the hallway, "2 a.m. You've been sleeping soundly. Do you need anything? A drink maybe?"

"Yes, that would be nice."

She leaves the room and returns with something that tastes like Gatorade. She tells me it is chock full of electrolytes, which I need, according to her.

"Anything else? How are you feeling?" She adjusts my foot strap, making me more comfortable, and lowers the head of the bed so I lie flatter.

I want to ask her if it's normal to hear someone talking in your head after being under anesthesia, but the voice answers my concerns: *Sarah, don't speak. Just rest. Since you're awake, we'll explain it when the nurse leaves. Relax. It'll all make sense.*

Afraid to talk, I simply bob my head when the nurse checks my vitals, charts them, and gives me another dose of Vicodin. When exiting, she closes the room's door more to shut the light out.

Without speaking, I deliberately think: What is going on? I demand to know. Now.

We understand, Sarah. Do you remember you willingly had our trial implant embedded into your brain? Do you know why?

Yes, I do—it was a beta test to allow your clients to enter my mind and see what I see, hear what I hear, and feel what I feel. You are paying me good money to do it, right?

Very good, Sarah. And we at Numen implemented the program in your brain, along with about a dozen other candidates. Unfortunately, two of the testers didn't work well with the device, and one is missing, which is no loss to us. You all signed a contract to be paid twenty-five hundred dollars every week that the device is activated in your skull. And you can void the contract at any time.

I do remember this part. They'd installed it about a month ago, and then it went live the same day that people were "taken," as Zoey says. But what's so weird is that I've never heard anyone speak to me inside my head. That wasn't mentioned anywhere in the contract.

Correct, Sarah. We didn't expect to contact you directly during the experiment, but now we feel it's imperative to bring you up to date about the outcome of your test.

Test? Did I pass? Am I going to get paid, or did I say the wrong thing or do something wrong? Was I too emotional or not exciting enough? Boring? I bet I was boring to them.

Oh, no, by all means, no. You were excellent. In the beginning, only ten viewers were online watching you. We surveyed them after the people disappeared. They all agreed they want more—a lot more from you! By the time you fell down the stairs, that number quadrupled.

Thus, we have a proposal. Now that you know we've been watching you, controlling your every movement, and can correspond with you telepathically, Numen would like your consent to continue to monitor your mind. We would like to offer you an addendum to your contract.

What do you mean you have control of me? Shouldn't you know already that I'm a control freak and must have things in order, the way I want them? You can't control me! No one can or will! Only I control me!

Ah, Sarah, you've misunderstood. We can't control you personally—you know only you can do that to yourself. We want you to be in control. But we can control things around you, especially if they're electronic or electronically related.

Although we could not unlock your front door deadbolt because Denny set it up manually, we could arrange for Zoey to be able to enter your garage door by releasing the code on our end. Did you ever wonder why your security alarm, which you set before you fell down the stairs, never went off?

I'm shocked. How did you do that? No, I never thought about it; I mean, the alarm does have a glitch every once in a while, but it never entered my mind because I was unconscious for hours on the floor in front of the stairs.

Yes, that's what we suspected. You were too out of it to think about it and may not have been coherent enough at that time to address the problem, so we assisted. And regarding your Alexa system—not the one you threw against your fireplace wall out of anger—we automatically turned up the volume in your kitchen refrigerator unit so Zoey could use it more easily while taking care of you. Consider the traffic lights that stayed green getting you to the hospital; you never had to stop and get involved with those hoodlums...we arranged that. We won't mention how we sped up the hospital's computer for Zoey or moved things along in surgery so you would heal faster.

Numen made and makes things easier for you. You can call it control, but it was to aid you, not harm you. And we can continue to help you if you agree.

A thank you is all I can think of to respond. I'm glad I'm still in control, and you're not.

Of course, and we're glad you are, too.

You did such a phenomenal job handling the world crisis involving the airplane crash—kudos to you for such an accomplishment. Please note that we made no changes to your top-rated photo. It was superb. And you dealt with Denny being gone and your injury amazingly well, which many wouldn't be able to handle.

Your fine work leads us back to the contract. Due to your stellar attitude and fortitude, Numen would like to offer you fifteen thousand dollars per full month that you allow us to remain active in your brain and continue to track you. Would you consider this option? We'd be so disappointed if you declined this excellent opportunity.

I don't know what to say. That's a big increase and quite an offer. It would be plenty to offset Denny's income that's no longer there. Such easy money.

Indeed, it is. With the recent issues facing the world, your finances may be strained and challenged in the upcoming days, weeks, and months, so it may be a perfect win-win solution for both of us.

True.

Due to such strange circumstances that we all, including you, never anticipated and what you've gone through, we've already deposited a ten-thousand-dollar bonus into your checking account. Also, we are in the process of erasing all student debt from both Denny's and your accounts. These incentives will help you face the next few days and weeks with more positivity, reassurance, and knowledge. It was fortuitous of Zoey to have you move those funds before the banks shut down. Clever of her to push you to do it.

Thanks. She's one special friend.

That she is. She's remarkable. Remember us saying we originally had ten viewers? Right before your surgery, we approached our database clients, and now we have over one hundred signed up. They want you, and they love your interactions with Zoey and Jeremy.

This isn't only good for Numen's program, but good for everyone who becomes a client. They can see, hear, and feel how a real, down-to-earth person—or even two strong women who are always in control—succeeds in this world, especially during the temporary turmoil. And Jeremy's sensitivity ranks high in the ratings with our female viewers.

Ah, we see you're starting to get drowsy. We can resume this conversation later if you prefer. But right now, if you want to accept our new proposal, state the words "I agree" aloud, and we'll arrange all the necessary paperwork and email you a copy of acceptance.

I guess I will do it. I mean, Denny's not here. Our baby's no longer growing inside me. I have my parents, sister, Zoey, and Jeremy, but that's all. Yes, it may be something I want to do. Yes, let's continue.

That's right. Say the words, Sarah.

Okay. "I agree."

Good job. Now remember, this is only between you and us. You can't tell a soul or mention it off-handedly to anyone.

But what about your clients, the people who've been in my head all this time? Aren't they hearing all this right now? About the contract? The money?

Oh, Sarah, Sarah. This conversation is currently offline. It's two in the morning, and we doubt many would be in your head right now as they know that when you dream, they can't tap into your thoughts.

When morning comes and you're awake, you'll be live again on our instant feed. And it can't be taped or copied—it's live and untraceable. So be careful with your thoughts about us and this conversation, or your contract may become void. You can mention the monitoring but not that we converse with you. All they know is it's one-sided viewing, mainly to protect you and them from meeting. And they, and we, love what we've been experiencing through you.

Okay. I understand. I'll do my best.

Thank you. Your bonus has been deposited, and we'll reach out again when necessary. May you heal quickly so you can continue to be one of our best team players.

Yes. Thank you.

Goodnight and sleep well.

But wait. I do have one or two last questions. What do I call you? And what if I need to contact you? Is there a way I can do it? Like if there's an emergency or something important comes up where I must talk to you?

Great questions, Sarah. We are AGI—artificial general intelligence, which mimics the human brain. We go by Numen, which is a Latin word that means "divine power presiding over a thing or place." And your implant is named Dios.

I get the divine power bit, but Dios as in God, the Creator of all? Surely you know by now, I want nothing to do with any type of restrictive religion. I don't believe in it. You know that!

Of course, we don't reference the name to God—which is only a proper pronoun if you think about it. There's a god in almost every religion. What's the difference between the Jews' Yahweh or Messiah, Christians' God or Jesus, Hindus' Vishnu, Brahma, and Shiva, or Islams' Allah or even their prophet, Muhammed? They're all one type of god to be worshipped. No, we don't believe that way; we agree with you.

To be truthful, we're more in line with your sister's beliefs: that each of us can become a god, our own god, one who's in control of ourselves, yet free to let others be gods themselves. We feel there's no ultimate distinction between humans and a god or any other person of spiritual enlightenment. Or artificial intelligence, for that matter.

That's better. I can accept a god or gods. We all want to attain that here or in the afterlife—if that exists. That's what control is all about. Aunt Amy and those self-righteous Christians believe there's only the straight and narrow path to salvation. I don't believe in Heaven or Hell.

I guess Dios is better than Diablo.

Ah, your mind is so creative and clever in its thinking; that's exactly why we chose you to be our tester, and what a fine choice we made.

No, we don't think calling our program "Devil" would be apropos. Dios applies to what we are. We do, however, chuckle at your charming thought process.

But let's get back on track. For the sake of anonymity, call us simply "D," so the viewers do not understand who you're talking to if you happen to mention us unintentionally.

Also, you may have forgotten this, so we'll reiterate it. When you initially signed the contract, we explained that the program is designed so that you have some privacy. Anytime you're in a precarious situation, such as in the bathroom, dressing, showering, or even looking in the mirror, the feed is blocked out from the viewers' view. They'll never see you naked or exposed. We want to protect you to the fullest. If you need to contact us, go into the bathroom or your bedroom closet or stand alone in front of a mirror, and the live feed will be muted. Understand?

Yes. I had forgotten that part and was concerned. It makes me feel more comfortable knowing I'm not vulnerable to your clients.

All right. Sleep well, our Sarah.

You, too. If you do sleep.

I close my eyes and force myself to succumb to the dream world, even if it involves drowning at the bottom of a lake.

"Rise and shine, Sar!" Zoey enters my room, bringing with her three colorful, helium-filled "Get Well" balloons. She walks over to the window and pulls the drapes open to their furthest point, glances down at the parking lot below, and mumbles about how she's not a morning person and hates pretending to be cheery. She continues her pseudo greeting, "It's glorious outside as my mom would say. But you've heard that saying before from me. And how's my favorite friend feeling today?"

All right, you, the ones here watching and hearing me right now. I'm known as ValleyGirl to you, but my name is Sarah. I'm glad to be back in your viewing life. Thanks for putting up with me the other day—and sorry that when I fell down my condominium's stairs the live feed got all messed up and went offline for a while.

To bring you up to date, I'm alive and somewhat back in control, although my body is busted up a bit with a broken wrist and foot. But I'm here for you now, and hope you stay engaged in my videos. I'll do my best to make it interesting, okay?

Zoey ties the balloons to one of the drapes' end cords and lets them bounce against its fabric and ceiling. Then she walks over to me and halfway hugs the right side of my body.

"Couldn't be better," I reply. "Now that I'm doing opiates, I can't go wrong."

"How's the pain from one to ten?"

"Maybe a three or four if I move my hand. Foot's okay for now."

"Sorry about last night and not staying. The nurses said you were out of it and would be most of the night. Amir said it wasn't worth me sleeping in that chair again, even with your dirty blanket cushioning me."

I tell her I understand and thank her for the balloons and all the help she's been giving me. Of course, I ask her about her dinner date.

"Terrific. We hit it off, although the hospital food was lousy. Going out on a real date later this week—we hope—if he can get it off. He's been working nonstop with all the strange medical incidents."

It's nice to see Zoey looking more relaxed. Viewer, do you have a friend or friends like that who you want so badly to meet the right guy or girl? I'm not a matchmaker, so I'm glad she's interested in Amir.

"But I can't stay. Work called me in. They finally want us to attend a meeting about going completely digital. My friend says there'll be no cash distribution by any bank here in America, and, I believe, in Europe and the rest of the world. You can turn cash into a bank, but not take it out. It can only be applied as credit. And yes, the banks are still shut down to the public during the transition. I get the privilege of ramping up all the computer systems and putting online security in place."

She adds, "And on a more interesting note about Amir: I told you he was born and raised in Israel, right? Well, since they're still involved in that war over there, he was concerned about me being Arab—that there could be issues with our family and friends. I kept telling him I'm not Palestinian but born and raised Muslim in America. Not that it or any religion matters as I no longer follow any. And my parents are dead anyway. I have no brothers or sisters. And I don't stay connected with my cousins either. He was telling me all about his lineage, and how he and his rather large family of six siblings are from the tribe of Judah. Yeah, he's all about history. I say it's all about who you know."

"That's great, Zoey. I'm glad you two hit it off."

"We did. And he's down to earth. A real talker, not a pompous imbecile who only prattles on about himself. Oh, by the way, do you know if you'll be out of here today?"

"I don't know yet. My nurse said the doctor's doing his rounds shortly, so we'll see."

"Well, I doubt I'll be here to help you, and your parents, as far as I know, are driving down still. Maybe you can ask Jeremy to get you home?"

"Yeah," I reply, but I hate to ask him to do another thing for me. Will he want me to reciprocate? Will he expect more than I'm willing to give? Is he going to go all mushy on me again like he did when we entered the hospital? Hmm. What do you think?

"Okay, I better get a move on. I brought your phone charger in case you need it. Text me once you know what's up, and we'll figure it out. Right?"

"Sure, thanks, Zoey. You're the best friend ever."

When she leaves, I turn on the television and peruse the channels. Everything is news. And more news. Depressing news. Tragedies fill the screen. All about the other day's disappearing act. Now they estimate that in the world, all children under the age of ten are gone. Zippo. No longer around. Millions of adults are missing. Gone. Every continent, country, state, city, town, suburb, or rural area—all have missing people. Gone. Maps are color-coded, displaying findings. Videos of people disappearing on Ring cameras inside and outside their houses. Videos of employees at fast food joints to high-end restaurants, bars, businesses, retail and outlet stores, malls, and food stores. Gone. Pictures of empty seats in schools, office and government buildings, and churches. Gone. And photos of entertainment venues, stadiums, and parks with discarded clothing, jackets, shoes, and purses left behind. Nonsensical and bizarre. Unbelievable and without understanding.

Hey, Viewer, what do you think about all this? Who is missing in your life? Someone close or a friend of a friend? It's weird, isn't it?

My memory recollects everything—the argument with Denny about me not believing in God as he does or did and him stomping upstairs; the little girls' barrettes, shoes, and socks in the sand by the swings; the horrific stab of pain when I lost our baby; the golden retriever dragging his leash when I met James after the plane crash and meeting his over-the-top mother when she stopped by; and pious Aunt Amy's emailed apology stating she won't preach to me anymore. And my dear husband who is missing, leaving me alone.

Dr. Tsai interrupts my sad trudge down memory lane. "Glad to see you're awake, Ms. Colton. How are you feeling?"

With a nurse at my side, they check and chart my vitals. I tell her I'm doing better than expected, and the pain isn't horrible.

"Looks like you're still bleeding heavily according to the nurse. Our staff OBGYN doctor should be stopping by to see you. Due to the blood loss, we don't want you to get lightheaded and collapse, especially at home. If he thinks you're all right, we'll release you. Does that work for you?"

"Sure." The thought of going home sounds wonderful, although I'm leery of the idea of passing out while alone at the condo. And then there's that whole "we" brain thing. Oh yeah, I correct myself—the "D" insert in my brain where you viewers are watching it live. Right now. Right this second.

I pause for a second and acknowledge everyone watching me online. Thanks to you who have been here from the start—when this implant was turned on. Thanks for being here throughout my journey. I'm glad you're a part of it—a part of me—now. I wish I could have a reciprocal conversation with you. And I heard more of you have recently joined me. Welcome aboard and enjoy the ride. You may not know what's happened in my life, but I'm sure you'll pick it up piece by piece as you get to know me.

However, do be aware that I, Sarah Colton, like to be in charge and in control.

All. The. Time.

You may or may not like me. Sorry if you don't, but I'm going to be me. No pretension here. And hopefully, you won't be bothered by my strong, sometimes misconstrued as obnoxious personality.

"Great," my doctor responds as she gently touches my braced arm. "Let me check your wrist, and if the pain isn't too bad, maybe we can switch you to a non-narcotic."

She undoes the immobilizer and checks the incision, explaining that she's concerned about it swelling, so she may have to put a cast on it later if I can't keep my arm still. There's some pain, which I tell her is tolerable. She explains I'll need physical therapy once things are healed a bit. She moves to my foot, telling me how the cast may itch and how to protect it when bathing, and then she adds therapy appointments to my to-do list.

"I will have staff follow up with OBGYN. You also should get checked by an ophthalmologist. I'll set up an online follow-up appointment with your primary doctor in a few days, and I'll stop by tomorrow when making my rounds."

"Good. Thanks, Dr. Tsai. I appreciate it."

She and the nurse leave together, and instantly my phone rings.

Seems there is too much activity in this hospital room. Would you agree?

"Sarah! How are you doing? It's Dad and Mom!"

"Much better. Thanks."

"Well, we'll make this short. We have a little glitch on our end getting down to California, dear. Here, I'll let your father explain."

"Hi, Cupcake."

The phone has lots of static again. Maybe it's due to the earthquake. That or they need to upgrade and get better phones.

"We're back home in Springfield." He lets out an audible sigh. "We tried to get to the 5 Freeway, where it connects to Eugene, and then head south. But the offramp from 126 to the 5 was completely shut down. There's a new sign blocking the road that states, '20 Minute Neighborhood Applies: Only Residents Allowed'—a spin-off of what's working in other parts of the world where you can only walk or go within fifteen minutes from where you live, designed to help the environment and lower emissions. I'm sure it's a great idea, but what an atrocious time to implement it when so much other stuff is happening. Guess in these cities, you need some sort of permission to leave or go into the area."

Daddy continues, "Anyway, we tried driving down Glenwood to hook up to the 5, but the overpass had collapsed due to the quake. So, we tried the 226, which is Franklin Boulevard—which has plenty of large buckles in its asphalt that we had to maneuver around. I've never seen traffic so backed up. I was thinking we could take the 99 down. But I tell you, there are crazies out there. Rednecks in trucks with guns kept diverting us to side streets or telling us to go back where we came from."

"Oh, sorry, Daddy," is my feeble reply.

It must be so frustrating not to be able to go where you want. Here I'm restricted in my walking, yet I can still get an Uber to drive me safely to the store, right?

Viewer, yes, you here with me—are you having any issues like this? What do you think?

"Needless to say, after going through those two Cascadia quakes and many aftershocks without extreme damage at our house, your mother was beyond herself. She heard through one of her colleagues that several of U of O's buildings collapsed, including her earth sciences office at Cascade Hall. We should be thankful, though, since the devastation in larger cities like Portland, Vancouver, Olympia, Tacoma, and Seattle is insurmountable. She and so many other scientists had been warning for years about this catastrophe, but who would have imagined two huge quakes happening minutes apart in the Pacific Northwest?"

Mom interrupts, speaking in her professorial tone, "Well, geophysicists have determined that Seattle's ancient network of shallow faults that sliced through the lowlands of Puget Sound the other day involved one of the most devastating earthquake-related phenomena. Soil liquefaction causes buildings and infrastructures to sink, float, and tilt, while the ground might spread and crack, settle, or even initiate a landslide, causing more damage to the city."

I wonder if any of you viewers live around there, or do you have loved ones dealing with it?

"Regarding the trip, dear, we tried whatever way we could," Daddy says. "There's too much damage, plus people are getting so ultra-protective that we didn't want to chance it, especially if we have to drive down the 5 to get to LA. What else would we encounter? Going only a few miles out of town was a nightmare as it was. I can't imagine how it is elsewhere. Less than ten miles took about two hours to get home. It seems cities and towns are shutting down, not wanting anyone to come in or go out—at least, that's what we see in Oregon."

Mom adds, with a noted panic in her voice, "And tell her what we saw, about the girl!"

"Barb, let's not upset our daughter. She's got enough on her mind."

"She needs to hear how sickening it is out there, Bruce." Mom's practically sobbing. I hope her emotions and stress don't agitate her asthma.

"Okay, dear. Well, there was this female, I'm guessing in her twenties..."

Mom interrupts again, "She had to be in her teens. She looked young." Another sob escapes over the phone.

Daddy starts talking again, "And, well, there were these guys. And she was walking down the street with no clothes on when we drove by. And one guy was pulling her by her pink hair."

Mom corrects her husband: "Yes, she was naked! Well, she had panties, socks, and shoes on. No shirt, pants, or bra."

"And, well, what could we have done? If I stopped, I feared the others would gang up on us. I didn't know what to do. My job is to protect your mom, so I didn't stop. Maybe I should have?"

Do you hear the sadness and remorse in his voice?

"After going through both those earthquakes, I'm not thinking so well, I guess."

"Daddy, I'm sorry. You did the right thing. You protected Mom. You had to do that—you had to keep both of you safe."

"True, and in the rearview mirror, I saw she was standing up again and talking to the guy. At least, he let go of her hair. Maybe she's okay now. I hope so," he solemnly answers.

"I'm so sorry, you two. What a tragedy." I hurt for them. And more for the girl. Don't you?

My dad says, "So, we're home. And safe in our small cul-de-sac. We plan to hunker down and not leave the house for now. I hope you understand. Maybe next week when we're supposed to fly down, depending on when Eugene Airport opens again, and we're allowed to fly. As of now, all airports are closed. We want to be with you, to help you get better, but we can't see a safe way down yet."

"I understand. I'm glad you're home and expect things to start calming down. You made the right decision, both with the girl and returning home. It's okay. I'm going to be fine. Zoey and Jeremy are here to help me. Besides, I'm your daughter, and you know I can survive almost anything."

Mom agrees, "You're so right, Sarah. We'll be fine. As I was telling your sister, it'll all make sense and work out. Her babies may be missing, but there's a reason this happened. We need time to figure it out. Let's keep a stiff upper lip, and try to get through each day at a time, okay?"

Yes, we can overcome this tragedy. We're strong. We're courageous. And we have the control and power to survive this new world that surrounds us. And you who are watching me right now—you viewers, also, are survivors. You've also witnessed this, so you know we need to band together to figure this out and move on.

After the phone call, I stare at the tiles in the ceiling, pondering if I should try to sleep or touch base with people. I'm wound up about my parents' encounter with the girl and the gang, so I doubt I would sleep anyway.

I pick up my phone, scroll down to Aunt Amy, and leave a simple message. I briefly talk to my sister Silvia, who's still hoping for her little ones to reappear somehow in their cribs. She's resilient; she'll bounce back, too.

I leave a short voice message for Denny's friend John, a cop who told us to stay home when everything fell apart the other day. I report that Denny is missing, I've been injured, and am currently at the hospital, hoping to go home later today.

I check Facebook to see if Denny's brother in Israel has posted anything new; he hasn't, so I one-handedly send him a text message about his brother. It takes forever to do as the phone has to rest on the table while I type in each letter. I will use voice-enabled texting for future messages.

With my desire to converse with another human, I decide to call work. Jeremy's probably out scouting someone to do a video interview, even if it'll be without me. Maybe talking to my boss will satisfy my craving for personal interaction.

"Hi, Brittany," I say as cheerfully as possible when the flirty receptionist at *Valley News* answers. "How's it going there?"

We don't care for each other, so she answers in her usual one-word responses. "Busy."

"Yes, I could imagine." I act friendlier. "Is Carl around?"

"Yes." She puts me on hold and a minute or two passes.

"Ah, my top journalist!" Carl seems chipper than the last time we talked, after his wife was almost driven off the freeway when a driverless car sped past her.

"I am she," I say with a grin on my face. He can't see it, but I bet he knows I'm smiling.

"What a good job. Syndicate said, and I quote, 'It's what the country needs, something positive during a polycrisis.'"

"Doubt I've heard that word before—polycrisis," I comment.

"It's the latest buzzword, so I did a bit of research on it. The term was originally coined by French theorist Edgar Morin and co-author Anne Brigitte Kern in their 1999 book, *Homeland Earth*. In early 2023, the World Economic Forum—or WEF—discussed it in its Global Risks Report, stating that the world was on the brink of a 'polycrisis' by explaining its relationship to issues in nature, security, and public health. From what I understand, polycrisis is a time of great disagreement, confusion, or suffering that's caused by many different problems happening at the same time so that they together produce a big effect. Well, I'd say the other day's event ranks up there with its many disasters."

"Yes, I'd agree with that one." There's not much to add to his statement. "Oh, thanks for the flowers; they're lovely."

"You're quite welcome. My wife loved hers, too."

"Is Helen doing better?"

"Yes, she is. The sedatives helped."

Another nurse enters my room and, without talking, removes my leg strap, gently resting the bulky foot cast on the bed; the hunk of plaster completely covers my foot to right below my knee. She looks at me for a response, so I offer a positive nod as I keep talking to Carl.

She leaves and returns, this time with a plastic pitcher of water and a matching cup. She fills the cup and nudges it to me, urging me with her brows raised, which I obediently do.

"Oh, about your photo. The kid—James somebody? Are you going to contact him? A follow-up article will drive interest further in your picture."

"Great, Carl! I do want to talk to him. He talked about his seatmate, a guy named Eddie, who disappeared in front of him. With the boy being only fifteen, the ordeal had to be nerve-wracking."

"Yes, you told me about it. You've got my approval. Maybe when you're up to it, you can interview him, even if it's over the phone. We can have Jeremy connect with him for pics if needed."

"Okay, I'll reach out to the kid; I have his contact info."

"Good. Well, I should get back to work. It's a zoo here, and it will be for weeks, if not months. You take your time healing, but I'd love for you to come back whenever you're ready. Even if you work remotely for a while, okay?"

"Sure, Boss, count me in. I'll get back to you once I get out of the hospital. Oh, one other thing before I hang up." Yes, of course, I'm going to ask him about all these disappearances and happenings. This is my job, my livelihood. Viewer, don't you want to know, too? "What else have you learned about all the missing people? What does the Source say now?"

"It's interesting. Seems half the public still thinks it is a potent virus that infected certain people instantaneously around the globe, making them disintegrate. The other half believe it involves UFOs or UAPs. You know how Congress has been releasing NASA data about Unidentified Anomalous Phenomena all the time? Maybe it gives merit to the idea of them snatching away us humans, who knows for what purpose."

"Hmm, that's odd, but maybe conceivable. Wish I knew more about the topic."

"Ditto, dear."

I hear over the phone his name being paged.

"Well, it looks like I'm being needed somewhere in this crazy maze. Sometimes I feel like a mouse on one of those exercise wheels, and I can't get off. Helen keeps telling me I need to retire."

"You do, but you love your job too much."

"That I do. Okay, talk to you soon. Let me know when you get antsy and need some work."

We say goodbyes quickly. I put the phone down on the table and plop my head back on the pillow.

I don't know about you, but I'm not the type who likes to laze around all day; being bedridden is not my norm. I get restless easily and always have. To me, inactivity is a waste of time.

And I don't want to start thinking about what to do about Denny. Should I have a memorial or a ceremony? Would you do that with your spouse or loved one? What if you had no body to bury? There's too much to consider, isn't there?

After dozing off and on for several hours, mainly out of boredom, a new doctor enters the room in the afternoon and introduces himself as Dr. Chandler, OBGYN. He looks at my chart, and we discuss my menstrual cycle, pregnancy, and loss of the baby. He states that he's concerned about me getting something called menorrhagia, so we must keep an eye on my bleeding. A prescription is ordered.

With the aid of a nurse, he helps swing my casted leg off the bed, dragging the rest of my body along to assess if I can stand up alone. I rapidly fail his test as my knees collapse, and both personnel assist me back into bed.

He mercilessly insists that I spend another night in the hospital and has the nurse make sure I take my next Vicodin. With little emotion, he confirms he'll be following up with me again tomorrow and wishes me well. The doc has rather cold bedside manners, doesn't he?

I'm devastated. I don't want something to be wrong with my insides, especially with my uterus. What if I want to get pregnant again in a few years? What if something is wrong inside me?

What would you do? Wouldn't you feel scared, Viewer?

It seems if it's not one thing, it's another. Just let everything go back to normal. Please.

I don't like this. I want to be in control.

Resolved to lie here and do nothing but wallow in my self-pity, I spend the next hour or more frustrated and fretting about everything.

While I'm still in bed, one of the aides helps me get out of the stiff hospital gown and change into my sleeping shirt.

Still discouraged, I nibble a little on my bland dinner when it's delivered, and then I fall asleep when the meds kick in once again.

I sleep soundly—maybe ten hours—unable to remember my dreams and without any strange interruptions.

~ Day 4 ~

When I wake up around seven a.m., I feel more refreshed than I've felt for several days, if not weeks. It'll be a good day; I can feel it in my bones. The worst of this nightmare is over, right?

Do you feel that, too?

After I finish a decent protein-packed breakfast, Nurse Carol enters the room with a better attitude. Maybe people are starting to adjust to the new way of the world. Although it's been less than one hundred hours since the big disappearing act, we all must move on; we've no choice.

Oh, Viewer, are you at that point yet, or are you still depressed and wondering what to do next? Either way, it's time to move on and use the past to make a better tomorrow.

Carol checks my vitals again. "Heard you were out cold last night."

"Yes, I must've needed it. Sure, the meds helped, but I haven't slept like that in a long time. It was like when I was a kid. The kind of sleep you think has been only a few seconds or minutes, but it's been hours. Wish I could always sleep like that."

"Oh yes, wouldn't that be divine?" she replies.

After she removes my catheter, she asks if I'd like to try getting out of bed and going to the bathroom.

I acquiesce. It's odd trying to walk with a what-feels-like-ten-pound weight only on one of my feet. And awkward because the thickness of the cast on the bottom of my foot offsets my hip and back.

Carol gets me into the small, attached room, and I do my business and brush my teeth with the toothbrush that Zoey thoughtfully provided. The nurse also cuts the extra pair of sweatpants on the left leg so I can wear them later.

It's also odd being unable to use my left hand since it's bracketed in metal, material, and Velcro.

Viewer, I'm unsure what you are, but I'm right-handed, yet I'm surprised how often my left hand is needed in assisting the right one. The pain level of both operated-on appendages is noticeable but acceptable.

After returning to bed, I'm exhausted from the feat, but I'm pleased with my progress. Carol says both Dr. Tsai and Dr. Chandler will be making their rounds within the hour. After my nurse pulls out a hairbrush in the bag Zoey left me, I try to look somewhat presentable.

I've got this. I'm done with this place and ready to move on.

According to the clock on my phone, both doctors enter my room at ten straight up. They have a more positive look on their faces: they are not scowling. Do you notice that with everyone I'm encountering?

"Good morning, Sarah. Good to see you up and more active," announces Dr. Tsai.

While she grabs the stool and clicks into my electronic chart, Dr. Chandler asks about my bleeding and says he heard I was out of bed earlier and had no issues. I tell both of them I want to go home.

"I'll release you, but if you see any infection or problem, give my office a call promptly," answers Dr. Tsai. "We both feel you can go home and recuperate there safely."

After Dr. Chandler concurs, they sign off my chart, authorizing me to leave the building. I'm more than joyful to get out of their hair. I thank them for taking good care of me. They confirm my wound care regimen, medications, post-surgical precautions, and many appointments I need to make for follow-up visits.

When Carol comes into the room, they give her the go-ahead to release me, on the condition I find someone to take me home.

Well, duh, of course. I'm in no position to drive with only one good hand and one good leg. Seriously? And the meds. No doubt I won't be driving anywhere for a few weeks, especially since my convertible VW Bug is a stick-shift; there's no way I can position my fat casted foot in my car now.

Once the three of them leave, I send a voice-text: *Zoey. Pick me up?* I hope her Audi A5 Coupe has enough legroom to fit my larger-than-I-want-to-be body.

A few seconds later, she replies: *Sorry, no can do. All day mtgs. Ask Jeremy.*

I cringe a little, but I know he's my only hope.

Me: *K. Thx.*

Zoey: *Will stop by later when you're home. Luv.*

Me: *K.*

Next, I contact Jeremy, who rapidly answers that he'll be here in less than an hour.

He's a good friend, and he means well. I feel bad, as I don't want to take advantage of him. If there was only a way to let him know I want to keep our relationship platonic. That's all.

As you can see, I'm seated in a wheelchair with flower arrangements and balloons in my blanket-covered lap, and that blanket has seen its share of hospital dirt and grime. I'm dressed in a solid black T-shirt and sweats that have had one leg cut off.

My aide escorts me out of the hospital and carries a pair of crutches, a tote of my personal belongings, and another bag of prescriptions and medical supplies.

Dear Jeremy has pulled his Suburban to the front of the building's doors and plays the perfect prince, getting me comfortable in the front passenger seat and making sure the dirty throw protects my body.

As we head back to my townhouse, I note the crack in the windshield and ask him when it'll be fixed. He simply shrugs.

I see there are still a few cars left abandoned on the roads. Most of them have shattered windows or missing tires and hubcaps, and some have doors left open. I'm guessing thieves are making a killing with the discarded bounty left behind due to the disappearances.

Feeling like I'm in a one-sided conversation, I bring up Denny—how much I miss him and that I have no clue what to do about it, where to start, or how to start.

I feel like I'm talking to only you, Viewer, not to Jeremy because he makes no effort to reply. My husband is gone. Should I cry? Be sad? Be mad? What am I supposed to do here? What would you do? Can you help me?

Jeremy doesn't respond to my rambling. Instead, he turns up the volume on the car's radio when Taylor Swift's "Bigger than the Whole Sky" song begins. I know she's one of his favorite performers.

Without a spoken word, he's pensive, not his easy-going self.

I wonder what's up. "You okay, Jeremy? You don't seem to be thrilled to see me."

"I'm okay. Got lots on my mind. I like this song, though." He cranks the radio's volume up further. His silence continues to fill the vehicle when the chorus sings.

He's probably thinking of me. Am I the "you" in the song? Or maybe it's the goodbyes Swift sings about? Does he feel our friendship has ended? I hope not; I do cherish him, but I'm not interested in a romance with him.

Viewer, what do you think? Do you have a friend who wants or expects more in a friendship? What do you do to shut that person down without hurting his or her feelings?

I break his concentration. "Did you go to work this morning?"

Only after the song ends does he barely whisper the words, "No, I had to deal with some stuff...parents."

"Oh, I'm so sorry. I forgot. You said you lost them."

"Yep."

"You never told me how you found out."

"It was bad, Sarah. It was so bad."

As he turns onto Rinaldi Street, he looks over at me with bloodshot eyes. It's the first time I've noticed them since my accident. He looks like he is ready to burst into tears.

"Oh, Jeremy, I'm so sorry. Do you want to talk about it? They say that helps." I want to reach out and touch him, but I can't with my wrapped-up left arm. "Let me help you."

Then it dawns on me that I may want to rethink how he's been acting toward me, shouldn't I? Maybe he doesn't have ulterior motives; maybe it's all about his parents being gone. Maybe I was wrong? Is that arrogant of me?

"I found Dad. Well, I found both of them. It—it was sad."

My friend, a friend who usually confides in me about everything from his ex-girlfriend's abortion to his cousin being incarcerated for selling drugs, is struggling. He's heartbroken, and here I've been so insensitive to him, dealing only with my issues that I've ignored his pain.

When we are almost at my complex, he is still tight-lipped, refusing to convey his feelings or what he is going through. I know his lack of communication is for me; he cares so much for me that he disregards his self-health. Yes, sad.

"Jeremy, I know you don't want to talk right now. I get that, but I'm telling you—you're going to tell me what happened. I'm your friend, so you must. And if you don't want to tell me, then promise me you'll tell someone else, okay? You need to and should talk about it; it will help you move on."

He only says, "Um-hmm."

He pulls up next to our garage door.

"What's your code?" He asks mechanically as he exits his vehicle. He offers me no time to reply, so I wait until he walks around to my side of the car and opens my door.

"You don't have to be rude about it. I know hurt can make one snotty—I've done that to you plenty of times, so don't play that game with me."

"Sorry." He's resolute in his avoidance. "Code?"

Sighing, I recite the numbers that coincide with C O L T for Colton.

"Thanks. Wait a sec."

When the overhead door opens, I notice Denny's and my car parked side by side. But my car looks like it has tears on its roof.

"What happened to my car?"

"I had parked it overnight in the overflow area when we moved you in Adam's van and didn't think to move it back. But when I dropped Zoey and the wheelchair off later, we went to put the car back, and someone had slashed the convertible's fabric. I'm sorry. That was the only damage we found. We're guessing the person got spooked and left because nothing was taken or damaged in the interior."

"Ugh. Another thing to deal with." I'm getting frustrated with ongoing problems that seem to be escalating. How about you, Viewer?

"Yeah. Do you now see why I haven't dropped everything to be put on hold for hours with an insurance company to fix a crack in my windshield? There's so much to do. You'll see when your head clears from those meds. Denny being gone will make you realize the hoops you have to jump through are all unimportant. What matters right now is the here and now."

I'm glad he finally is talking again—yes, depressingly, but that's reasonable. I want to know about what happened to his parents, and he's going to tell me before the day is out.

After explaining to Jeremy where we keep a spare house key hidden in Denny's toolbox in the garage, my chivalrous friend helps me into my house. It's almost comical as we work ourselves between both cars, being sure not to bang the left side of my body against my car's door handle. When we get to the step that enters the condo, he picks me up and carries me over the threshold, sarcastically commenting on my extra weight due to my foot cast. He delivers me to our long couch in the great room.

The act of being helpful seems to be one of my friend's endearing characteristics as his overall physique improves.

With the day half spent, Jeremy and I work well together with me dictating how to rearrange the great room, so that I won't have to traverse up the dreadful stairs that caused my pain.

Since Denny and I have one of those fancy split electronic beds that adjust with the click of a button and can be separated by undoing a bottom bar, Jeremy—by himself—drags downstairs my half of the thick, upscale mattress and sets it on the floor. After he empties an old bookcase Denny had in college that was kept in the garage, he lays it face down to use as a platform for my mattress.

When he's done playing the role of a mover, he demands that I take a nap on my new bed, which I gladly do.

While I snooze, he goes food shopping, including buying a bake-your-own pizza and salad. When he returns, he tells me that shopping was a nightmare with people fighting for food and fewer employees available.

Thinking only about myself, I find it demanding to understand what has been happening outside my world for the last several days.

Throughout the hours, I constantly thank him, yet never push him to discuss his parents. He puts Carl's get-well flowers on the dining room table and swaps out the dead tulips on the kitchen windowsill with the white ones Zoey gave me.

When Jeremy sets up my laptop nearby, he suggests I order one of those rolling knee scooters from Amazon because the crutches are hard to handle with one of my arms being out of commission. And he opens the delivered shipment of the new Alexa and sets it up.

No, there's no way I can thank my dear friend enough.

Viewer, could you? Can you think of something special I can do to reciprocate for all he's done? Let's think about that one.

With the use of one crutch, I hobble into the kitchen and attempt to get out plates, forks, and napkins for our meal while Jeremy sticks the pizza in the oven. He stops me and forces me to slide onto one of the kitchen's tall metal barstools. He cracks open a can of La Croix, pouring it over a lot of ice in two glasses he retrieved from the cupboard. He always likes lots of ice, so I'm glad he feels more comfortable being in my home.

After a few bites of pizza smothered in chicken, mushrooms, and cheese, I determinedly insist, "Okay, now's a good time to talk. Time to tell me about your parents."

Jeremy slows down his chewing; the Adam's apple in his throat goes up and down as he swallows. "All right. I left work and raced over to Encino right after that odd noise happened. It was crazy driving the five miles. Mayhem everywhere. People standing in the street, dazed as if not knowing what to do. Men and women sitting on the sidewalk curbs sobbing with their hands holding their heads. Accidents. Cars on fire. Young women screaming."

He fiddles with his pizza slice, picking off a mushroom and eating it, then continues, "I remember driving by Lemay Street Elementary School on Vanowen Street. Many adults were standing outside, in the parking lot, on the sidewalks, looking dumbfounded. And the wailing. That's still stuck in my head."

I'm thankful Jeremy is willing to talk, but I'm unsure if I want to hear these details. I can't imagine being a mother—or if I had my child who I lost—and he or she disappeared. No way.

"One lady came up to my Suburban, holding some clothes and shoes, screaming at me, 'Where did he go? Did you see my little boy? Where is Mateo? Can you help me find him?'"

"How sad." I readjust in my chair, wondering if my discomfort is physical or emotional.

"Yeah." He eats a forkful of salad and adds, "When I got to my parents', I couldn't find them. I looked through all the rooms in the house and saw nothing askew. No clothes were lying around like everyone mentions right off the bat. Nothing. I started to panic, trying to guess if they went somewhere, but both their cars were parked in the drive. Then I heard water running. I rechecked the kitchen and both bathrooms, but I couldn't find the source. Yet I knew a faucet was on somewhere, so I ventured into the backyard. And—there I found the hose on, its nozzle spurting liquid all over Mom's prized roses. It flooded the bed to the point that water was running down the patio toward their bedroom slider, along the side yard cement walkway, and into her vegetable garden. I turned the water off. Mom's pink shirt and black tennis skirt were discarded by the hose; her shoes and undergarments were stacked under them. I picked up her watch, necklace, and wedding ring, leaving the clothes where I found them."

He puts his hand in his jeans pocket and pulls the jewelry out. "I can't let go of them, Sarah. This is what I have left of her."

I wobble off the stool, hop on one foot around the counter, and offer a one-arm hug. We cling to each other to grasp any comfort we can, wanting the personal contact to strengthen and keep us standing. We hold on tightly as if nothing else matters.

When we finally release each other, Jeremy is crying. Not sobbing. Not gasping. Tears are running down both sides of his face. Seeing him so distraught, I start to sob.

After he wipes his face in the crook of his arm, he grabs a nearby napkin and gently dabs my eyes, being extra careful around my swollen one.

"That's not all. There's Dad."

"Yes?" I blink away the moisture that threatens to collect again.

"I looked around the backyard, but he was nowhere to be found, including the garden shed. I couldn't find any of his clothes left anywhere after rechecking everywhere multiple times. I looked for what seemed like hours on hours, trying to figure out if he was home when it happened or not. His car was there! Both of my parents' cars were in the driveway. I checked his shop, where I thought he would be because he's always tinkering out there. Then I walked our entire property and fence line. Perhaps he was making sure things were secure. Nope. Not there. When I texted you saying my parents were missing, I was beyond hopeless. None of it made sense, especially since I couldn't locate my father."

He puts his fork down and looks at me. "About a half hour later, when I was standing in their dark living room looking out their front window at the lights in the Valley, I realized that the only place left I hadn't checked was the garage. So, I walked across the breezeway to it."

He takes a swig of his drink, and pauses, presumably not wanting to continue. He stares at the granite counter and calmly says, "I found him; I found Dad. He had hung himself from the rafters."

"No, Jeremy! No! Oh, I'm so, so sorry." I grab him and hold him tightly, so tightly it hurts my wrist, but I don't care. We're both crying again. This poor guy. He must be so broken.

"Yes. The only thing I can piece together is that he must've seen Mom disappear and was so distraught over it that he walked into the garage, never thinking about turning off the water, and put the noose around his neck."

He lets out a breath of air and adds quietly, "I've told you how Dad depended on Mom for everything and how he would get depressed from time to time. It must've pushed him over the edge seeing her go away like that. He mustn't have known what to do. I can only hope he didn't suffer too long."

"Oh, Jeremy."

It now makes sense; this is why he's been acting so protective and caring of me. He needs me as much as I need him. We'll get through this. We must. We have each other. He had to go through the agony of doing something with his dad's body—like waiting until the police came to confirm it was suicide. He must've been torn telling me about it over the last few days. How heartbreaking.

Are you crying, Viewer? Tell me you wouldn't want to be in his father's shoes. Or in Jeremy's. Horrible.

Thankfully, there's a knock on the door that distracts us from the deep stab of emotional pain.

"About time, Jeremy," Zoey says as she enters with a couple of shopping bags hanging on her arms. "I thought you'd need dinner, so I picked up Thai. Took forever. One of the people in line said restaurants are having trouble staying open, all because of the missings."

"How sweet of you." Jeremy kindly helps her with the bags as he quickly glances at me.

I chuckle. These two friends of mine are truly remarkable, aren't they? And Zoey, dear Zoey, doesn't get upset after we explain we already ate the pizza and salad, remarking that both food choices make great breakfast and lunch meals. And that doesn't stop her from grabbing a fork out of the kitchen drawer and sampling all the boxes she purchased, exaggerating the marvelous taste of each one.

"Jeremy, Sarah said you helped arrange things here—my, you did a fantastic job. I love how the bed and platform fit perfectly by the bay window; you can still use the long couch and table. Where did the loveseat go?"

"We stuck it in the dining area. See it in the corner? I turned the table sideways so we could shove the smaller couch out of view."

"Smart of you. Glad to see a man with muscle also have aesthetic qualities."

He smirks. "Thanks, Zoey, but I don't think that'll attract a woman."

I enjoy their bantering; my girlfriend usually makes anyone feel at home with her vibrant personality.

"So, here's a question," she says. "How will Sar bathe? She's going to start smelling soon."

Jeremy replies, "I put a bunch of clean towels in the downstairs bath. Yeah, I know there's no shower there, so maybe I can carry her up the stairs in a day or two, and you can help her in the shower."

"Great idea. I was going to suggest those dry hair shampoos. And moist towelettes. We can order them on Amazon if needed."

I protest, "Seriously, you two are concerned already about my hygiene? I greatly appreciate all you're doing, but it's above and beyond. Really."

"Yes, because we love our dear friend," says Zoey.

After we clean up the dishes and put away the food with my minuscule contribution—more like instructions on where things go—the three of us sit down in the great room, with me resting on the bed, and my back leaning against the bay window's shelf so that my leg can be supported with pillows.

Zoey has helped herself to a bottle of Shiraz and offered Jeremy a glass; she pops open another La Croix for me, insisting I get completely off the Vicodin before I can touch the hard stuff. You bet.

She takes command, as usual. "How are we going to work this, you two? I can offer to sleep here at night, but who can keep an eye on Sar during the day? You have to work, right, Jeremy?"

"Yes, but I'm taking a week off to deal with family stuff." From the way he says it, it's obvious he doesn't want Zoey in the loop about his parents. "Since I live close by, I can come by during the day and keep a close eye on her."

"Wait up, guys," I demand. "I have a say in this, and I can get around pretty well. Yeah, I'll need help showering and maybe food shopping at first or getting to those doc appointments that I can't do online, but I'm not bedridden. I can move around downstairs quite easily."

"Gotcha. That's settled. Jer, you'll do days, and I'll do nights." She adds, "And let's swap phone numbers, Jer, so we can keep her on our schedules. Deal?"

Jeremy agrees, and each one logs into their phones and adds the other to their contact list.

Zoey explains further, "In a few minutes, I'll get some clothes from my house and return, and we'll get you to bed. You must be exhausted, Sar."

My friend stops from getting up off the couch. "But wait! Before I go, I've got to tell you about work. Jeremy, this is privy info, but since you're Sarah's friend, I'll share it if you never divulge that I'm the source. I don't want to lose my job over it."

She continues, "The other night Sar and I moved our money around to protect ourselves, so—since the banks are shut down—you won't be able to do that part. I hope you have enough funds tucked away for the next several weeks or months before the CBDC—Central Bank Digital Currency—is fully implemented."

"Yeah, I have several accounts and cash." Without making eye contact with either of us, Jeremy stares at the red liquid in his glass, adding, "from my parents who are gone."

"Sorry to hear that, Jer. Is it okay if I call you that?" Zoey asks.

"Sure, but I do have a question. If my parents are no longer around and I'm on their bank accounts, can I access their funds? Is it legal to do that?"

"Are you a named beneficiary, or are you listed on the account?"

"My brother and I are both named on the accounts—I believe it's a trust fund, so can we tap into it at any time?"

She explains, "Yes, if your name is on it, you can access all of it. However, if it is under a pension or TSA, you'd have to submit a death certificate to touch any of the monies. And if your parents disappeared, well, then it may not be allowed on those types of accounts for months or years."

I wonder if Jeremy will mention his father. I'm sure he could get a certificate on him, but it might take a while.

Zoey adds, "If your parents did online banking, then I'm sure you can go move funds around when things open back up. But that isn't happening anytime soon."

"I see. Oh, I have one other question. What about Bitcoin accounts? Are they still viable? Will they be accessible?"

"Yes, for now. They're like GoFundMe; they're decentralized so anyone can set them up and run them—and charge any outrageous fee they want. But I think that they'll be deleted and eventually banned. Centrality will become the norm through the CBDC, so everything can be monitored."

"I see. Thanks." Jeremy seems a bit more relaxed. Maybe from the wine or knowing he can access some of his parents' funds.

"Back to my work today," Zoey says. "I learned quite a bit by being in meetings. In a day or two, our bank and most likely any US bank will open on a limited basis—like only at the drive-through or automatic deposit sites. This is so they can accept cash, any form of it like bills or coins. With our bank being the biggest in the country, we are offering ten percent instant interest on any cash deposited within the next thirty days. If you drop two grand into our bank, you will have twenty-two hundred dollars added to your account. This is a great way to cash in the money while making money. Although, I must mention that it's treated as interest, so the added amount will be taxable down the road."

She pours herself more wine and adds, "The idea is to get rid of all cash and go completely digital, so this incentive should work well for both the banks and people. Initially, our government will be subsidizing the payout to the banks to give customers a piece of the pie by turning in their cash. And why get rid of the cash? Mainly it's about corruption. If no cash and every transaction can be traced, it'll stop the underhanded black market and drug deals because paper money will be worthless. Sure, it'll float around in backstreets for months or even years, but the dollar as we know it today will be dead if it's in physical form."

She turns to me and says, "I was wrong in my summation the other night when I expected cash to be king, but it's not going to be. However, if you have silver or gold—like when we talked about your coin collection the other day, their value may soar as it's considered a commodity and worth something. If anything, when the stock market reopens in a few—that's what I heard—I'll be buying futures in both gold and silver. However, purchases won't be allowed until banks can process the paperwork, and who knows when that will occur. It'll all be interesting. I'm still not sure I'm on board with the whole thing. It seems there's something strange going on behind the scenes, but I haven't figured it out."

Jeremy asks, "So what you're saying is I should turn in all my cash and any of my parents' that I find?"

"Yes, and do it right away to make sure you get the extra ten percent. I think our bank will set the benchmark, and others will follow within days."

"Thanks, Zo—if I can call you that?" he teases.

"Yes, we'll all be the one-syllable friends then."

She gets up and tells us she'll be back in a few minutes because she must go collect her things from her condo.

When she is gone, Jeremy cleans up our glasses but leaves Zoey's half-full one on the counter. He asks if I need another Vicodin. I better take one, and if I get a good night's sleep, I tell him, I'll start weaning off them tomorrow. The last thing I want is to be addicted.

By the time Zoey returns, Jeremy is already standing by the front door, ready to leave, although it's only a little after nine o'clock. After we both taunt my neighbor that she's a night owl while the majority of normal people feel more productive during the morning, we confirm that he'll be back around nine a.m., hopefully by the time she's awake.

The poor guy has done so much for me and has gone through so much; I wish I could help him. I wish I could make him happy and carefree again, but I think it's going to take a while.

Viewer, do you have any friends like that who you want to help, but you don't know how?

Once Jeremy leaves, take-charge Zoey has put sheets on my bed, brought down the soft comforter from our bed, and added my pillow to the cozy retreat. She goes back upstairs and pilfers our bathroom for soap, deodorant, toothpaste, and Kotex, carrying an armful of accessories downstairs and organizing them nicely next to my prescriptions in the half bath.

During one trip upstairs, she hollers down from the staircase asking which pajamas I feel comfortable in. I request my down-to-my-knee gray bed shirt, so we don't have to deal with my bulky foot cast.

She helps me undress in the downstairs bathroom and gets me ready for bed, including handing me a warm washcloth that feels wonderful on my face and body.

When she leaves to discard my used clothing into the washing machine in the utility room, she allows me some privacy in the small, enclosed room.

D. Are you there, D?

Yes. We are.

Good. How am I doing? I haven't talked to you in almost two days. Is it okay now?

Yes, the monitor is off. Don't start talking out loud as Zoey may think you need her.

I could see that happening. Thanks for the reminder.

You're doing great. Your ratings are spiking upward, and more clients are engaged in viewing you. Any concerns on your end?

Not really. I wondered if I'm boring, that's all. I'm used to being more in control of my surroundings and my go-get-it attitude, yet I feel stifled due to my injuries and these meds.

That makes sense. You're fine. If you need the drugs or are in pain, take them. We've got you covered. We'll make sure nothing bad happens to you. You know that.

Thanks. Oh, any chance I can tell Zoey about this program? I think she would be a great candidate for an implant.

No. Not yet. We've vetted her but are unsure of her loyalties. Although she works at the bank, we don't think she's that receptive to the digital currency issue—at least not yet. And she quoted the Bible, which seemed uncharacteristic of her.

I agree with that one—Zoey was brought up Muslim, so I've no clue why she said it either.

We'll keep monitoring your interactions with her and see if there are any other red flags.

What about Jeremy? Would he be a good choice? I hate to see him suffering so much. It might help him out of his funk.

Again, it's a no for now. He's fragile and highly emotional. Perhaps when he has a better grasp on his parents'—especially his father's—deaths, we might reconsider.

Okay. Keep me posted. It's good to talk to you. I'm becoming more receptive to this idea of you and the viewers in my head. To me, it's a form of control.

Yes, we're in agreement wholeheartedly. You're the perfect choice for this project, and we appreciate everything you're doing. Now, get some sleep. Tomorrow is a new day with new opportunities. And Sarah?

Yes?

Did you notice your bathroom fan is fixed? We did that.

No! You did? The screeching sound everyone hates is gone! Amazing. Oh, I love you more and more. One less thing to deal with now that Denny's gone. Thank you. Thank you.

You're welcome from Numen. Good night.

When I exit the bathroom, Zoey has a quizzical look on her face. I'm smiling from ear to ear, but I don't respond as she gets me to bed, deadbolts the front door, and has Alexa turn off the lights and set the alarm.

As she retrieves her glass of wine and climbs up the stairs to our extra bedroom, she asks me for our internet password as she'll be working and won't be sleeping for hours.

~ Day 5 ~

I t's eight in the morning according to the chiming clock on the mantel above our double-sided fireplace. The rest of the condo is silent.

Using one crutch, I limp/hop quietly to the restroom, once again amazed the annoying fan is magically fixed. I use a clean washcloth to wipe the "sleepy men's sand," as Daddy calls it, out of my eyes and take my required medication.

I'd feel better if I could get used to this heavy cast. I'd undo the straps on my arm immobilizer, but I don't want to see any pins sticking out of my body or gore today. No thank you.

Dragging my left foot behind me, I sneak into our kitchen and choose a coffee pod. I select Dark Magic, a bold, intense dark roast that ensures I stay awake, and insert it into the Keurig. Next, with only using my right hand, I pull out four eggs from the refrigerator, two at a time. I set four pieces of Trader Joe's multigrain bread in the toaster and start making breakfast.

Tell me, Viewer, are you hungry? Are you the type who eats three meals a day or are you a grazer like Denny was? Oh, how I miss my guy.

There's a soft rap on the door, so I ask Alexa to unlock it, knowing it must be Jeremy since he's always early. Then I remember Zoey set the bolt, so I hobble over, unlock it, and greet my friend. After entering without speaking, he points upstairs. I signal in the affirmative. Yes, Zoey's still asleep.

As he holds my good elbow and directs me into the kitchen, he whispers, "Feeling better? You look like you got some sleep."

"Yes, I was making breakfast. Do you want Zoey's since she's still asleep? I could always make more when she wakes up."

"You bet. I'll cook. You go sit down. Are scrambled eggs okay?"

We both seem much more relaxed. Almost as if we'd both jumped over a large hurdle that didn't fall down and neither did we.

He gets out three plates and silverware and goes to work, reminding me that his brother is an executive chef at a fancy hotel in Chicago. During high school, Jeremy learned how to cook due to Dylan's practicing and testing recipes on the family.

They're stepbrothers since Dylan's father married Jeremy's mom a year after Dylan's mom skipped out on them. Dylan and his wife moved out of the Valley a few years ago.

As he preps, we talk about what needs to be done today. He mentions he should go to his parents' house and find their financial documents, plus see if any bills need to be paid.

I tell him that I have no doctor appointments for the day, and I wish I could check up on Aunt Amy, who lives off Sepulveda Boulevard.

The conversation is normal, almost how it was before the disappearances wrecked our lives. We talk about work and who's missing.

When I bring up Brittany-the-flirt, he gives me a dead stare and blurts out, "Don't set me up with her, please, ever!"

"Jeremy, she's cute and fun. She may be the perfect one for you."

We must have been enjoying ourselves and laughing loudly because Zoey comes down the stairs, her hair a mess and wearing the same clothes she had on last night.

She says groggily, "I need coffee! This is too early for me."

Jeremy, ever so helpful, picks up a cup of already steaming hot liquid and walks it over to her as she stands at the foot of the staircase. "Here you go, Zo. And your breakfast is almost ready."

She pads over to the other barstool next to me and sits down, running her fingers through her long, untidy black hair.

"And you say I'm a trainwreck, Zoey?" I interject as Jeremy places two plated dishes in front of us, turning them at a perfect angle to view from our side, complete with toast encompassing eggs and three slices of avocado displayed perfectly. "You are the mess, girl. Look at you. You didn't even bother to change."

She starts to backpedal. "I—I fell asleep. I never sleep in business attire. I don't think I've done this before." She seems confused. "Amir and I were texting half the night.

Good thing he likes late hours like I do. Time must have gotten away from both of us; I fell asleep. I'll have to check my phone to see which one of us texted last. It's still upstairs. This is so not me."

Jeremy tells her, "Eat first. Before it gets cold."

She digs in, as do I, while Jeremy stands on the opposite side, sampling his culinary creation.

"Jer, this is good—*really* good."

"The secret is water," he says. "Most people add milk to their scrambled eggs, but my brother taught me that adding water essentially steams them, and as the water evaporates during cooking, it yields a fluffier scramble."

"Well, I usually pass on breakfast, but this is marvelous. Thanks. Well needed."

After breakfast is over and the dishes are cleaned up, Zoey goes upstairs and quickly gets ready for work.

When she comes downstairs, she carries my UCLA sweatshirt, underwear, a sports bra, and a pair of Denny's drawstring sweatpants with one leg cut off. She helps me with my clothes in the bathroom, and she's out the door at 9:37 a.m., which might be later than normal for her.

As she leaves, she tells us she'll be back around six, and we'll decide then if we want to eat last night's meal or get something else.

"Zo sure is a bullet," Jeremy comments. "More like a whirlwind. Does she ever stop?"

"Rarely—but she's a good friend. I depend a lot on her. She's one-in-a-million."

"That she is. So, what do you want to do next? Carl texted, asking how things are going here."

I say, "Oh, I've got an idea. And you can help! Remember that James boy from the crash? The one in my photo?"

"Sure. The fifteen-year-old, right?"

"Yes. I didn't go into much detail since Carl only wanted it in bullet format, but I did reference his seatmate who disappeared during the flight. Having the guy evaporate right in front of him freaked the kid out. Carl and I talked, and he wants me to do a follow-up. Let me text the teen and see if we can meet him or have him come here and maybe do an interview at the crash site in the field behind my condo. You know, make it all about surviving the devastating fallout of the crash."

Jeremy says, "Do you think he'll want to revisit where it happened this early? I mean, would you want to stand next to that burnt-out fuselage and rehash the horror? Or would you want to go upstairs to Denny's office and revisit all that angst you felt when you realized Denny was gone?"

He continues, "That's what I'm struggling with today; at this minute, I don't know how I can go into my parents' house alone. I'd only go there if you're with me. Dylan said he can't come help me out either—all airports around the country are still shut down, and he hates driving."

"Yes, I see what you're saying," I say. "What if I text James, see his response, and then we'll go from there? If he's up to it, we'll have him come here—and see if he wants to go out in the field where the plane hit."

I add, "Then maybe tomorrow, I'll have more energy to get out of the house, and we can swing by Aunt Amy's and your parents' places. How does that sound?"

"That makes sense. Physically take it easy today, and tomorrow maybe we can venture out. Yes, text James, and let's see what happens."

In less than a half hour after contacting James, he responds, and we set the time to have him come to my condo at two o'clock. In the meantime, I sit on the couch with my laptop, my foot cast resting on a pillow on the glass table while Jeremy transports his video equipment from his vehicle into the great room.

While checking emails and online news sources, I turn on the TV above the mantel. There are only a few visuals of the mega earthquakes in the Pacific Northwest, most likely because there's no electricity or 5G available in the big cities of Olympia, Tacoma, and Seattle, which have received most of the damage. A tsunami hit the shores of multiple islands in the Puget Sound.

My phone rings; I notice it's Denny's friend, who's a cop in Burbank.

"John! How are you?"

"The bigger question is how are you, Sarah?"

I update him on my accident and that I'm back home, getting used to being a gimp with a worthless hand. He tells me how he's pulling twelve-to-fourteen-hour shifts and that things are crazy in the Valley, especially at night. Mainly gangs confronting nobodies. It's beyond controllable, and the police know it, so they back off because they don't have enough workforce.

He tells me, "If Denny's one of those who disappeared, you need to go online and report it."

"How? Where?"

"There's a new website—I think the OWL or something like that set it up. Go to *themissings.com*. It's a global site where all those who've disappeared are being collected and tabulated. Put in as much info as you can."

"OWL? Who's that?" I question. "Maybe 'O' for Only, One, or Our? 'W' could be for World, and 'L' maybe for Liaison, League, Lobby, or Lord. One World League?"

"Beats me," he says. "Get online as soon as you can and file a report. The site went live a few hours ago, so most people don't know about it. Do it before the president announces it tonight in his speech, and the site overloads and crashes."

"Okay. Will do."

"And Sarah, be careful out there. Stay home, as I advised you earlier. Don't go out unless you must. Do you need anything? I can stop by, if so."

"No, I've got plenty. I'm being well cared for." I tell him briefly about Zoey and Jeremy.

"Okay. I got to go. We're going to have a press conference in an hour about the Valley falling to pieces."

"Is *Valley News* covering it?" I ask.

"Probably—if they have the manpower. The more who know about it, the merrier."

When we hang up, I tell Jeremy about the missings site and jump online to fill out the form.

After I enter Denny's Social Security number, date of birth, address, et cetera, I'm asked to input his physical description, when he disappeared, where he was when it happened, if I was present during it, and if any proof of the disappearance, such as clothing or jewelry, was left behind.

It takes forever to type with one hand, but I'm faster on a keyboard than on a phone.

Feeling as if I'm displaced and writing a fictitious story, I wonder if you, Viewer, would be affected by filling out this form. Would you only have to file for one person or many?

Jeremy drags out his phone and reports his mother's information but not his father's. I hear him sniffle several times, hopefully not rehashing the terrible experience of finding out what happened to both parents.

By the time we're done, I'm worn out. Jeremy fixes me a small salad and cons me into taking a nap. I'm proud that I haven't taken any Vicodin, but I do ingest three Motrin to ward off the throbbing in my hand and foot. I lie down and quickly fall asleep, lulled by Alexa playing soft classical piano music in the background, which Jeremy thoughtfully selected.

A gentle push on my shoulder pulls me out of my slumber.

Jeremy's rousing me. "Time to wake up, Sarah. It's one-thirty, and James will be here soon. We don't want you to snore through your interview, do we?"

He helps me to the bathroom, where I comb my hair and put on a little makeup. He asks me if I want to put on a nicer-looking shirt, but we decide it's best if I'm not in view during the video or still shots, since I might become the focal point due to my battered body.

James arrives precisely on time and is taken aback by my appearance. It takes several minutes to explain the past several days of my life. Introducing him to Jeremy is a good segue. Both males seem to instantly bond, which is a plus.

There's a look on the boy's face that I didn't see when we first met. Maybe I didn't notice it, but he seems more reflective, more observant as his eyes dart back and forth around the room. Most likely going through the crash has made him change. I can't put my finger on it, but something's shifted in him.

When all formalities are over and we all settle in the great room, I ask, "James, did your mom drop you off or did you have any issues coming over?"

"No, ma'am—I mean, Sarah. I rode my e-bike over; it gets me everywhere and is easy to ride on most streets if I avoid the congestion and gangs. My stepfather gave it to me for my birthday last year. I like it because I can get around faster than taking an Uber."

"That's cool," cuts in Jeremy. "And you don't have to buy gas."

They talk about how fast it can go and if it's hard to pedal.

"In five months, I'll be getting my driver's license. My mom and stepdad said they'll match any money I have to help me buy a car."

"Out of school now?" Jeremy engages him in a way that's not pushy or condescending.

"School. Well, they're closed due to the missings. No kids in elementary school and about half in middle school. With the teacher and staff shortages, the LA County Unified School District shut down all thirteen hundred schools for now. Wonder how long it'll be until they reopen."

I hadn't thought about that—no schools are open. Why would they be as parents and families deal with their loved ones' disappearances?

Viewer, are you dealing with this? Do you have any kids in school who were not taken? How are they dealing with it?

"So do you work?" asks Jeremy.

"Yeah, just weekends at California Pizza Kitchen on Tampa Avenue, or I did. I mean—if they're still open. I haven't checked. Too many stores and restaurants have their doors closed, especially at the mall. I heard gangs took it over."

I look at Jeremy. He looks at me. I know this kid enjoyed talking to me about journalism at the crash site. He's a bright boy. And intelligent. Way up there on the maturity level.

"Jeremy and I could put a good word in for you at *Valley News*. Would that interest you?"

"That would be awesome! I would love to be an intern or something. I'd even do it for free."

"No. That wouldn't be necessary, but we'd be glad to help," adds Jeremy as he glances at me.

It's settled. We both could make James our "Project Feel Good" after all the bad that surrounds us. And it would be easy to twist Carl's arm to get him to give the kid a job, even if it's menial. It would be a good start in the news world.

When I ask James if he wants to talk about the crash, he flinches slightly but agrees. I sense he's cautious and still shell-shocked from the event, but he appears to want to put it behind him by talking about it.

Having been through some of it with him and experiencing my horrors, visiting the crash scene is probably the best therapy to center both of us back to living life.

Together we leave my condo, solemnly retracing our steps through the nightmare we went through—past the swing set, cross the side street, and into the field where the Boeing 737 crashed and 123 lives were lost. Respectfully, Jeremy tags behind us, giving the two of us the space to reverently remember the fiery accident.

During the video shoot, Jeremy handles the only survivor with kid gloves, prompting him to stand a certain way by the side of the plane. We both agree not to shoot in front of the opened fuselage, where the torn seats and devastation would trigger sickening memories for both James and me. Thankfully, the strewn body parts that continue to give James and me nightmares are gone from the weeds and California poppies.

The video takes only a few minutes to do, with me asking brief, concise questions about James, his name, age, where he lives currently, and how he was flying from San Diego where his dad lives to Bob Hope Airport. I touch on what the boy witnessed and felt when the strange sound occurred and when people disappeared including the pilot, and the plane turned on its side. I don't focus on the crash itself, but how the teen came to when he was videoed on my camera and his hand moved. We briefly mention his seatmate.

The shortness of the tape, in my opinion, is perfect, because the less time standing in that field, the better for my psyche—and probably James's, too.

As I limp with the one crutch back to my condo, I direct the conversation to my interviewing goal by asking James, "You mentioned Eddie, the guy who sat next to you. I want to know more about him. Can you talk about that?"

Jeremy trails behind us but has his boom mic close enough to capture our conversation.

"Yes, he was my seatmate. A cool dude. Older than I am, but we got along well. I'll miss him, although I barely got to know him. He loved sports, including basketball—just like I do. That was what we talked about the most. He arranged tickets to next week's Lakers game for me since he couldn't go." The boy's steps slow down when he mentions it.

"Yes, you said that," I say.

"His email did go through. I can pick them up at the game. I don't know, though. I mean, I'll be sitting in a dead guy's seat. I don't know how I feel about that."

"Oh, James. He didn't die. He disappeared. You know that. You saw him go."

"I did, Sarah. That was crazy. Seeing him and then not, right in front of my eyes; it was like watching a *Star Trek* movie where the person slowly dematerializes, but more instantaneous and no swirling particles. I still can't believe how it happened. It was totally weird."

Yeah, that's true, but why is he saying it with calmness in his demeanor? As if he knows something I don't.

All three of us stop on the sidewalk, right in front of my condo, where there's a potted rose bush next to a little iron gate to our patio that has a metal table with two matching chairs.

I put my good hand on the kid's arm. "It's okay, James. I know. My husband Denny is gone, too. I found him. I found what he left behind, including his contact lenses, the crown of a tooth, his watch, and his wedding ring. I know what you're feeling. I know. And I'm sorry, so very sorry."

I look at Jeremy, wondering if he will mention his mother's disappearance, but he doesn't.

James doesn't reply, but we start walking again. As we approach my front door, he says, "Yes, and I told you what Eddie said. He talked about God; he said it was God who changed him, who made him whole and complete."

"Yes, I remember you saying that—and me telling you he was wrong. There's no God, and you need to forget what he said and move on."

As I put the key in the door to unlock it, James blurts out, "No, Sarah, you're wrong. You're the one who's dead wrong." His tone is firm and uncharacteristic for someone like him to confront an adult like that.

I again look at Jeremy; his eyebrows are raised as if wondering what'll happen next.

"Sure. You can say that, but you don't mean it," I add as I enter the great room, putting my keys down on the nearby half-moon mahogany table.

"We'll see about that," replies James.

He turns to Jeremy, as if for support or agreement. "What do you think? Do you think there's a God, the Creator of the Universe?"

"Yes and no or no and yes," replies my friend. "What is God? He's whatever you want Him to be. I do think there's a Superior Being who created Heaven and Earth, yes. But I don't think a Deity can control us."

"See, there you go. No God," I add.

"Fine. Be wrong. But let me tell both of you this, right before Eddie disappeared, he told me to read the Bible. And that's exactly what I've been doing. I told my mom and you that I would. Started on page one in Genesis about Creation and have already done the first five books, called the Pentateuch. And you know what I've learned? There's a God. Period."

I contest. "Fine, James, it's great you're reading the Bible. I never have and doubt I ever will, but please do it with open eyes. It's all a mystical, unbelievable story. It's fabricated."

He shakes his head. "No. It's. Not."

The conversation is getting heated with his stubborn determination and my frustration over the topic.

Jeremy enters the kitchen, turning a deaf ear to our impasse.

Viewer, what would you do to shut this down? Do I let him continue or what?

James leaves me alone sitting in the great room on the couch and heads into the kitchen and focuses on Jeremy. "Have you ever heard the verse John 3:16? You know, they use it on signs everywhere, especially at sporting events?"

"Uh-huh," Jeremy replies mindlessly.

Based on his response, maybe he also wants James to cease his sermonizing.

"It's easy. 'For God so loved the world, that He gave His only begotten Son, that whosoever believeth in Him should not perish, but have everlasting life.'"

"Yes. I've heard it, James. So, what's the point?"

"Just asking. People always stop at that verse, but I like the next one: 'For God sent not his Son into the world to condemn the world; but that the world through Him might be saved.' The two verses are beginning to mean a lot to me. Especially since Eddie gave me this before he disappeared."

He pulls out a key fob from his pants pocket and tosses it to Jeremy, who misses the catch. The thing clatters on the kitchen island's countertop.

This piques my interest. Does it whet yours, Viewer? Do you know what it could be?

I don't say anything, waiting to see Jeremy's response.

"It's got a flash drive," James says as Jeremy picks up the USB drive and inspects it.

"I see that. What's it got on it? It says *RaptureKit.com* on its side."

"Only everything I've wanted to know, Jeremy—about God and Jesus and other stuff—like the future of the world. That's the one Eddie gave me. It has a massive 32GB to put in your computer, and you'll have everything right there! It's got videos, files, Bibles, tracts in different languages, sermons and teachings, and lots of articles about what to do after the Rapture, which happened when so many disappeared days ago!" He's ecstatic talking about it, as if he's obsessed.

From the other room, I try to stop him from ranting, but he ignores me.

"And get this—the info is free online. I've downloaded the files to other flash drives, and I'm going to give them out to everyone I meet. Yep, that's what I'm going to do, and no one can stop me."

Seriously? This boy's gone mad. He reminds me of Aunt Amy and her incessant preaching and proselytizing. No, it's worse! This teen can't be saying these things, believing them. No.

"James!" I vent as I stumble over to the kitchen island and stand next to him. "Don't get involved in this stuff. It's nonsense. I know, I've lived with it for years; it's dribble."

"No. It's not. Do you know the ABCs of eternal salvation?" he retorts. "I do now, and it's easy to believe. Admit you are a sinner. Believe in Jesus. Confess Jesus as your Lord—how simple is that?"

"Oh, stop it," I say. "Here are my DEFs on the topic; and listen carefully. 'D' is for deceiving as the Bible says that all have sinned and death is the penalty, and that can't be true; it's hearsay to give no hope to people. I'm certainly not a bad person, and neither are either of you."

I glimpse at Jeremy, and he's smirking.

"'E' is for exclusionary because it leaves out certain people or groups: If you don't believe specifically in Jesus dying on the cross for your sins by shedding His blood and rising on the third day, you go to Hell. And 'F' is for fatuous because Christianity shows a lack of good sense or intelligence; it's foolish to believe its stories like the Flood, the Red Sea splitting, Jesus's resurrection, et cetera, and there's not enough to prove them except for some book man has written."

With emphasis, I add, "Oh, and I'll add 'G' for gaslighting because Eddie has manipulated you by psychological means using the Bible to gain power and control over you."

I think that one hurt because James is only shaking his head back and forth, not speaking.

But I'm on a roll. "Want me to keep going? I'm sure I could cover every letter of the alphabet more than once."

Yeah, you can see this is a hot topic for me. Can't you?

Now Jeremy is grinning. I knew he would take my side over this newbie to a religion he knows little about.

James is mute. He should know better than to debate with me about religion, any religion. But I don't want to argue; I only want to put him in his place, like I just did. I like him, but not what he's currently pushing.

Finally, James backs down when Jeremy asks him who his favorite basketball team and players are. Thank goodness calmness fills the kitchen again; I'm relieved.

We play nicely for about twenty minutes more, and then James says he must get home. His mom wants him to help her in the kitchen since their housekeeper disappeared. His mom doesn't like to cook. Yeah, I can't see the boy's mom knowing how to make scrambled eggs, with or without adding water to make them fluffier.

When five o'clock comes around, Jeremy turns on the TV to 24/7 news and our president makes a brief statement. He begins by apologizing that there are no definite answers to why millions have disappeared, but he reminds us it is his top priority. He urges us citizens to calm down and support our country—our world—as we accept a new normalcy. He tells us the military and all local police forces have the authorization to keep the peace in our cities, no matter what the cost. After mentioning to report online those loved ones who are missing, he concludes his message by reiterating we need to band together and help each other deal with the grief and tragedies we all are facing.

Throughout the short talk, OWL's website flashes across the bottom of the screen.

During the speech, Jeremy uploads James's video and I write my article involving Eddie. The words don't flow the way I expect, most likely because I'm still miffed at James's religious declaration. I try not to lash out at the kid between the lines. After reading it aloud to Jeremy, where he catches my subtle digs but tells me it is acceptable, it's forwarded to Carl.

By six, Zoey texts that she'll be late—like after seven—so she insists we go ahead and eat. We pull out the Thai food and reheat it, with Jeremy adding a pile of fresh veggies to the khao pad with shrimp. I try to help him cut the mushrooms and carrots, but I run out of steam and am banished to the couch once again.

As we converse across the room, he sets the table in the dining room and lights two tapered candles. While eating, we talk casually and comfortably, like good friends reminiscing; we discuss his parents and brother and Denny along with my family.

We both question whether we need to have memorial services for our loved ones or arrange for a plot in a cemetery. Jeremy tells me Dylan and he decided to have their dad cremated and his ashes sprinkled on their property. Jeremy says he'll make some kind of marker with both parents' names on it to place nearby.

But I don't know what to do about Denny. Having none of his remains does not give me any closure. I miss him so much yet do not know what to do or think.

What would you do if you were me?

After dinner, both Jeremy and I are asleep when Zoey arrives at 7:30 p.m. He's stretched out on the couch, and I'm wrapped cocoon style on my bed with my casted leg sticking out of the comforter. The television still has the news playing, something I enjoy falling asleep by.

"I hate to wake you two, but it's not even eight!" She startles both of us.

Jeremy gets up, seemingly uncomfortable that he had sacked out on my couch and was awakened by a woman. He stumbles to the bathroom while Zoey puts her briefcase down, goes to the fridge, and scavenges for food.

As usual, she grabs a fork from the drawer and samples the left-over Thai food, commenting between bites how good it tastes and that it's full of vegetables. By the time she completes her feast, Jeremy returns to the great room and informs us he needs to leave.

"No, you can't yet," my girlfriend says. "Sar must shower. It's been almost a week. Look at her. That stringy hair has to go. Jer, can you help me get her up the stairs?"

I look at Jeremy, who is blushing.

"No, you won't be assisting in her undressing and dressing. We only need your brute and brawn for the task of getting her to the bathroom. Please," she implores.

He accepts the task, with an obvious sigh of relief.

The several attempts of the two of them trying to carry me by each holding my thighs or Jeremy cradling me in his arms would make a funny sitcom. The easiest way to tackle the job without hurting my leg or hand is for me to ride piggyback on him, with my good arm wrapped around his neck and Zoey directing my derriere. We climb the stairs carefully.

I glare at the final top step where my stupid sock slipped, forcing me to tumble.

When we pass Denny's office, I'm thankful the door is closed. I'm not one to go down memory lane, especially when I'm not ready to deal with its aftermath.

Zoey helps me remove my clothes, and I waddle into the shower with the abundance of plastic trash bags she has put on my protected extremities. The warm water feels wonderful, including when she washes and rinses my hair, being careful not to let soap run down into my puffy, bruised eye. She's right: This is what I needed. Afterward, I feel exhausted but so fresh and clean.

Before Jeremy leaves, I climb onto his back and am delivered back to my bed. Zoey offers me Vicodin, but I refuse, only accepting more Motrin since I'm determined to fight the pain.

After inspecting my swollen eye and declaring it has gorgeous hues of blue, she gently kisses me on my forehead like Daddy does and says goodnight before turning off the lights and heading upstairs. I quickly fall asleep, not fretting about James and his ridiculous flash drive.

~ **Day 6** ~

I t's three in the morning per the mantel's clock.

I can't sleep. I've never been a good sleeper, and having my leg bonded in plaster doesn't help the situation.

Since I'm thirsty, I get up for a drink but first use the facility, hopefully quiet enough not to stir Zoey. But the light flowing out of the upstairs guest room may mean she's awake or has fallen asleep fully dressed again. Maybe she's still texting Amir.

I feel bad we didn't get to talk much last night.

After picking a glass out of the cupboard and filling it, I gulp down the cold water. I look out the kitchen window and see the swings and...the swings that started everything when those girls went missing.

As I head back to bed, I ask D—Are you around?

Of course, we're always here for you.

Good. So nice to hear your voice again. It's comforting at times not to feel alone. Zoey and Jeremy are wonderful, but I'm starting to miss my husband. I want to get used to being able to talk to you; it's encouraging to know someone is nearby, anytime.

Yes, that's how we designed it: to make you feel in control and a part of us, always.

Thank you. I do wonder, though...

Yes, we can see you're troubled. Your heart rate has spiked. Is it about Jeremy and his feelings for you?

I don't think so. I understand he's lonely, but it's in a different way. I want him to think of me as a sister, not a lover.

That makes sense. I think he's getting the gist of things. Remember, he's hurting—maybe more than you are, having lost both parents.

Could your restless mind be about James? Do you find his new beliefs discouraging?

Yeah, maybe that is why I feel down. Like I'm not good enough. Like my article had no substance. My heart wasn't in it, so it didn't read well. Do you agree?

Don't worry about trivial things. It'll all work out. You did fine. And maybe it's good that it wasn't one of your best works.

How can you say that? I only want to do my best and be the best. And this article, it's trash. It's not up to my potential.

No, we disagree, Sarah. It's perfect. It's well written.

You wait and see. If James is into his religion, this may be the best way to counter him—by not giving him the accolades he desires. If no one raves about the article, they won't idolize him or praise him for being the only survivor, which he had no control over anyway. And if he has no platform to preach his flawed beliefs, then isn't that better than him being personified and glorified? See, it's perfect how it's working out.

Oh, I understand. You don't want him to get noticed because then he'll be able to spew his God and Jesus lies more. Yes, that's a great strategy! I never considered that angle.

Correct. We have it and him under control. You need not worry.

Okay. But you're not going to hurt him or cause him any harm, right? I mean, he's an innocent kid.

We have it handled. You did well, especially with your alphabet retort. That was priceless and so debate-worthy. Now go back to sleep. Only hours until it's morning and a new day.

After dawn arrives, I'm awakened by Jeremy's soft knock at the door. When I open it, he enters with three cups of Starbucks coffee and three choices of breakfast sandwiches that he tells me he had to wait in line for over an hour for. Knowing Jeremy likes the sausage one and Zoey would pick the egg white one, I select the bacon, gouda, and egg. What a nice treat.

Zoey clatters down the stairs in a huff and with motivation. "It's a great day, guys! I'm early for once because I have to run over to my place and change shoes. Sar, do you think this skirt's too short? Jer, do my legs show too much? I must look professional since I'm sitting in on a meeting with the head honchos, and I need to make an impression."

Jeremy looks at her, but he doesn't reply. Instead, he hands her a sandwich, for which she appears grateful. She takes a bite and heads to the door, explaining she hopes to be home around five for once.

Of course, I tell her she looks marvelous, but she could find something a few inches longer and maybe pull her hair back into a bun instead of a ponytail. She's stunning any way she looks, but if professionalism is the goal, notch it up a bit.

After she leaves, Jeremy and I plan our day. We'll first hit Aunt Amy's duplex ten minutes away and see what's up there. Then we'll go over to Jeremy's parents' house so he can look for their financial papers. On the way back and if I'm up to it, we'll stop by and see Carl at the office.

Since Zoey didn't select my wardrobe, I ask Jeremy to go upstairs into Denny's closet and find a pair of loose black drawstring sweatpants. He also locates one of my husband's button-up collared shirts to put over my bulky arm. This time, we only cut a little slit on the pants to fit them over my foot cast. Dressing myself is a little more complicated, but I feel funny asking a guy for help. I roll up the shirt's cuffs and put on a little makeup, so I don't look dorky.

Before we leave my condo for our excursions, Amazon delivers my scooter and Jeremy quickly assembles it, showing me how I can get around more easily without my foot holding me back.

After popping a couple of Motrin and climbing into Jeremy's Suburban, I feel alive getting out of the house.

The warm, cloudless sky makes the sun brilliant, so I don my oversized sunglasses to filter the glare and hide my bruised face.

Once Jeremy puts the scooter in the back, we head toward Sepulveda Boulevard. It's already over seventy degrees out, and only a few cars are vacant on the sides of the wide street. Since it's morning, only a handful of stores appear to be open, and there aren't many people around.

"Turn left at the light and then an immediate right. Her duplex is the white one with the black trim; she's on the right side, so park in the driveway since her car is probably in the carport."

Jeremy obeys my directions, and when we arrive, he asks, "What will you do if we don't find her? Have you heard from Denny's brother yet?"

"I don't know. If she's not there, then I'll have to file another OWL report. If she's there, be prepared for her fire and brimstone sermon. She has no tact whatsoever and will leave you feeling lambasted. I did text Hal, but he's in Israel—or was. Who knows?"

"Do we go knock on her door? If she's not there, how will we get inside?" After exiting his side of the car, he opens my door and gets my scooter out of the back.

"Oh, ye of little faith! I have Denny's keys, see?" I dangle the keychain in front of him.

"Ah, good. I'd hate to have to break the door down or crawl in through a window and have her neighbors call the cops."

"Nope. Keys work great when in your possession."

Using my newfangled scooter, I roll up the walkway and stop on her front porch. When I knock on her front door, there's no reply, so we unlock it and enter.

It's so quiet inside that we can hear a clock ticking. There's nothing amiss in the living room, so I roll down the hardwood hall to the kitchen.

Her cat Isaiah warily greets us by meowing. I go into the tiled kitchen and check his self-feeding and watering bowls; only a few dry kibbles remain and maybe a half inch of water. Oh my. I forgot about her cat—a cat I've never liked. He scratched me once because I shooed him off my lap, and we've never gotten along since then. And whenever I visit, Aunt Amy knows to keep him away from me.

While Jeremy checks the rooms, I search through Amy's cupboards and find the cat food, replenish the feeder, and add water.

"Sarah, come in here!" he calls to me from the adjoining dining room. "Look what I found."

I let out a curse when my casted foot bumps against a chair leg as I enter the room on my scooter.

"Amy must have been on her laptop at the table," he says.

Her glasses are on the keyboard; her clothing is draped haphazardly on the chair; her socks and shoes are under it. Her watch, earrings, and a cross necklace catch my attention.

"She's gone." I pick up her glasses and set them on the table. "She, also, was taken. Looks like I'll have to file that report." I'm dumbfounded knowing another person is gone, even though I didn't care for her.

"Yes, and look here." He motions to the tabletop. "Here's her Bible. She must've been on her computer when it happened and was reading or studying something."

"Oh yeah, you better believe that." That's peculiar. I wonder if she had sent me that email about how sorry she was for the way she'd been treating me right before she disappeared. I still have it in my inbox. "Can we fire up her computer and see what she was doing?"

"Let me try." Leaning over, he slides the laptop in front of him, away from the Bible, and clicks on the blackened screen. When it asks for a password, he ignores the message and hits enter. The device instantly comes to life.

Hmm, was it set up without a security code?

In seconds, he tells me, "Yes, looks like she had her email browser open."

Just then her screen goes completely dark. As if it was disabled.

D?

"That was weird," Jeremy says. "The screen probably got shut down because I didn't use her password. Oh, well. I don't feel comfortable accessing someone's computer without them knowing, especially your aunt, whom I know little about."

"Interesting," is all I mutter.

"I wonder what she was reading in this Bible." Jeremy closes the laptop and swivels the book so he can view it, scanning the pages for any clues. A pink highlighted section on one side of the page catches his eye. He puts his finger on it and reads out loud:

For the Lord himself shall descend from heaven with a shout, with the voice of the archangel, and with the trump of God: and the dead in Christ shall rise first: Then we which are alive and remain shall be caught up together with them in the clouds, to meet the Lord in the air: and so, shall we ever be with the Lord. Wherefore comfort one another with these words.

"Woah," he adds. "So, you think your Aunt Amy was reading this page when the disappearances happened?"

"Could be—but what an odd coincidence."

"I've heard these verses before, but I never read them like this." He fiddles with the book's thin pages. "Kinda gives me the chills if it's true, huh?"

"No. You're not becoming like James, are you, Jeremy? You can't seriously think there's a connection between these verses in the Bible and what happened the other day, could you? Do you?"

"Well, how do you explain that strange tri-sound we heard that this passage mentions—that we've never heard before or again? Or what about the people being caught up in the air and all the disappearances? I'm not saying I believe it, but people are gone. Was it synchronicity? I'm baffled, that's all."

He shuts the Bible and returns it to its spot on the table.

"Stranger things have and do happen, Jeremy. When I found Denny, he was listening to some tape that mentioned Jesus and forgiving sins. I was so mad that I threw Den's headphones against the office wall. That's why I avoid that room—I don't want the memory of my meltdown. Denny's gone. Amy's gone. And your mom's gone. Gone. I don't think they are coming back, either. And there's nothing we can do about it. We must move on."

I reverse the scooter into the kitchen. I'm not upset. I'm worn down, beaten by all of this. As Zoey had said, it just won't stop. I'm drained. I want everything to go back to normal—any kind of normal that I can get used to. Call me selfish, but this is getting to be too much.

Viewer, do you feel the same? Like me, are you tired of it?

I glance over at the cat, who is finished eating his allotted meal and licking his paws. At the minimum, someone is getting what he wants.

Jeremy walks in and looks at the animal, who slinks over to him and is rubbing against his leg. "What are you going to do with Isaiah?"

"Well, not keep him. That's for sure. I hate that thing. And he hates me."

Jeremy picks up the feline and pets it. "Well, you can't simply leave him here alone."

"Why not? It's not my cat!" I bark.

"Because that's not nice. I—I'd never leave a cat all alone. Poor guy. He's been in this empty house for days. If you don't take him, I will. And gladly. It'll give me something to love and care for."

"Great. You keep the cat, Jeremy. Don't tell me you don't want him in a week from now when he destroys your furniture."

"He won't do that. He's old." He snuggles up to the critter.

I'm touched by his compassion. I don't know what to do with a pet, having never had one.

"All right, Eyes—yes, E Y E S." He spells the word out. "That's what I'll call Isaiah for short. Let's find your crate, bedding, litter box, treats, and toys.

We climb back into Jeremy's vehicle, cat and his paraphernalia et al. I can't see this working out, but whatever—if that's what makes Jeremy happy, and I don't have to be involved, fine with me. One less thing to deal with.

We start the eight-mile drive from one side of the Valley to the other, but when we drive side streets to Victory Boulevard by Birmingham High School, it looks like there's a protest or rally of some kind as a couple of hundred teenagers are in the street, blocking our passage. Several are carrying handwritten signs that state, "Goodbye, Believers" and "No More Jesus Freaks," or others declaring, "We're in control." Several have misspellings or are interlaced with profanity.

Jeremy has me use his phone to take some pics and a video and asks me to forward them to Carl, who's always looking for an interesting angle from today's youth, especially right now.

It takes us longer to get through their barricade, but we escape with no damage.

After we cross the 101 Freeway and Ventura Boulevard, which is deserted perhaps due to its many closed retail stores and restaurants, we head into the Encino hills off Havenhurst Avenue and wind through a street called Empanada Place, where it comes to a dead-end.

There's a thin gravel road that Jeremy drives on, and we take a couple of twists until we approach an iron gate around a fenced-in property.

He opens his window, keys in a password, and the gate opens.

I'm astonished. He had told me his parents were old school and liked living off the grid, but this makes me think of Charlie Manson's ranch in Chatsworth, where his gang lived during the Tate and La Bianca murders.

We continue on the lane with a few more short turns.

Sensing my apprehension, Jeremy says, "Oh, calm down. This is where I was raised. It's simply a house on some rural land in the Valley. Yes, a rare sighting in LA, but it was a fun place to live during my childhood because part of the property has access to Encino Reservoir. I can't tell you how many times Dylan and I would sneak over there and play in the water. Dad would get furious when he found out."

"It's so remote."

"Yes, that can be good or bad." He pulls up to a driveway and parks his SUV in between the house and detached garage.

I notice his parents' cars side by side in front of the building, but I don't mention them.

In the dry California heat, I gawk at all the land with its many trees and bushes that dot the hillside.

The first thing the guy does when he stops the SUV is remove Isaiah from his crate. It's almost endearing how he coos at the animal.

While carrying the cat in one arm, he pulls out the scooter for me with his other and brings it to my opened door, but the rolling device doesn't handle the gravel well.

Inside the Lincolns' one-story sprawling home, it's as neat as a pin. Maybe too simplistic and sterile looking for my taste.

Photos of the two boys are on the fireplace mantel, so I ask Jeremy about them as he puts Isaiah down on the dated shag carpet.

"This one here, that's when I was about five years old, and Dylan was nine." He moves on to the next one. "Dylan and I love fishing, so that one's at Lake Tahoe. Dad and Mom took us there often. We had a cabin there for several years until I went to college. By then, Dylan was at culinary school."

"Is this your parents' wedding picture? Your mom's beautiful."

"Yes, she was." He picks up the framed photo with care. "Since both had been married before, they tied the knot in front of a judge in Santa Monica and honeymooned in Santa Barbara. That's taken at a resort there. The lighting is stunning in that shot. The way the setting sun glistens off the water with them standing to the side makes it perfect."

It's nice to see Jeremy talking about his parents. I'm sure this is hard for him.

Wouldn't you have trouble doing this, Viewer?

I can't imagine going up to Denny's office again. Maybe I can have Zoey help me clean it out, eventually.

He picks up the cat and directs me to a back room, which, I'm told, was once his bedroom and has been turned into his dad's office. It's got the original wood paneling typical of cookie-cutter ranch-style homes built in the 1960s.

Jeremy says this is the only home he knows, as he lived here most of his life. More photos flank the walls, mostly of mountain and river scenes. One could tell his father loved the outdoors.

"Did you take these, or did your dad?" I ask.

"They are all mine. Dad enjoyed my hobby as much as I did—well, he loved to be outdoors, and he loved me capturing the beauty." He reminisces as he sits down at the desk, Isaiah resting on his lap.

He digs through the top drawer and locates a small black book. "I have to say that Dad was a perfectionist. He's got every password ever used in this. And it's in pencil, so I bet it's up to date."

"Whoa," I comment, "your dad has an old computer."

Its antique design takes over most of the desk with its large case.

"Yep, he only uses it for spreadsheets and printing out stuff. It isn't hooked up to the internet; nothing in this house is. That's why I couldn't live here when I was in college. Sometimes, it's cathartic to be in an electronic-free zone."

Viewer, can you imagine that? No online access? No electronic texting or messaging? Nope, not my thing. Would you go crazy without it?

In the desk's second drawer, a ledger is removed. Jeremy glances through the meticulous writings.

I don't want to know about the family's finances, so I keep myself busy looking at the many books about fishing, kayaking, and parks in America.

With a sigh here and there, Jeremy doesn't say much more, but he writes some notes on a pad of paper on the desk. He rips off the page, puts it in the black book, and sticks both into his back jeans pocket. After putting the cat on the desk, he takes the ledger, opens a filing cabinet, gets out a large manila envelope, and inserts the notebook into it.

Next, he opens a closet, pulls out some file boxes, and sets them on the top of a credenza.

I ask if there's anything I can do, but he says no.

With Isaiah warily watching us, swishing his tail back and forth, Jeremy gets down on his hands and knees to access a floor safe that's well-hidden under the carpet. He knows the combination because, in seconds, the safe is opened. He pulls out a bunch of cash and asks me to count it. He removes all the other contents, mostly documents and certificates, and adds them to the ledger's envelope.

I count the bills and report: "$15,820.00." Wow, that's quite a bit of cash to have lying around the house. But I make no additional comment. It's none of my business.

"Looks like we'll have to stop by the bank. Didn't Zoey say that ten percent starts today?" He finds another envelope to carry the bills.

"Yes. Good idea."

Jeremy's handling this rather well, don't you think? Maybe going through this with him will help me deal with doing it myself. I don't know.

We don't go anywhere near the garage, but while Jeremy carries the cat throughout the house, searching for more cash and coins, I roll my scooter into the backyard and immediately notice the fruit trees and grape vines standing in perfect rows in the middle of the yard.

I pick up his mother's clothing, go back inside, and discard it in her bedroom closet.

While I'm in the room, I peek inside one of the nightstands next to their bed. There's a Bible in it, so I carefully pull it out. A small picture of two boys falls out. It's like the one on the mantel when Jeremy was little, but this one is smaller with tattered corners. I put it back and wonder if she, too, had faith in a God who I don't believe exists.

Next, I retreat to their kitchen and open the fridge, which smells a little stale. I find a box of baking soda, open it, and store it on one of the shelves, hoping it won't get disgusting to clean the next time Jeremy visits.

So much to do. It's overwhelming.

"What will you do with the house, Jeremy?" I ask as I get back in his SUV.

Before he answers, he puts Eyes back in his crate and collapses my scooter, putting it next to the animal.

He climbs inside the cab. "It's paid off, so I'll probably get rid of my apartment and move across the Valley. I mean, this was my house growing up. There're too many memories to give them up."

"That's a good plan. If you update it—like add current day conveniences such as internet and cable—it'll be more valuable."

"Yeah, the land is a lot of maintenance, and it's farther away from work and you, but Eyes and I could do okay here, once I get rid of some of the things I don't want."

He continues, "Last night, I asked my brother what to do, and he doesn't want to sell it either, so maybe I'll pay him off and keep it."

I think about how all the people left must deal with the mess of those who have disappeared. It's too much.

Viewer, is your list of things you have to do growing, too?

We hit the drive-through at Jeremy's bank, waiting almost an hour in line, and he makes the cash deposit. He asks me if I want to stop by work, but I decline since I'm worn out and my leg is starting to ache. We swing by his apartment on the way to mine; I remain in the front seat of his car when he unloads Isaiah and the cat's possessions. I've no qualms with him keeping the cat and don't bother saying goodbye.

When we return to my condo, it's after noon so we grab leftovers for lunch. I remark how tired I am and want to nap.

I tell Jeremy that I don't think it's important that he stays, since Zoey will be home in a few hours, and I can fend for myself now that I have the scooter. He's more than contented to comply now that he has a reason to go home.

After downing more Motrin, I bid him farewell and go lie down on my mattress, turning the volume low on the television for background news.

Before I drift off, my phone rings, and it's my sister.

"Hey, Silvia. How are you doing?"

"Fair. I can't get over the fact my babies are gone. It makes no sense. I'm trying to center on the positive, but I see none. I try to think karma will right the world, my world, somehow. But I have no closure."

"Yeah, it's hard," I tell her about visiting Aunt Amy's house, leaving out the Bible and email stuff. She thinks it's good that Jeremy took Isaiah. I mention his parents and the bonus banks are giving, plus the website to file missing reports.

"Thanks for the info. I'll get on both of those tomorrow."

We talk about our parents being stuck in Oregon, unable to travel, and how the Pacific Northwest has been devastated by the earthquakes. There's little positive news, and we both know it.

She says, "Oh, I'm going to email you some e-book links. They promote mindfulness involving being calm and learning to accept the unknown, especially during these trying times. I got them downloaded yesterday, and they're helping me look forward not backward."

"Thanks. Usually, I don't care for those books, you know that, but maybe I can skim through one or two."

Without thinking, I add, "I think I'm depressed. I'm despondent, probably because I'm overwhelmed with all the tasks of what to do, and I have it easier than others. I can't imagine being in Jeremy's shoes and dealing with everything about his parents' property from now on."

My sister doesn't confront my feelings but says, "At least, he wants to move into it. Imagine if he had to sell it. Think about all the mortgages that are going to go unpaid and homeowners defaulting on their loans. How will the missing people change the housing market? And what about the insurance issues involving them? Then think about the missing children. In Tom's and my case, we no longer have our babies, but Jack and Jasmine were adopted less than a year ago, so it's not like we raised them and knew them well like other parents. But oh, I do miss them. It breaks my heart."

"Yes," I respond, bothered about the idea of having a baby, our baby, and knowing he or she no longer exists. Which further depresses me, but I won't mention a word to her.

"But," Silvia adds, "I saw this article online. China has been making AI children—realistic-looking humanoids that can interact with you and act like a child who has the abilities of a three- or four-year-old child, with skills such as cleaning up, fixing things, and responding to commands. I told Tom, and he thinks we should investigate it, like get on a list now. With the entire world having no kids who are that young and us not being able to get pregnant, we had better order one soon. What do you say? I wonder what Dad and Mom would think."

"Hmm," I say, "that's something to consider, and it would help relieve some of the paternal and maternal angst after all the kiddos disappeared. And our parents would probably accept it, hoping you could get one soon."

We talk a little more, but I tell her I need a nap, so she lets me go.

After checking my wounds, including my swollen eye that now has tinges of greens mixed with the blues, I snuggle down in my comforter and have restless thoughts about robotic children who go berserk and take over the world.

I wake up around four and text Zoey, asking what her plans are. She quickly responds she's already on the 5 Freeway past the Getty Museum, whose parking lot is empty, so she should be home in less than an hour. We discuss dinner, and she suggests raiding her freezer and bringing something over to my place.

While scooting around the condo, I put my dirty laundry in the washing machine and start it, empty the dishwasher, and wipe down all the kitchen counters.

The key fob James gave Jeremy is left on the bar. I consider throwing it away as it has no use to me, but I push it aside, setting it next to our coasters. Maybe Jeremy wants it, but it should be tossed.

Zoey arrives a little after five with a bag of supplies. "How about steak? Does that sound good with asparagus and a salad? We should probably eat this stuff before it gets bad. I didn't want to stop at the store. It's almost been a week, and it's still a mess out there. Plus, I heard store shelves are not getting restocked...or maybe it's a rush on food. Crazy people." She starts putting the food away. "Oh, where's Jeremy? Upstairs?"

When I tell her he left me alone for a couple of hours, she's enraged. I counter that I'm a grown woman and I can easily take care of myself, then explain what I have done the last hour. I don't mention I haven't turned the laundry over. I also say she doesn't have to sleep here anymore, but she insists she wants to stay tonight.

Next, we work side-by-side preparing our meal. She tells me her meeting went well with the bosses and, on the QT, they will be setting up a digital card system for everyone to start using by the end of the month.

"Zoey, do you think this will stop all the hacking and stealing of identities?"

"Of course not, but it may deter it. However, it'll have info on the cardholder that includes their fingerprint ID to make it harder to duplicate. Also, within two or three months, they will expand to a visible tattoo with a chip that is inserted into the back of the hand to eliminate all thefts."

"Ha. But what if someone cuts off my hand, takes it, and scans it?"

"Funny you should mention that, as it was brought up. They explained that VPR, known as Vascular Pattern Recognition, which uses what's called near-infrared light to reflect or transmit images of blood vessels, has advanced its biometrics to include a human chip designed to work only with live blood, so it is tapped into the vein. No blood, no clearance on scanning the chip, which includes a tattoo on the skin that can be easily recognized."

"What do you think about it?" I question. "I mean, isn't that, like, prophetic from the Bible stuff Aunt Amy preached? Like what they call the 'Mark of the Beast'?"

"Well, I'm not completely gung-ho about it. I see its value but wonder if the system is getting a bit controlling. Seems we are all becoming slaves—if not to our electronics, then to the system that makes them."

She gets out a spatula from a drawer and says, "Oh, I didn't tell you—when I was walking over here from my place, I ran into Gus—you know, the pool guy with the nice tan?"

"Yes, didn't he ask you out once?"

"He did, but I told him I was unavailable. I mean, c'mon, men who maintain pools don't have much potential."

While I'm setting the table, a doorbell ring interrupts us, so Zoey answers it.

I rarely hear someone ring our bell—everyone I know always knocks unless it's a stranger.

"Hi, is Sarah here?"

Zoey is startled. She stops, then turns to me saying a young man is asking to see me. It's James. What's he doing here?

I tell Zoey to let him in. He enters, and I introduce the two.

Courteously, Zoey asks James if he would like some dinner.

Immediately, I evaluate if it's the right move.

He replies, "Oh, I'm sorry. I didn't realize what time it was. Thank you for the offer, but I better not, ma'am."

Zoey stops in the middle of plating the food. "Ma'am? Please, I'm not an old biddy. We have plenty of food. What male teen would turn down a steak? You're a growing boy and need the protein, kid. Please come sit down with us, at least."

Shaking my head in disbelief that this young religious fanatic is in my home, uninvited, I give up and join the conversation.

"James, have a seat next to me here in the dining room. We're talking about Gus, our complex's pool man. Anyway, Zoey, why did you mention him?" I return to the conversation as she pulls the roasted asparagus out of the oven.

"He's so mad! He says someone, obviously a male, left their swimming trunks in the jacuzzi—it must have been days ago. And they got sucked into the pump and broke the entire motor. I mean, who leaves their clothes in a pool? Who knows, maybe he was taken?"

She looks at both of us without talking and then soberly adds, "Yet, as I told you the first night when the disappearances happened, I wonder if it's we who are untaken."

I don't speak. The last thing I want to do is get James started on his Jesus talk.

But he puts his two cents in, saying, "Untaken? Yes, I guess I would say I'm untaken, too, like from the Rapture. Perfect description, Zoey. I—"

Flustered, I immediately cut him off. "James, why did you stop by?" I'm not ruining this meal by talking about religion.

After grabbing the third steak that was meant for Jeremy, Zoey places full plates of food in front of us and retreats to the kitchen to get hers.

James asks, "You know that flash drive I gave Jeremy?"

Yeah, that bunch of nonsense that belongs in the trash! But I hold my tongue and reply nicely, "Yes, is there something wrong with it?"

One can only hope.

"Oh, no, I need it back."

Zoey sits down with her plate. "What's this about? Did I miss something?"

I give her "the look." Yet, she pays no heed to me, giving James full attention.

"It's a USB drive with a bunch of Bible stuff on it, including what happened six days ago. And there's this video on it called *What Tribulation Saints Need to Know*, plus one on the Mark of the Beast, which is all about this man—the Antichrist—who says he can save us by establishing permanent peace."

He takes a breath, then continues, "But I know better; I know what happens next, because it was predicted two thousand years ago, and it's all coming true right before our eyes. After researching, I discovered the truth for the first time in my life, and I found answers that make sense. It's coming, and this gadget explains it all."

Smiling, he adds, "I'm so glad I turned my heart over to Jesus and believe He died on the cross, shedding His blood for my sins. I am—"

Suddenly, there is a loud beeping sound. It's the smoke detector!

I'm astonished. Are you, Viewer?

Zoey runs into our utility room and gets a broom.

I question her actions as I hold my hands—yes, including my wrapped hand—against my ears, wishing the noise would stop, but thankful it forced James to quit his sermonizing.

Zoey pulls out one of the bar stools at the kitchen counter, moves it by the oven, and climbs up on it. She wields the back end of the broom at the high ceiling's detector, trying to hit the little red button. After multiple tries, she hits her mark, and the unit goes dead.

Relieved the noise is gone, I calmly say, "James, please don't talk about God or Jesus in my home, or you will be uninvited here. I don't appreciate your proselytizing. You may be hyped up on your beliefs, but I, for one, want nothing whatsoever to do with them. And I'm sure Zoey feels the same."

If he's going fanatical on us, there's no way I'm going to pitch Carl to hire this kid.

Zoey climbs down off the chair and puts it back, along with returning the broom to where it belongs.

James replies, "Okay, Sarah. I understand. But please, I do need that flash drive back, if you still have it. It didn't download everything when I copied it, so I want the original again."

I motion to him its location by the coasters on the bar.

Without eating a bite of food, he gets up, retrieves the flash drive, and says casually, as if there was no disagreement, "It was nice to meet you, Zoey. Thank you for offering me dinner, but I think I should go now."

He leaves without another word, closing the door quietly behind him.

"Whew," Zoey sighs. "What was that all about?"

"The boy has found religion and is turning into a zealot. I had to shut him down, quickly."

"Oh, I see. He sure is enthusiastic about it," she replies.

"That is true, dear friend. And you know I don't go there, ever."

"Yep, that's true, too, Sar."

After we finish our meal, bag up the untouched steak, and clean up the kitchen, I'm still a little agitated, and Zoey knows it. She gets out the bottle of red wine she brought and pours herself a glass, then she gets out a second glass and offers me two small ounces, which I greatly appreciate.

When we settle in the great room, with both of us on the couch and me with my cast resting on a pillow on the table, she asks how my day was. I walk her through the hours, mentioning Jeremy finding all the cash and getting the bonus. I tell her about Aunt Amy and finding her clothing, but I omit all Bible talk. She agrees that the cat needs a home and approves of its new owner.

We talk for hours, mainly about her work and my pain level being incredibly low for someone who fell down the stairs. When she says that it "must have been a God thing," I shake my head, and she apologizes for the faux pas.

While on her second or third glass of wine, she intersperses Amir into her conversation—he did that, he did this, he's so wonderful—on and on. They hope to go out in two days, so maybe she'll cut back on the infatuation stage where one wants to know everything about the other and tell everyone he or she knows how perfect the person is for them.

When it's a quarter to midnight, we're talked out, so we both head to bed.

What a full day it's been.

I head to the bathroom to change into my pajamas. After brushing my hair, washing my face, and putting on moisturizer, I stare at myself in the mirror.

D? D, you had me going today!

Clever of us, wasn't it?

Twice, right? You shut Amy's laptop down and set off the smoke alarm. All remotely.

That we did, dear.

And I see what you mean about Zoey not being fully committed.

Correct. She's on the fence. Let's help her swing to our side, right? And you're the one who can help us do it.

Yes, and I'll do my best.

But it's James who bothers me the most. What will you do with him?

Don't you worry. We're working on that, and you may be the one to help us out.

That would be my pleasure, D.

Good girl. Oh, and your numbers are through the roof! We've tripled your viewing stats, something no one else has accomplished. We're all quite proud of you. You're doing an excellent job.

Thanks for the accolades. I like it when I do the right thing and help others; it makes me feel good.

There's a pause in our conversation. I wonder if D has left without saying good night.

No, we're conversing offline. We've agreed to send you a fifty-thousand-dollar bonus to thank you for your loyalty and persistence. It'll pop up in your bank account in the morning.

Wow, fifty-K? I didn't expect that. Thank you! It's so nice to be appreciated! You guys rock!

No, you deserve it. It's all about you and what you're accomplishing—for us. Thank you.

Good night, D of Numen.

Good night, Sarah Alexandria Colton with the handle of ValleyGirl.

I smile. You know everything. No one uses my middle name, not even my parents.

After I take a couple more Motrin, I crawl into my makeshift bed, realizing what a long, emotional day it's been.

Tossing, turning, and not able to sleep, I text Jeremy, telling him to enjoy his cat Eyes and to not come over until after noon because this girl is sleeping in for once.

~ **Day 7** ~

It's after 2 a.m., and I'm still not asleep.

I hear the air conditioner click on, meaning it's still warm outside.

For any late-night viewers here online with me, you know how you get overly tired, yet do not go to sleep?

I've got that problem bad right now. I'd get up and do something, but I don't want to wake Zoey by moving around. I try to count things in my head, as that usually works, but I give up.

Do you ever have that issue where when you lie down, your body doesn't seem to sink into the bed? As if it remains floating and not settled in. I've got that now. Plus, my casted leg is starting to itch. I want to move my toes, but they're confined. I want to flex my fingers, but I'm afraid to, like that'll make me step back in my healing process and force my hand to be put in a cast.

After scrolling with my right thumb through the news on my phone, I get weary of the glare and set it back down on the glass coffee table. I stare out the bay window that holds my prize orchids. I could get out of bed and water them since it's been about a week. But I'm too tired to move, to make the effort with my clunky cast.

The moon shines into the room, making it bright, so I adjust my blanket to cover my head. Maybe that's why I'm so wide awake—a full moon can make people wired, can't it? I could ask Alexa or research it online, but I lie hidden under the comforter, wanting to shut the world out.

I reflect on my husband. Denny was a good man; he genuinely loved and cared for me. I miss his embrace, his laughter, his love. I miss him. A sadness fills me. He's no longer here; I'm the one stuck in this darkened world, with no one to love like a soul mate, a partner—no husband like Mom and Silvia have...no, not even a cat as Jeremy does.

Depression soaks in and finds a home. I cry, mainly out of loneliness, but also out of despondency. There's little to be interested in, to care about now. How will I go on? How will I live? Does any of this matter? What's there to look forward to when my world has gone wrong?

By six o'clock, I finally doze off, thrown into a dreamless state of nothingness.

When I awake around nine, it's Zoey's heels clicking on the stairs that alert me. "Ugh! I'm late—late again!" she complains. "I've got another meeting at ten that I'll never make it to. Why do I do this? I need to rethink staying up late at night; it serves no purpose."

I greet her and try rolling over, but my cast is too heavy to rest on my good leg.

"I get this email, apparently at seven, stating I'm needed to work on implementing another new program. This one copies China's already established social credit system that was designed to make sure individuals and businesses comply with the country's laws and regulations. They monitor all transactions, both financially and socially, to rate their trustworthiness, reducing availability to one's credit and leading to fewer opportunities if they don't conform. They want the world to accept the concept to encourage sustainable climate goals, so America is getting on board."

"But how will it affect us—the banking clients?" I ask.

"If you don't pay your bills, are late in paying them, or are behind in alimony or child support, the bank will suspend your account. Freeze it. And give you an insufficient credit score that will affect every aspect of your life."

She opens the fridge, grabs a piece of sliced Swiss cheese, sticks it between a folded piece of bread, and takes a bite. Yuck.

She speaks, "But what bothers me is how they'll be able to judge you. Think about it. Let's say you love to drink whiskey, so you buy a bottle every week at the liquor store. What if you start drinking too much, buying it every couple of days instead of weekly? Will this social system void your credit card when you go to buy a new bottle? Will the card work at a different store? And if you can't use cash, how are you going to get the one thing you crave?"

She picks up her briefcase and stuffs her face again with the sandwich.

"Uh-huh," she says with a sigh. "It's all about control, and you know how we both feel about that."

When she's at the door, we talk about her not staying at my house tonight. She tells me that she's taken the sheets off the bed upstairs; they're on the washing machine. I wish her a good day, almost thankful again that I have a few hours completely to myself before Jeremy arrives.

At 9:30 a.m., a text pops up on my phone reminding me I have a video appointment with my primary care doctor in half an hour—an appointment I never made, but, like the banking system, healthcare now also controls me.

Knowing I'm dressed like a slob, I quickly go to the bathroom. Since I have no way to get to my closet upstairs and Zoey didn't bring me a clean wardrobe, I head to the utility room. When I see the pile of bedsheets on the washer, it dawns on me that I never turned the laundry over yesterday. I pull out the dampened clothes and put them in the dryer, hoping a few will be dry enough to wear during my online call.

I enter the kitchen and quickly do as Zoey does—grab a fork and forge through the last of the Thai food. I notice the forgotten lasagna in its sealed container. Thinking it's probably had its day, I put it in the sink to discard later.

Rushing back to the dryer, I struggle to put on one of Denny's work-logoed T-shirts and a pair of sweat shorts. The clothes are damp, but they're not too wrinkled.

With ten more minutes left until the call, I fire up my laptop on the kitchen counter and wait. I ponder if I've enough time to get my mail, which has not been picked up for over a week. I glance at the scooter and make my move; I pick up the keys on the table by the door and roll down the sidewalk to the end of our block of condos, where the mailboxes are located.

"*Hola*," I say to the Hispanic woman at the collection of boxes. I've seen this lady before; she lives on the opposite side of our unit, and we've occasionally talked with each other, always using the Spanish greeting.

"*Hola*. Oh my, you've been hurt! Are you okay?"

Oddly, her left arm is also wrapped up.

"Yes, I fell down my stairs. I'm healing better than I thought. What about you? What happened, if I may ask?"

"When the missings happened, I gashed my arm," she explains. "My grandchild disappeared while in her highchair. I tried to pull open the table part, and the metal bracket cut into my thin skin. My husband bandaged me up; hopefully, it won't get infected."

"I'm sorry." I open our box.

There's nothing in it. I notice there's nothing in hers, either. Yet taped to the metal containers are more than a dozen flyers. Mostly children with their names and pictures plastered on them. The plea to immediately call if you see them breaks my heart. Three other posters state, "Warning: the Rapture has happened."

"*Si*." She must have noticed my pause seeing the flyers. "Yes, so sad. I feel horrible for my friend's daughter. She couldn't find her two children. They were on the playground. She's still convinced someone took them."

No, not those girls—the ones I watched on that horrid day. Swinging and enjoying life, and then they were gone. I don't respond. I can't.

"Poor Marcia. She had a breakdown. She's in the hospital."

I nod, not knowing what to say.

Another flyer flaps in the breeze. A boy: eight years old. Blonde hair. Blue eyes.

After a minute of dead air, I ask, "Have you seen the mail carrier? Or do you know if maybe our boxes got hit again?"

"No, haven't seen them. I heard they stopped delivering because it's dangerous right now. Maybe next week they can deliver two or three days."

I reply, "Oh. Isn't their motto, 'Neither snow, nor rain, nor heat, nor gloom of night?' Guess a worldwide tragedy doesn't apply here."

"*Si.*"

I shake my head. Another problem to consider.

We say our goodbyes, with me telling her I have an appointment in a few minutes.

When I return to the condo, there are two minutes to spare. I move my body and the laptop over to the couch, put my leg up on a pillow, and let out a cleansing breath from all my rushing.

Clicking on the Open button online, I'm surprised to not see my regular doctor. Instead, it's Amir!

After greeting one another, he says, "Sorry, your primary hasn't been on staff for a few weeks. He and his wife went to India to visit her family with their children, and he was expected back at work yesterday, but no one's heard from him. So, you've got me."

I give him a big smile. "Ah, but it's nice to see you. I hear Zoey and you are going out again—tomorrow night, right?"

"Yes, that's the plan if I don't get called in. I asked for the evening off and told them not to put me on call, either." What a sweetheart; he cares about her.

"So, what about you? How do the foot and leg feel? Any issues we need to discuss?"

"So far, so good," I tell him. "My leg is starting to itch, and I don't like the feeling that my toes are restricted. And my hand is acceptable. It tingles a lot. Is it okay to move my fingers?"

"The itching is normal, and so is the feeling—or lack of it—in the toes. Your hand may be healing, so I'd recommend being cautious about moving the appendages as little as necessary for another week or two."

"Okay."

He asks, "Any other concerns? Are you sleeping?"

"Actually, no. The last two nights, I've been restless. I want to get up and move around, but it's too much work."

"I could order you a script for Zolpidem, which is Ambien, or you could try over-the-counter Melatonin."

"I'll pass on the prescription. I may have the herbal supplement; I'll try that instead."

"Good. Anything else to note?"

I feel a bit off sharing things about my personal life with this new flame of Zoey's, but I know the value of mental health, so I say, "I've been forgetful, which is not me. I think I'm depressed. I've suffered it before and worked it out in therapy, but this feels different—almost a forlorn feeling of hopelessness."

I briefly explain the shooting of the governor's son with the boy dying in my lap, saving James during the plane crash, losing my baby I had just learned about, and then my husband disappearing.

"My. You need something to center you from the teeter-tottering of volatile emotions."

"I confess—I took one of my husband's Ativan when I learned he disappeared. I'm not sure the drug did anything, but I didn't have an allergic reaction to it."

"That's an anti-anxiety med; I want to prescribe Sertraline, also known as Zoloft, and see how that works for you—it's for depression and normally takes a couple of weeks to kick in."

"Will it make me tired? I don't want to walk around like a zombie."

"No, not at all. Patients tell me they feel less of the high highs and low lows, so it helps them manage the day-to-day things. I'll start you on a mild dose, and we'll see how it works, okay?"

"Sure, as long as it doesn't alter my personality." I smirk at him on the screen. "I don't want to be dull. I aim to be like Zoey."

He laughs, and we finish our conversation, with him giving me an open-ended prescription to fill whenever I'm ready and me wishing him good luck on the date tomorrow night. I give my condolences about his mother dying, and he tells me his three brothers in Israel are helping his father and sisters deal with the loss.

He also tells me that, unfortunately, his youngest brother in the IDF (Israeli Defense Forces) was recently injured in the war and is recuperating at his dad's house. Since his mother is no longer alive, his father is playing nursemaid, which might be the best thing right now to keep him occupied.

I like Amir. He's bright and funny, and he seems to be compassionate and considerate of others. Although I see a tinge of reservation in his demeanor—almost a cautiousness—I approve of his relationship with my best friend.

After the appointment ends, I finish folding the now-dry laundry and move Zoey's sheets to the dryer. I clean up the kitchen, putting everything back my way instead of my guests' haphazard methods. I dump the left-over lasagna in the trash compactor, rinse the container, and stick it in the dishwasher. Finally, I add water to the flowers on the kitchen sill and dining room table and hand-water my orchids in the great room.

When all my domestic tasks are completed, I hop over to Adam's house.

I pass the lemon tree in a large clay pot situated between our two light blue doors angled ninety degrees from each other. With a couple of green lemons growing on the plant, it seems to continuously emit a fresh smell, but it needs to be watered.

When I knock on Adam's door and he answers, he's wearing a dirty T-shirt and boxers, appearing as if he woke up recently; his eyes are red and glassy. He offers a disoriented hello.

"Sorry to bother you, Adam, but I have another favor to ask you. You were so helpful last time—a godsend. So, I hate to ask again, but I think you're the only one who can help me." I try not to sound like I'm pampering his ego.

"Sure, neighbor. And don't you look spiffy with that cast get-up and arm wrap? Do you hurt much? Need some drugs or something?"

A red flag pops up in my head when he says it. I know he's a pharmacy tech with a lot of knowledge about medications, but it's the way he says it—like *he* has the drugs or something.

"No, well, sorta. I need a prescription filled, and I can't drive to pick it up. I guess I could ask Jeremy, but I prefer not to."

He must've read between the lines on my wording. "Your secret's safe with me. You put the Rx in at the Walgreens on Nordhoff Street and pay for it online, then when I go into work today, I'll process it and bring it to you."

"Are you sure? I mean, it's not an inconvenience?"

"Not at all, I have to be there from noon to nine today, so you're not putting me out at all. There's such chaos out there at the stores that are still open; you don't want to deal with it. I'll take care of you."

I offer my thanks.

"Yeah," he adds, "yesterday at work, UPS was making a delivery to the store, and the driver got accosted by a couple of thugs who took a bunch of his packages. We tried to patch the guy up, ya know, putting an antiseptic and dressing on his wounds. Anyway, he said Amazon now has two people in each of their trucks, and one is armed! That's crazy. He said they still make shipping products their priority, but they may no longer get your order there the next day—possibly a day or two later, to keep their staff safe during the crisis. I can't believe the rise in crime. I pack heat now wherever I go."

He rubs his eyes, saying, "Oh, and I've been staying overtime to keep up on the scripts, so I may not be home until ten or eleven to drop your prescription off. Is that okay? Is it something you need to start taking immediately?"

"No, it's not that important." I know he'll be able to see it's for depression. "Why don't you drop it off tomorrow morning, please."

Grinning, he replies, "Your wish is my command, lady."

With more small talk, I mention that I should water the lemon tree and my potted abracadabra rose bush by my gated patio. He tells me to wait while he leaves for a few seconds. When he returns, carrying a large, filled pitcher, he waters both plants.

With nothing else to chat about, I thank him for his graciousness and limp back to my home, thankful I've got such an odd but helpful neighbor who waters plants.

Inside my den of safety, I go online and order the meds, paying for it on my credit card, while wondering if Big Brother is also tracking my mental health.

With half an hour left until Jeremy comes over, the doorbell rings again. I instantly rule out Zoey and Jeremy, the door knockers.

Unexpectedly, it's Adam, now dressed in khaki pants, a polo shirt, and a light blue lab coat. Gone are the glassy red eyes.

It's obvious he's got something in the palm of his hand, but it's hidden from my view, as his arm is turned downward.

As he stands at my doorstep, he informs me he's on his way to work; he wants to run an errand and then start early since they're short-staffed.

Oddly, he's whispering, looking down the walkway, as if to see if anyone is coming. He asks me outright if he can come in for a second. Confused about his demeanor, I comply but wonder why.

He's inside the condo, standing next to the half-moon table.

"What's up?" I ask, almost afraid to know.

"Two things. First, you know how crazy it's getting out there, right?"

"Mm-hmm. The world's turned upside down," I silently question where this conversation is going.

"I want you to be protected, Sarah. I want my neighbor safe."

He pulls his arm up and opens his hand. It's a gun!

"Um, what are you doing with that?"

"It's a single stack Glock G43. It's my dad's—or was. I've got an identical one. So here, it's yours."

He hands me the weapon, shaft pointed downward.

I don't touch it. "Adam, I don't want it! I don't like guns."

"I figured that, but you need to be safe, and this'll protect you. It's small, lightweight, simple, yet effective."

He tries again to give it to me, but I refuse.

"The chamber has its magazine already loaded. It's ready to go."

He ignores my refusals. I keep shaking my head no.

"See how small it is? It's easy to carry in your purse or stash in your car. Just point and shoot."

Now I'm vehemently wagging my head from side to side.

"I anticipated you not wanting it, but you must be prepared—we all must be." He turns and opens the small drawer in the wall table and sticks the firearm inside, closing the compartment's door afterward. With a look of satisfaction, his eyes crinkle at the corners. "That settles that one. See, it wasn't that bad. Now grab it when you need it—if you need it."

I stumble over my words, surprised I agree to have a gun in my house. "O-okay, but I hope I never have to use it."

"Of course, but I feel better knowing two people—not just one—are now protected in this complex."

I expect him to take his leave, but he reaches into his front lab coat pocket.

"And here's the other thing." He puts a joint—yes, marijuana—on the table.

I'm more than mystified. Not at the joint, but that he plopped it down without care or concern. Or my approval.

"If you're ordering meds for something—I'm not judging you, but this may stop you from feeling over-anxious and edgy. It's been helping me more than I expected. And I have more if needed, of course."

All righty. This guy's got a different side to him than I expected. Maybe the loss of his dad put him over the top.

What do you think, Viewer?

He says, "I would rather be a hero than a villain, so if it's survival of the fittest, I aim to help my neighbor."

Then he abruptly declares he's off to work, while I visualize him in a seedy back alley, trying to score some pot from shady men in oversized dark leather coats and carrying small black guns.

When he leaves, I force myself to ignore the elephant in the drawer that I want to forget. I shut the table's drawer more tightly and hide the joint behind Denny's wallet and phone that I haven't touched since last week.

I spend the next half hour on my computer doing quick, easy tasks, such as cleaning up my emails. I go to *themissings.com* and file what I can on Aunt Amy and then check my online banking. There's a large balance in checking—which it shouldn't have if all the banks are still closed. Snickering to myself, I wonder if I'll need to contact an accountant come tax season.

I voice-text Daddy, Mom, and Silvia in our online group, giving them an update on my doctor's appointment, but I don't mention my prescription or the questionable drug. I ask if any of them have received any mail or Amazon boxes and get negative replies.

Also, I go on Facebook to check if Hal has responded; he has not, so I send another message about Amy's disappearance. I question mentioning the Bible verses she was reading, knowing they would stir up a hornet's nest.

I call Carl to give him an update, but Jeremy's arrival interrupts it.

While on hold as Brittany contacts our boss, I let my co-worker into my house. He appears more contented, maybe from taking care of the cat.

I point to my phone and mouth "Carl" as his voice echoes into the room.

"Hi, Boss! Jeremy and I are here on speaker. We wanted to touch base to see if anything's going on."

"Great to hear from you two. All doing well, considering?"

"We're hanging in there." Jeremy beats me to the answer.

"Yeah, it's a learning curve, but we're dealing with it." I try to convince myself.

After Carl checks on my health and well-being, he says, "Have either of you been to the stores lately? I hear there's been a run on those with food. Helen left her cart in the parking lot, without even going inside. I want an article about it. Are either one of you up for it yet? I know you, Jeremy, are off work still for a few more days, but..."

Jeremy interrupts him. "Got you covered on that one already, Boss. I had to go to Petco before I came over to Sarah's. What a mess. The store still has some stock, like cat toys and generic dry and wet food, but all the high-end items are gone. I'm unsure if they were sold out, stolen, or even kept in the back somewhere. Only out of curiosity, I took a couple of still shots of the empty shelves. I'll be glad to send those over; maybe you can use them."

"Great. Thanks, Jeremy. Good job for thinking about the news wherever you go, whatever you do."

"That's not all. You'll want to hear this." Is he teasing us with the story? He does this sometimes, and it drives me crazy.

"Cut to the chase, Jeremy. I don't have all day," demands our boss.

"Okay, okay. I walked to Vons Supermarket next door and stopped by a trash can, checking my phone for texts. In the parking lot, there were three males—guessing in their late teens to twenties—on mopeds or e-bikes. They also had AK-47s strapped to their backs, same as that gang we saw under the overpass, Sarah."

"Yes, I remember, they were hassling the homeless who camped there."

Jeremy continues, "Right. Well, these guys were just as intimidating. I pulled out my phone and started a video. I safely stood by a pillar, a little out of their view, and kept my camera down by my waist. Next, there were two similarly dressed guys on their bikes coming out of Vons. Yup, riding them out of the store! Full bags were strapped around their arms as they raced out of the automatic doors. All five bikers took off down San Fernando Mission Boulevard, screaming and laughing."

"Wow," I say. Going food shopping is no longer safe.

Carl is silent for a few seconds. Then he adds, "'There is a way which seemeth right unto a man, but the end thereof are the ways of death.'"

"Boy, that's a true saying," says Jeremy.

"Yes, I had to look it up online. My mother used to quote this verse; I didn't realize it came from Proverbs 14:12 in the Bible."

Of course, I cringe at Scripture being referenced, but Jeremy draws me back into the conversation by saying, "After the incident, I went inside the store and taped a few of the customers' responses. They all seem scared and concerned. Yes, a lot of shelves are empty. People are panicking by stocking up on anything they can get their hands on, afraid the food chain has been suddenly disrupted. One couple was in tears—you'll see it in the video. The husband has celiac disease, so they've got to be extra careful, finding only gluten-free food, which is getting harder to procure."

"How sad." I sense this is getting increasingly out of control. Mainly because people aren't working together to help the greater good.

Viewer, what do you think? Are you experiencing these shortages? Have you had to deal with any?

"Yes," interjects Carl. "Helen said she's heard the same thing, about there being no food." He adds, "Great job, again, Jeremy. But I must go, so I'll pick and choose from those pics and videos if you send them to me. Knowing your disdain for writing, can you have Sarah assemble some bullets for me?"

"Sure," we both reply simultaneously.

"Oh," says Jeremy, "sorry, I had to use my smartphone camera during it all; it may be grainy, but it's better than nothing."

"No worries, and thanks. Get to work and let me know when you two want more of it. And Jeremy?"

"Yes," he answers as he looks quizzically at me.

"What were you doing in the cat aisle at Petco?"

Jeremy explains, and Carl chuckles; he can't believe the guy has a pet, either.

When we hang up, I go to my still-opened laptop and type in the information Jeremy gives me. I send the data to Jeremy's email, and within minutes, we fulfill our mini-project.

Since we both haven't eaten lunch, Jeremy walks into the kitchen, opens the cupboard, and pulls out a can of tuna.

As he puts together another amazing edible mixture, we talk about food shortages, shipments, and how Amazon is determined to deliver its goods by being armed. Since food is the current topic of the hour, we decide we should go over to Aunt Amy's house and rummage for it, bringing back whatever staples we can find to keep a good stock here.

Ten minutes later, we're driving over to Amy's duplex. Sepulveda Boulevard is emptier than our last drive. With no school, only a few businesses open, and not many commuting to work, it reminds us of COVID days when everything shut down. Although it's eerily quiet, it's almost a relief not to see people.

After I give Jeremy Denny's keys to move Amy's Toyota Camry, he unlocks the car with the fob; we both notice its gas panel's lid is open. We think someone could have stolen her gas. Shaking his head in disbelief at the desperation of thieves, he moves her car to the street and backs his Suburban into her driveway.

When he goes to unlock the nearby kitchen back door, we both notice it is ajar. It looks like someone has taken a tool or something to the lock and door jamb.

I give my friend a "should we go inside?" look, and he nods in the affirmative, intertwining the keys in between his fingers so they stick out. It's a pathetic weapon, but, at least, it's something.

I didn't bring my scooter on this trip—I had completely forgotten it. So, my good hand stays in touch with Jeremy's back as I drag my casted foot along the cement. I'm getting used to walking without a wobble, even though it's uncomfortable with its plastic heel insert forcing my hip upward.

When we enter the home, silence abounds. There's no movement. Some of the kitchen cabinets are open.

Jeremy picks out a Santoku knife from the kitchen counter's butcher's block. Letting go of Jeremy, I select a cleaver, noting there's no pointed end to stab someone with.

We slowly, quietly tiptoe into the living room. I make sure not to thump the cast on the wood flooring.

The flatscreen is the only missing object.

Jeremy motions me into the dining room.

The laptop and phone are gone; the Bible remains closed on the table.

We silently walk down the hallway.

Without entering, we see the first bedroom has its nightstand open with its contents spilled on the floor. A closet is open with some clothes discarded.

No one is in the room.

We stop by the single bath. Jeremy points his knife at the closed plastic shower curtain. He rapidly pulls it back as he wields his knife in the air, prepared for the attack. I stand, ready as I can be with a broken foot and wrist.

No, nothing there.

Only two bedrooms left to check. The tension in me ramps up. I stumble when my cast—the outer left ankle side—whacks into the hall wall, making a cracking sound.

Jeremy growls and rushes to the end of the hall where the two bedrooms intersect at a T. He glances back and forth quickly, and then he gives me a thumbs up that all's clear.

We both let out exhausted sighs.

Amy's bedroom has no bedspread on the bed. Her jewelry box is empty; her bureau drawers' contents have been dumped.

The other room, which holds a sleeper sofa, coffee table, small rolltop desk, and chair, appears messier: several desk drawers on the floor, the closet open with papers strewn about, and books removed from their bookcase and tossed on the carpet.

I enter the room and notice in the closet that there are stacks of books—maybe a hundred in neat rows, except for one row that has been disturbed and spilled into the room. All black leather-bound Bibles. Bibles! Grr.

There's a small business envelope resting on top of one of the uniform stacks. On its front is my first name—yes, Sarah. I drop the cleaver and pick up the note.

No, not now. I refuse to read this now. I know what it's going to say. I should throw it away or burn it, but I stuff it in the side pocket of my shorts.

"Find anything?" asks Jeremy. "Looks like this room got hit the hardest. Can you tell if anything's gone?"

I point to the stack of Bibles, tossing him one that he catches. "There's a ton of these. Want one? Like they're worth anything."

He puts the book on the coffee table, ignoring my comment. "I think whoever it was did a grab and go—they entered, searched for electronics and jewelry, wrapped them up in her bedspread, and split, off to another victim's house."

With no bad guys in the house, we retrace our steps back to the kitchen, where I mention the carport has a storage unit behind it; I tell him to use the key on the keychain to see inside the outbuilding.

Meanwhile, I open all the cupboards and pull out everything edible that has a decent shelf life, organizing it on the dining room table.

When I haven't heard from Jeremy for a while, I duck my head out the back door. He tells me he found a treasure trove of MREs (Meals Ready to Eat) and canned goods in sealed plastic containers, dry goods in burlap sacks, toilet paper rolls, and a myriad of untouched but highly organized supplies.

I wince, realizing Aunt Amy was a prepper who was prepared for a catastrophe like this, something Denny and I never thought about.

After four hours of purging the house, we head back to my condo with the Suburban fully loaded.

We decide to put his SUV in my garage overnight but remove all perishable items by storing them in the extra refrigerator/freezer in the garage. The last thing we want is our precious cargo to be stolen. We also agree that he takes my car to his apartment for the night, and hopefully, thieves won't hit it again.

Right when we turn onto the side road to my building, both our phones ding simultaneously. I pull mine out; there's an emergency update that an atmospheric river is approaching in the next four to six hours that will contain high winds and an abundance of rain.

Aha. Here we go again! Southern California is known for its earthquakes, Santa Ana high winds that often cause fires, and triple-digit temperatures, but, seriously, more rain? Sigh. Double sigh.

By the time Jeremey switches the cars around and makes us fajitas, using the untouched steak from Zoey and Amy's fresh vegetables and tortillas, it's after six o'clock, and we are exhausted.

When the kitchen is put back in order, Jeremy collects my car keys and bids me goodbye, mentioning Eyes has been alone most of the day and he doesn't want the cat to be afraid during the storm.

Although fatigued from all the physical work, I'm happy we accomplished so much. By seven, I take my smelly, dirty clothes off and put them in the washing machine, remove Amy's note from my pocket, and place it on the half-moon table, still not interested in knowing what it says.

After wiping my body down with a wet washcloth, I'm back in my pajama shirt with my face clean and my teeth brushed, wanting to veg out and watch the news or an old movie, hopefully dozing off at the same time.

Adjusting the now-clean white couch throw on my body, I try putting my cast on the sofa under a stack of pillows instead of on the glass table. It's a challenge to get comfy; I try several positions using pillows holding up my arm and under my head.

I turn the television on to a channel that specializes in global news. The newscaster speaks:

> Klaus Schwab of the WEF is continuing his plans for 'humanocracy,' which is the fusion between our physical, digital, and biological dimensions. Our new 'Intelligent Age' will be driven by the Fourth Industrial Revolution, where humankind will enjoy many more opportunities and possibilities due to technology. We hope to see a new dawn of human civilization—one that harmonizes technology with the needs and aspirations of humanity and where artificial intelligence, robotics, the Internet of Things, 3D printing, genetic engineering, and quantum computing become the foundations of daily life, yet are guided by respect for human values, creativity, and the natural world.

After asking Alexa to lock the door and turn off the lights, I consider the broadcaster's words. What he said was a mouthful, wasn't it? But the idea of a new world where everything clicks and works together with the help of technology would be ideal. It's like we are getting a second chance to restart the world and make it better this time.

Don't you agree, Viewer?

The television screen flickers as the wind howls outside.

Looking out the bay window, I see water running down the glass. The rain has arrived, and it's getting nasty outside.

A text pops up on my phone. It's Zoey: *Storm has hit. Staying onsite at the Bunker Hill office to shelter in place. Will sleep in tenants' suites. Don't like Downtown LA, especially this high-rise. Safer than hydroplaning on the 101 or driving my Audi through flooded streets.*

Wow. This must be quite a downpour.

OK. Be safe. Keep me posted, I reply.

Will do. I'll look for food in the downstairs shops.

Now that I've mastered the voice-texting option, it's easier to converse, so we message back and forth for a half hour.

Zoey tells me Amir wants to take her out tomorrow to a nice restaurant, but none of them are answering their phones, so they're considering other options.

I tell her about my doctor's appointment—not mentioning Zoloft—and our conversation about his family.

She writes that Amir's older brother walked off his job as an officer in the IDF, saying something about how he wants to be something like an Israeli missionary. Amir is upset as he knows their father is not happy about it, and neither is his injured brother, who had his leg blown off kicking an IED away from some Palestinian kids in the Gaza Strip. Yeah, war and its repercussions are a nightmare.

When we end the texting, I call my parents.

Without Daddy being on the line, Mom tells me that the neighbors in the eight homes in their cul-de-sac are banded together and have blocked their street entrance with their SUVs to deter other vehicles from entering. One of the men wants to set up around-the-clock guards to secure the area, yet she doesn't think there are enough of them to do it, and my father is against the idea.

I tell her what we gleaned from Amy's house, and she agrees it's a good idea to stock up. Since Daddy has always been a collector, she believes they have plenty of goods in the basement that should last weeks, if not months.

I hang up the phone, hoping this all is temporary. I'm frustrated due to all the negative news, so I get up and go to the bathroom.

D? Time to talk a second?

Yes, Sarah.

Am I going to be okay? It seems like the world's falling apart around me. I don't like it.

Understandable. Hang in there. It won't last forever. Things will go to a normal state soon. You must be patient.

But I don't like it. I feel lost. And my body being broken doesn't help. I can't do anything. I can't sleep. I can't get comfortable. I'm not me like this. I'm overwhelmed with everything that needs to be done, yet I don't know how to do any of it. And there are crazies everywhere. I don't know how much more I can take.

We know. It's been rough for everyone.

But am I safe here? In my own home? It's been a week since the world shifted with the missings, and look at all the disarray that's occurred so far. How much more can we take?

We're here for you; we'll always protect you. You know that. And now you have protection, thanks to Adam.

I hate guns. I'll never touch that thing.

Never say never, Sarah. You don't know the future. You don't know what you're truly capable of. You're only going through a rough spot. The anti-depressant will help center you and bring back the real you. All will be fine—you need to believe that. You need to believe how strong and determined you can be.

I've got such a foreboding feeling. I feel lost. Alone. Will I be able to survive this? Will I be able to handle it all and take care of myself?

Yes. You'll be fine. You are fine. And you have plenty of money to stay safe and alive. You have Numen; we'll be on your side as long as we work together as one entity.

Thanks for the encouragement. Maybe tomorrow I'll feel better once I start those meds. Yes, tomorrow's a new day.

That it is. And things will get better. Be patient; wait and see.

After my escalating viewer ratings are praised, we say good night, and I climb into bed, hoping things will start to improve.

Sleep continues to evade me, mainly because of the lightning and thunder that accompany the torrential downpour and swirling winds buffeting the nearby window.

~ Day 8 ~

It's 12:05 a.m., and I'm still awake. The long hours of listening to the pounding rain and wind give me jitters, so I toss and turn.

At 12:08 a.m., my phone lights up the room.

Jeremy: *I need your help.*

Me: *What's wrong?*

Jeremy: *A tornado took off my apartment roof.*

Me: *No! We don't get those in LA, do we? R U OK?*

Jeremy: *Water's everywhere. Glad I'm on the bottom floor. Can't stay at my parents'. Nowhere to go. Can I crash at your place?*

Me: *Yes. Come over. Now! Wow.*

Jeremy: *Eyes too?*

I pause before I respond: *Yes.*

He thanks me and says he should be over in less than an hour, once he can gather up the cat's gear and his prized video equipment, most likely stated in that order of priorities.

When there's a faint tap on my front door, I limp over and unlock it. My friend is drenched, carrying his beloved cat in his crate in one hand and a bag of cat supplies in the other.

He hands me the bag and puts the crate down, asking me for permission to open it. Warily, I consent, and the cat is more than happy to be freed. The furry thing immediately rubs his body and tail around Jeremy's sandals and bare legs.

My friend removes his wet shoes and sticks them next to my clogs under the half-moon table.

"Go in the bathroom and get dried off with those towels on the rack, please. Now. Then go upstairs and find a dry T-shirt and gym shorts of Denny's." I snap the commands. Seems I have no reservations about telling this male friend of mine to go through my missing husband's closet. Have I come that far in the grieving process?

While he completes his assignments, he explains how the storm has devastated most of his building and everything is soaked.

Eyes has made himself at home by jumping up on my mattress. I shoo him away, but he retreats to the wood bay ledge where my orchids are kept. Glaring at the feline, I reiterate that I'm the owner of this home, and I'm the one in charge. Not him.

"I've never been through a tornado. It was incredible. There was this deafening rumble, then a terrifying screech that sounded like nails being ripped out of the walls, and then loud thuds of flying debris hitting things. Poor Eyes was terrified."

Now dried off, Jeremy looks better. He takes the cat bag into the kitchen, assembles its contents on the floor by the refrigerator, and sets up the litterbox in the utility room. "Where is he, anyway?"

My eyes gravitate to the ledge at the bay window, and I grumble. The cat is wedged between two large white pots and staring placidly at the two of us.

The storm rages on.

Right when we both sit down on the couch, there's a flash of lightning that's ultra-bright, followed immediately by thunder that tremendously shakes the windows. The lights blink off and on while the glow ring of Alexa flickers.

Jeremy jumps off the couch and runs into the kitchen to look out from the window above the sink.

The feline, emitting a loud hiss, scampers over and sits on my lap. I try to move him off me, but he won't leave.

Not wanting to be scratched, I become a statue.

"Wow. That bolt hit the swing set!" Jeremy screams. "Both seats are toast, and their plastic has melted. The metal is all blackened. I don't think they're on fire. Looks like none of the other playground equipment was touched."

"Amazing." I remember how that swing set was the beginning of the horror.

Then, to make things more dramatic, the electricity goes out.

Jeremy sighs. "Great." Sarcastically, he adds, "Time for a little romance with candles?"

With my direction, he gets a flashlight out of the kitchen bar drawer. He brings it, along with the two candles from the dining room table and an electric lighter over to the glass table. Light is added to the dark room.

I thought I was on edge before. No. I'm amped up now.

Denny and I have gotten used to the Valley's rolling blackouts, so emergency items are always readily available in our home. He kept telling me he wanted to install a generator in the garage, but he never got around to it.

Whenever the electricity goes out, I feel a loss of control. I don't like it. I need to calm down, and alcohol may not be the best choice. And having this lump of wet fur plopped on my lap doesn't help. I refuse to pet him.

"I've got an idea," I say as Jeremy heads to the couch. "Go to the half-moon table. You'll find a little something behind Denny's wallet and phone; it may help our nerves, or, at least, mine."

He picks up the joint Adam gave me and turns to me, smiling, "No way. This'll definitely help, but I'm not so sure Eyes will take a puff."

I explain where it came from, and we both acknowledge the guy has some unique characteristics. As Jeremy lights up and hands me the joint, he carefully removes his cat, who had gotten quite comfortable on my thighs.

After a couple of hits, my tension and stress have taken a well-needed vacation. Also, Jeremy is more relaxed, more mellow. This may have been the smartest thing we've done during the crisis.

"Oh, how's my car? Any more slashers stop by it?" I tease.

"Naw, I parked it next to a Mercedes; that one got hit, but yours didn't."

"Cool. Plus, they probably saw the stick shift and didn't know how to drive it."

We talk about how we both learned to drive a stick, our first experience taking drugs, and our worst experience being on drugs or drunk. Thoughtless stuff.

As Jeremy pets his cat, he starts singing, "I've Only Got Eyes for You," followed by naming all the different singers who sang it going back to 1934, which include the Flamingos, the Lettermen, and Art Garfunkel, to name a few. His uncle was a fan of the song, so he repeated its words and history often when Jeremy was a boy.

Of course, we challenge each other with songs containing the word "eyes" in their title: "Can't Take My Eyes Off of You" by Valli, "Gypsy Eyes" by Hendrix, "Lyin' Eyes" by the Eagles, "Ocean Eyes" by Eilish; it goes on and on.

By three a.m., we decide we're done and blow the candles out. Yes, the electricity is still not working.

Viewer, what's it like where you are? Are you okay? Does pot relax you like it does me—or do you even use the stuff?

Jeremy takes the throw, adds some pillows, and lies down on the couch with his head near my bed. I stretch out on the mattress.

In the dark, the rain continues to dump on my condo. The sound is loud and annoying, but in the room, it's too humanly silent. Alone silent. Too dark. No electricity between us. Lonely.

"Jeremy? You still awake?"

"Uh-huh."

"You're welcome to come over here. It's much more comfortable than that couch. I know, I've tried both, and that one's not cozy."

"Do you mind?" It's timidly spoken.

"No, come on over." I pathetically croon some of the words of the 1965 song by the Drifters'. "But you'll have to crawl over me because I can only lie on my left side. The cast is too heavy to sling over my right leg."

Awkwardly, he climbs over the end of the mattress and wedges himself between the bay window ledge and me. The animal copycats Jeremy's entrance but reclines on the windowsill.

"That's better. Thanks, Jeremy."

My good hand grabs his wrist and pulls it around my waist; I hold it to my stomach, and he cleaves to me as we both fall asleep. The human touch we both yearn for soothes and comforts us. There are no words to explain it.

Finally, I'm at peace and the calmest I've been for days.

No. Not the doorbell.

I see my bed partner leap off the mattress, quickly working his way around me, trying not to touch my cast.

Still half asleep, I get up as best as I can and look at the clock. 10:25 a.m.

Jeremy rushes to the door and opens it partially.

Adam is standing outside.

"Oh, hi, Jeremy." He sees my friend's casually dressed and barefoot. "Is Sarah available?"

"Here I come." I attempt to get off the bed, but my legs haven't woken up yet.

"Um, sorry. I didn't know you two were a thing. Not that I'm inferring anything; that's none of my business."

Jeremy is not thrilled about my neighbor's insinuation. "No, Adam. It's not what you think. My apartment roof blew off in the tornado last night. I had to go somewhere."

"That makes sense. I heard about one touching down in Mission Hills. Several died. So close by."

"Yes. My apartment is history."

When I'm closer to the front door, Jeremy opens it wider. "Oh, Sarah, remind me to check my video camera. When the electricity went out last night, it was awfully dark outside, but I did manage to take two videos showing the sky cracking with lightning. I need to go back over today to videotape the apartment damage."

I nod my approval, then give our guest my full attention. "Adam?"

"Oh, yeah. Here's the prescription I picked up for you. It's all there."

"Thank you." I grab the bag but don't look inside it. I'm embarrassed discussing my medication with these two men.

Neither one speaks.

Adam breaks the ice: "Glad the power came back on this morning. At least, it wasn't out long. Still, parts of the Valley are without it."

Jeremy says, "Yeah, that's good to hear. I'm sure Mission Hills is still blacked out. It went off at my place before the tornado hit."

He and Jeremy chat for a few minutes until Adam says, "Well, I must go; work's calling me again."

He rubs his nose as if wiping away moisture.

For a mere second, the thought of him snorting a line of cocaine fills my head.

Viewer, did you catch that? No, I'm not trying to accuse him of being a druggie, but I'm starting to wonder. Are you?

As Adam leaves, I thank him again for helping me out.

When he's gone, I don't mention the medication to Jeremy, but take the bag into the bathroom, read the bottle, and ingest the first one to make my days ahead look brighter.

As I enter the great room, Jeremy declares he's hungry and is already whipping together French toast and feeding his cat.

Our conversation is light. We know we did nothing to be ashamed of last night. It was needed—a healing of our tattered souls. I don't want it to be uncomfortable between us, and I doubt Jeremy does either. We're friends—*only* friends.

According to the man's explained routine, he asks, "Alexa, what are the five most popular news items for today?"

She replies:

> To date, over one point five billion children are considered to be missing around the world. Almost eighty thousand people died in the two Pacific Northwest mega-earthquakes days ago, which have an estimated damage of over three hundred billion US dollars. China has bombed Taiwan again, causing multiple casualties. The dollar has dropped over twenty percent since last week with the Dow Jones also plummeting eighteen percent since the market opened yesterday. In local news, the County of Los Angeles suffered an unusual tornado last night, killing seventeen people.

We listen to the news silently, offering our respect to those who have lost their lives.

Later, we map out today's chores: collect items from Jeremy's destroyed apartment, take videos/pictures of the building's damage and surrounding areas to send to Carl, and unload Amy's loot, putting it upstairs in Denny's office where it wouldn't be noticeable by anyone visiting me.

After breakfast and changing our clothes, I explain to Jeremy that I will not allow his cat free reign in my house when I am not here. He knows I am serious, so he puts Eyes in his crate, repeatedly telling him to be a good pet and that we will only be gone for an hour or two. The animal and his crate are placed on my bed, angled so Eyes can look out the window.

We take Denny's BMW X3, because it has more space in the back than my VW and we still haven't emptied the Suburban.

We note the damage done by the storm around my complex with trash cans displaced in the side street, palm trees blocking pathways, large eucalyptus trees uprooted, and phone cables down.

When we arrive at Jeremy's place, it's more of a disaster. The three-story building has no roof and one side of the twelve units is gone, its entire side wall of all three floors missing. It looks like when Silvia and I had a dollhouse and could view each room.

When I ask Jeremy if anyone died, he says none in his building, but he heard a family of seven didn't make it in a building that collapsed two blocks over.

I say, "Oh my, your place is totaled. Feel free to stay at my house until you can figure out what to do next."

"Thanks. I'd stay at my folks', but, like I told you, I can't be there alone, yet. My apartment mess is another paperwork bad dream. How much more can I take? It's getting ridiculous. I feel like I'm hanging on by a thread. Insurance companies are going to hate me."

"Yeah, I know. And none of it makes sense. As Zoey said, it just won't stop."

With it still lightly raining, I wrap a plastic trash bag around my leg and use my scooter to follow him through the damp house, complete with soaked carpet that squishes whenever you step or roll on it.

Before we pick up some of the possessions of his life, he takes videos of the inside and outside of the building. I grab a few stills with my Nikon that I brought along.

For over an hour, we work silently as we gather up his important memories and stack them in the SUV. Although it's mainly his cherished video gear, we add to the collection all perishable and non-perishable food.

On the way back, he says, "Do you think it would be wise to keep all the stuff at your house? I mean, my parents have all that secluded land and buildings. It's off the grid. We both could easily live there."

"I don't know. It's a good idea—like a safe house that we could go to whenever needed. But I'm unsure if I want to live that remotely. I mean, c'mon, your dad doesn't have internet."

"I understand where you're coming from, but I worry about your place being broken into since it's at the end of the building. What if someone came in through your bay window or broke in through the garage? And then took all the food we've collected?"

"Let me think about it, okay?" I speak the words tersely. "Okay."

By the time we get back home, we have two fully loaded vehicles. I agree we need to put it all someplace safe, so I concur most of it should be moved to his parents' house.

When we enter the condo, Jeremy immediately releases Eyes from his prison; the cat did fine and didn't seem too riled about being confined. Then Jeremy uploads our videos and pics, and I send Carl text messages about last night. I'm sure Jeremy will also use the information when he contacts his insurance company.

Knowing I can't be one of the drivers, our first run across the Valley is with the Suburban. Jeremy insists on taking Eyes in the crate. I question the decision because I think he is already getting too attached, but I understand he doesn't like my no-cat-rooming-in-the-house-alone rule.

We decide to try the 405 Freeway, but we must get off at Victory Boulevard and backtrack because the Sepulveda Basin is flooded due to the storm, blocking the freeway interchange to the 101. Jeremy has to drive the SUV around a tanker truck that has jackknifed on Woodley Avenue.

When we get to his parents' gate, he tells me the password in case I need it. Well, it's not like I'll be driving anytime soon, but I appreciate his thoughtfulness.

Instead of parking the SUV in the driveway between the house and garage, we bear to the right and take a narrow windy road to an extremely large—we're talking huge—shop with several tall doors and a metal roof. Nearby there are other outbuildings such as a pole barn and a couple of carport areas covering some vehicles and farm equipment.

Jeremy pulls up to one of the large doors, gets out, uses a key to unlock the lock, and gets back into his vehicle.

When we drive inside the building with a completely cemented floor, there's a motorhome at one end of the building, flanked by a fishing boat, a speed boat, two kayaks, and two ATVs. The other end of the shop contains an office with stairs leading to the second floor.

After turning off the car's engine, he says, "I'll show you around."

"I didn't know your parents had all this! It's wonderful and so spread out. It's like living in the 1960s with all the dated decor."

"Yes, it was fun growing up here with all the toys. As I said, Dad loved the outdoors, and Mom loved to watch us enjoy it. Such great memories."

A shadow of sadness covers his face until he puts Isaiah's crate on the ground and lets the cat roam inside the shop. Curious, the animal smells the cool, flat ground, but he stays within a few feet of Jeremy the entire time.

My friend leads me to the office, and we step into a room with a desk and lots of filing cabinets with more framed photographs of nature on the wall. Of course, Eyes follows closely behind us.

"Upstairs is a mini-apartment, complete with a small kitchen and full bath. Dylan and his wife stay there when they visit."

Next, he takes me to another area where there's a locked door. After he opens it, he escorts me inside. It's a storage room with shelving from the ground to the high ceiling. It's packed more than half full of labeled boxes.

"We'll put Amy's and my stuff here and sort it later."

Although I'm disabled and can't lift anything, I stay by the back of the Suburban and line up Amy's boxes, sealed plastic containers, and crates so Jeremy can put them into the storage area with a hand truck. Eyes trails Jeremy's every step.

When we are done, he scoops the cat up in his arms. "C'mon, let's look outside. We won't go far because the scooter won't work that well on the gravel or dirt."

To the right of the building are several walnut and oak trees. One of the oaks has a treehouse in it, complete with wood slats hammered into its trunk to use as steps.

Jeremy sees where my attention wanders. "Yes, Dad, Dylan, and I built that. Isn't it cool? I read once that forty percent of Americans had a treehouse growing up. That seems high to me. Did you?"

"Hardly, but that's pretty cool. I've never been in one."

"Well, once your body heals, that'll be a priority."

With one arm holding the cat, he points to other parts of the land: an orchard, a vineyard, and a barn. He tells me they had horses at one time when they were young. His mother loved them.

When the short tour is over, Jeremy returns Eyes to his crate, and we take the SUV back to the front of the house.

"I think we should switch cars since mine's getting low on gas. Stay here, and I'll get Mom's keys for her Prius. We can use that one for a while. But, if you can, maybe you can get your scooter out of my SUV?"

While he's gone, I do as he suggested, noting both his parents' cars are still parked in front of the garage.

As he comes out of the house, he hits a fob. His mom's car trunk opens, and I slide the scooter in while he deposits Eyes and his crate into the back seat. He opens the crate door open, yet Eyes stays inside it during the entire drive.

On the way back to my condo, there's not much traffic. Again, Jeremy brings up moving to the Encino house. And again, I tell him I'll think about it. I'm not ready to make a big move, not yet.

Don't push me, Jeremy.

Since his mom's car is a hybrid and can be plugged in when it's low on gas, we determine it should be kept in the garage with the BMW, so neither gets stolen. Jeremy moves my VW to the complex's parking lot, and we hope it won't get more slashed and trashed.

After grabbing a quick lunch of sandwiches made with meatloaf from Jeremy's freezer, we begin the second trip to his parents'. This time we take Denny's SUV. Again, Eyes becomes a crated passenger.

While driving down Haskell Boulevard, a school bus whizzes by us, weaving in its lane.

I quickly pull out my phone and aim its camera at the bus, which looks like it carries a half dozen rowdy teens out for a joyride. When we stop at a red light, we're parallel to the bus.

We both think it's a stolen vehicle, as no adults are visible on board.

I keep the camera on my lap while our car idles, hoping the teens don't look down and notice it.

When both vehicles start at the light and pass the wide cross street, the bus driver loses control and veers into our lane. It sideswipes the length of the Beemer, scaring all its occupants, including a screeching cat.

Yes, I've got the incident on video.

Jeremy hits the brakes on the SUV as the bus is floored, fleeing the scene while leaving a puff of black smoke plummeting out of its exhaust tailpipe.

While Denny's vehicle is stopped in the lane, Jeremy gets out and examines the damage, using several choice expletives. He checks on Eyes, who seems to have used up one of his lives and is somewhat calm. There's nothing we can do about the hit-and-run but send the video to Carl to see if the bus and driver can be tracked down.

Due to Jeremy's growing anger about filing more paperwork with insurance companies, the remainder of the drive is quiet.

When we get to the shop and Jeremy goes through the same routine with the cat, I inspect the mango-colored paint covering the length of the driver's side of Denny's car.

We unload the car and head back home, both of us tired of dealing with the onslaught of problems.

At my place, of course, the first thing Jeremy does is release Eyes, where the animal quickly runs to the utility room to do his business.

I ask my friend if he would help me up the stairs because I would love to take a shower. He permits it when I tell him he won't be involved in my disrobing or washing routine.

Again, I go piggyback on him up the stairs and take a cleansing respite of water running down my body, with some parts of it awkwardly protected. I smother moisturizer on all accessible parts of my skin and take two Motrin to ward off the sore muscles and pain from the broken bones.

My eye is now mainly green and yellow, and the swelling has dissipated a little.

When I'm dressed and done with my primping, I shuffle past the extra bedroom and notice clean sheets have been put on the bed. Did Jeremy do that? Hmm. Maybe that's a good thing.

After my housemate delivers me downstairs again, I sit at the bar and send Carl the bus video along with some details about the hit-and-run.

As I check my email, Jeremy makes dinner—simple cold shrimp and salad, since he's trying to use up the produce that is starting to spoil. He seems to be in a funk, but I ignore any hints about moving to Encino.

I text Zoey, asking about her big date tonight.

She replies, *No date. Later.*

Okay. Looks like two of my friends are in bad moods, but I'm not. I don't reply to Zoey. I'm feeling refreshed, albeit from the shower or even the Zoloft, I don't know.

When dinner is ready, Jeremy asks if we can eat in the great room so he can watch the Lakers game. I accede to his request, but I stay seated at the bar. Without saying another word, he places a large bowl filled with salad and topped with shrimp on the bar top, complete with a fork and napkin, and leaves the area. It's too much food, so I hop around to the other side of the counter, get out a container and lid, put half my salad and some shrimp in it, and seal it.

Next, I get on the scooter, rest the container on the front of the padded seat, and one-handedly drive to the front door. It's only then that I realize that Adam is still at work, so without looking at Jeremy, I return to the kitchen and put the extra meal in the fridge.

I hate the silent treatment, don't you? Denny and I used to do this, and it drove me crazy. Immature on both our parts. Well, it's not happening this time. No. Way.

After adding my fork to my bowl and covering it with the napkin, I carefully roll the scooter, complete with my meal, into the great room, being careful the napkin doesn't go flying off.

"Jeremy, I know you've had a bad day. No, I know you've had several bad days. And I'm sorry. None of this is your fault. And it's not mine, either. I didn't cause these people to disappear—including your mom. And I'm sorry about what happened to your dad, but it wasn't my fault. I wasn't involved in the tornado, or the Beemer being hit. This is life—sometimes bad things happen to good people. We can't control it, but we can control how we react. So, I refuse to go down when everything around us is falling apart."

I add, "You have Eyes now. You have me. Let's be friends. Talk to me, please!"

He stops eating. "I'm sorry. I didn't mean to lash out. I cherish our friendship."

"Thank you. I don't want us to shut down. I want the communication channels to stay open, no matter what happens around us. Okay?"

"Yeah," he says as he stabs his fork into the salad. "I understand. I'll try."

"Good. Now move over, and let's watch that game."

That wasn't as hard as I anticipated. See, I can control some things, although that one was rather minimal.

Do you play that game with someone where you have to give a little to get a little? Do you usually win at it?

While Jeremy flips to the proper channel, I ask him how people could go to a professional sports game during a worldwide crisis. He replies that money drives everything, including entertainment, but we both notice Staples Center isn't packed to the rafters with fans like normally. I would be scared driving to Los Angeles at night, afraid I might get carjacked. Everyone is trying to maintain a normal life, doing things they always do. A way to keep their sanity.

Meanwhile, I mindlessly check my phone as I have little interest in the sport.

It looks like an email came in from my doctor—the surgeon—checking on my healing status. I send an email to Dr. Tsai, replying that all's well, and that I'm off the Vicodin and only taking Motrin occasionally. Her note also recommends I click on a link to make my first physical therapy video appointment. I do, scheduling it for tomorrow morning.

When I look at the TV, the game's camera homes in on a gay couple being rather amorous—too romantic for PG-13 television. But the crowd is cheering and egging the males on as they go at it.

I go back to perusing my phone.

About five minutes later, Jeremy yells, "Did you see that? Isn't that the kid?" He points to the screen. "Yeah, it's James!"

Now my eyes are glued to the screen.

James is sitting with an older Black guy—I'm guessing his stepfather—and they're courtside, two rows up from the players' bench. Probably the seats Eddie gifted him.

The camera zooms in on the two of them while the announcer mentions that they have a special guest: James Hixon, the only survivor of a recent airplane crash. The fans applaud.

James's stepdad is beaming, but James is not. He has a pensive look in his eyes.

While the camera is still focused on the boy, he pulls a folded sign out of his jacket pocket and unfolds it, showing it to the camera, the audience, and all jumbotrons.

JOHN 3:16 is written on the placard.

The video continues to center on James while his stepfather tries to take the paper from him. Someone in the row behind them grabs James's arm that was holding the sign but misses as the sheet floats between the seats. The camera angle expands, and more people are coming over to James; food and empty drink cups are tossed at the two. A security guard rushes to them and escorts them out of the building while boos and profanities are screamed throughout the arena.

"Well, so much for his fifteen minutes of fame," Jeremy says.

"Yes, he's alienated a lot of people with that religious garbage. He never should've done that. His time's up. He's a has-been now," I add.

Yeah, he had this coming, didn't he?

During half-time, we clean up the kitchen.

I start another load of laundry and make two short phone calls to my parents and Silvia, never mentioning moving the supplies to Encino, as I know Jeremy's listening to each conversation. Dad reports Mom's asthma is acting up again, and she needs a refill of her inhaler. I suggest ordering it online, if possible, instead of having to pick it up.

When the second half of the game starts, Jeremy suggests I go on Amazon and order as many non-perishable goods as possible—large amounts of powdered and dry food, bottled water in bulk, more MREs, emergency bug-out kits, and any other stuff we deem important.

The task keeps me busy as I research the many available options, checking their differences and prices.

Jeremy offers to pay, but I tell him I've plenty of credit available, so I don't mind ordering, but I question where it should be shipped.

"Should I send everything here? Won't it get stolen if we're not home and it's left at my front door? Or if it goes to the Encino place, how will it arrive? I mean, there's a locked gate hidden off a dead-end street, so how will Amazon know where to put the boxes?"

"Got that covered. I'll text Sam at the UPS Store on Ventura Boulevard. Dad has had an account there for decades and knows Sam and his family well. Dad uses a post office box there. He has no known physical address listed, so he always has shipments sent there. Sam will let us know when the stuff arrives, and Amazon shouldn't have any qualms about not having to drive to a residence."

"That's a cool idea." I consider the number of boxes as I add more items to my cart. A while later, I state, "I've got over a grand on order." It's so fast and easy to spend money online. "Is that too much or not enough?"

"Order it, and let's see how it pans out." Then he adds, "But be sure to check each item's availability date. If it's made in China or some other country and is shipped directly from there, don't purchase it. Only select those that Amazon ships, not a third party. I'm sure the online mega-store will be more than happy to get rid of their stocked goods."

I examine all items in detail again, deleting over half of them and then doubling or tripling other products. In the end, I place an order to ship to the UPS store for over eight hundred dollars. Let's see how this goes.

After putting the laundry in the dryer, I change and brush my teeth in the bathroom. I quickly look in the mirror and ask D how things are going.

Fine, Sarah. You did well throughout the entire day. Sorry that we couldn't help with the bus incident. The young driver's poor skills weren't anticipated when we changed the light. But you're good; you've got over a few thousand viewers now. Excellent work in such a short period.

I've got a question.

Yes, how can we help?

Do you think I should move to Jeremy's parents' house?

We cannot make that decision for you. Remember, you're in charge. But do bear in mind, it's a secluded area. There are no cameras there. Sure, we use several governments' satellite surveillance systems and phone coverages, but Jeremy's father never used a computer or had Alexa, so you'd be out of reach in some ways. We're working on that issue currently.

Your ratings could be affected. If no visual or audio is available from your implant, you may not be as popular as you are now. So, make a wise choice that benefits you, not anyone else.

Thanks for your advice, and for not pushing me like Jeremy's doing. I want to always make my own decisions. I want to be in control of me, not anyone else.

Yes, we're aware of that, Sarah.

After I exit the bathroom, I ask Jeremy if we can watch an old movie. We end up with *Casablanca*, which I love and have seen repeatedly, but Jeremy never has.

Around 9:30 p.m., I hear movement at Adam's condo through the thin walls. I get up from the couch and roll my scooter to the kitchen to obtain the salad container. I tell Jeremy my intentions of giving something to my neighbor for his recent help, not bringing up my meds.

My roommate's engrossed in the movie, so I leave the condo alone and knock on Adam's door. I make sure I shut my door all the way, so Eyes doesn't escape.

When Adam answers, he's more than thrilled to be given a homemade meal. He's smoking pot, and the strong scent emanates from his home. Once again, his eyes are bloodshot, but he seems to be in a good mood, profusely thanking me for the food.

Before we part, he shares that he's been working ten- to twelve-hour shifts; he's looking forward to being off after one more day on the job.

When I return, Jeremy's still glued to the TV, as Eyes roams around my house.

The dryer beeps, so the cat follows me into the utility room where I fold clothes and he does his business again.

Settling next to Jeremy, we watch the remainder of the flick, with Jeremy caressing his cat and me drifting off to sleep.

Before the clock strikes midnight, I wake up, only to find the lights and TV off and the rest of the couch empty. Noticing a light shining from the upstairs bedroom, I go to my mattress, hoping to go back to dreamland.

~ **Day 9** ~

Jeremy thumps downstairs with a spring to his step, asking, "Sarah, are you awake? I want to show you something!"

I'm awake, but not up yet.

With my good hand, I brush the hair out of my face, including some stuck to the side of my mouth.

"Check this out," he demands as he stands next to my mattress with Eyes purring behind him. "Remember I told you I took two videos during the tornado, but they were too dark to send to Carl? Well, when I went to bed, I looked at them again, lightening up their frames. So, look at this!"

"What am I supposed to be looking for? It's a dark sky with dark clouds and maybe lightning strikes," I inspect the small screen on his phone.

"Now watch, I'm going to replay the video but stop the frame."

He hands me the phone again, and there's this object peeking out of a cloud. I try to enlarge it farther, but it doesn't work.

"Sarah, see that? What do you think it is? Does it look like a UFO to you?"

"Yeah, maybe. I guess. Weird, that's for sure. But couldn't it be someone's AI-created design that's beamed into the sky? Like techies are doing at concerts, firework displays, and arena celebrations?"

"Right, during the middle of a tornado, someone is playing with digital technology. I went on the internet and searched for UAP that night, and there were several pictures taken from the Valley, like at Castaic Lake, Woodland Hills, and Mount Wilson Observatory in the San Gabriel Mountains—all showing this same round disc object hovering in the sky."

As Eyes jumps up on my bed, makes his way to the bay shelf, and lies down, Jeremy continues, "In researching more, I learned there's a secret organization named Project Blue Beam that manipulates technology and stages events to control the population, trying to promote a new world order. So yes, these aberrations could be manufactured. What do you think?"

"You know I don't go for conspiracy theories, yet this Blue Beam thing makes me wonder. I can accept AI creating something like this to rule the world—and maybe for the better."

I add, "Carl said half the people nowadays think the missings were because aliens took them, but I can't figure out why they'd take all the babies and kids."

"To reprogram them? Co-mingle with us? To use as food?" he suggests.

"I hope not. And why so many disabled or elderly people? You would think the outsiders would target us, those healthy and productive in the prime of life, wouldn't you?"

"And how would they know to take the unborn?" he questions.

I cringe inside, knowing I had learned I was pregnant right before it all happened. Jeremy is unaware, and I'm not spilling the beans.

He adds, "I don't know, but they always say those from outer space may be more intelligent than we are. I think there's something to the theory, though. I don't think a virus could work that fast, but after reading so many articles online, maybe an alien abduction doesn't seem so far-fetched. Maybe it's part of the plan to merge us with them to make a better race. Even network news channels are starting to show coverage of these flying objects!"

I say, "Okay, I'll go back to my original thought. Were the sightings AI-generated or not? Technology has come so far, you know that."

He agrees and tells me more about his online findings, stating transhumanism could be a blend of aliens *and* humans, especially if mixed with technology.

By now, I've given him his phone back and gotten out of bed. I'm becoming a pro at adjusting to my casted leg as I step-drag-step-drag into the bathroom to change clothes.

"When you have time, research it. You're the journalist; I bet you'll be blown away with what you find," he says as I shut the door for privacy.

I take my second Zoloft and more Motrin, wash my face, brush my teeth, and comb my hair. While staring at myself in the mirror, I ask D what they think about alien spacecraft stealing people.

We wouldn't rule it out completely. It does make sense if you investigate it further.

What about AI tinkering with the concept? That's viable, isn't it?

That it is. But what will people accept and believe? Any of these options—a virus, alien invasion, or artificial intelligence are feasible ways that'll bring the world back to working with one another, caring about one another, and loving one another—that's what the new world order is all about: togetherness.

You'll see over time that this is only a step in the process of everlasting peace, be it between humans and cosmic beings or the new possibility of supertranshumans.

Okay, you might be right. I need to keep my eyes and mind open to these possibilities you suggest. Thanks for the talk.

Jeremy has started breakfast, sticking to his usual routine of asking Alexa to list the top five viewed news headlines of the day.

She reports:

> Swarms of locusts have destroyed farmland and crops in Africa, Brazil, and the United States. Organized by the One World League in Italy, the European Council, United Nations, and Omnilateral Commission are planning an emergency meeting early next week regarding the missing people, which will be attended by most

countries' presidents, prime ministers, and dignitaries. Insurance companies are refusing to pay out any life insurance plan, stating the missings were an act of God and not under human control. A new strain of Disease X has been detected and is twenty times more contagious than COVID-19, plus it has a higher death rate. In local news, flooding from the recent storm has created a health risk of leptospirosis.

We don't discuss him sleeping upstairs, which I'm glad about. He asks if it's okay if he leaves Eyes home with me for a few hours. He wants to return to his apartment to scavenge through the debris again and run a few errands.

He also asks if he can take the Beemer since it has more cargo space than his mom's car. I allow it. When he asks if the pussycat can remain uncrated, I give him a fake-sour look and agree.

Despite Eyes being in my condo, it's sublime having my house to myself again.

I open my laptop on the bar and file online reports with the police and my auto insurance company about my car and Denny's BMW, complete with photos. I also send an email to the insurance company about my husband's disappearance and let them know I filed on *themissings.com*. On a whim, I wonder if I will be the one left to handle Amy's estate, too.

At nine o'clock, I attend my physical therapy appointment online. The young Indian man is factual with a no-nonsense personality as he rushes through my exercise regimen. He's quick in his explanations, stating he'll be following up with an email of detailed instructions and repetitions. The entire call takes less than ten minutes, with him reaffirming how I must fastidiously do the movements to get the best results.

During the entire time, Eyes sits next to his bowl and watches me but keeps his distance.

I'm getting stiff sitting still. The therapist's admonitions echo in my mind: keep moving. Don't be stationary.

After hopping over to the table by the front door, I pick up Aunt Amy's envelope and return to the couch to read it. Again, Eyes follows me, this time curling up under the glass table. After opening the envelope's flap, I unfold one sheet of paper.

Dearest Sarah,

I'm sorry it's come to this day in history—and such a sad day it is for some. By now, you have found out that Denny's gone, and so are Hal and I. You're most likely confused, maybe mad, and upset, wondering where we've gone.

As I've mentioned before, this unbelievable event was what we Christians called the Rapture! All those who believe that Jesus Christ was God's only Son who came to Earth, died on the cross, shed His blood for our sins, and rose on the third day are now in Heaven, forever with our Savior, our Lord.

We only had to confess this and repent of our sins, which He freely has already forgiven us.

Now, if you're reading this, it's clear where you stand, and I'm heartbroken you never wanted to believe in Christ. But there's still time left to change your mind. Accept. Believe. Confess. So simple.

If you don't trust completely in Jesus, you'll face eternal damnation. If you do believe, you'll be able to go to Heaven, but you'll have to go through the next seven years or so dealing with unimaginable tribulations.

Here's what the Bible says will be happening soon: An extremely charismatic man will arise and promise safety and peace in the world, which is what everyone longs for with all the natural disasters that have happened. This man will establish a seven-year peace treaty with Israel to end all wars. He'll allow them to rebuild their temple so they can make sacrifices with the instruments, vessels, furnishings, and rare red heifers they already have. This man will appear wonderful and perfect.

Halfway through the seven years, he will revoke that treaty and demand ultimate obedience and loyalty to him and him alone. He will be killed, only to rise again later. He'll force all to agree to accept his special mark on their hand or forehead. Anyone who refuses will be put to death.

But there's hope. When the seven years are up, Jesus and we saints will come down to Earth. He will battle with this same man, the Antichrist, and God will win. In the end, all will bow down to the Almighty, but those who don't believe in Him will be sent to Hell for eternity.

I know you've heard this before, but time's running out for you, Sarah. Either you commit to Jesus, or you follow the Antichrist. It's one or the other. Which will you choose? The door is closing for you, Sarah.

Love, Amy

I put the paper down and shake my head at Eyes, saying aloud to the animal, "I knew she would do this—like she thinks she gets the last laugh by writing this note."

Eyes stares at me, not bothering to blink. So, I keep the rest of my thoughts to myself.

I don't care what Amy thinks or believes. Right now, right this minute, I would consider the virus or alien abduction over this hogwash for the missings explanation. I'm numb to her antics, her evangelism. It means nothing to me; now that she's gone, she means nothing to me. I refuse to consider, think, or reread any of her asinine, foolish words.

And this time, I'm not angry or want to throw something as I have in the past when I've had to deal with this woman. I don't care what she thinks.

I'm Sarah Colton, and I'm in charge and in control.

I get off the couch and head to the kitchen, the cat at my heels. After opening the trash compactor, I toss the letter, complete with its envelope, into the bin. Done. I'm so done—with Amy, with her piety, and with anyone who pushes religion down my throat. From now on, I'm going to shut them down the instant they open their mouths. Done.

With the incident behind me, I decide I need to be a good patient and flex my muscles more, so venturing upstairs is in order. I'm tired of wallowing in my self-pity and physical limitations.

I bravely and slowly ascend the stairs. Yes, I'm being extra careful as I do it backward, sitting down as I pull my body up each step with my good arm and drag my bad leg behind me. My wrist hurts a little, but I ignore the pain and concentrate on the muscle movements the therapist drilled into me. At the turn, I pause and catch my breath, wondering if going down the stairs will be any easier.

And wouldn't you know it, Eyes is always two to three steps below me.

When I land in the hallway, I crawl to Denny's door, open it, and enter. The cat follows. There's nothing to see here now except for broken glass from when I threw Denny's prized headphones against the framed photo of his friend John and him on the eighteenth hole at Pebble Beach.

After picking up most of the debris and discarding it in the trashcan under the desk, I put the broken picture on a side table and brush any remaining particles on the floor to the corner, hoping the cat won't eat or step on a sharp sliver.

I crawl over to the filing cabinet that houses our personal information and pull out our living will and all other pertinent documents. Placing Denny's discarded clothes and shoes on one of the upholstered green wing chairs, I sit down at his desk, fire up his computer, and fill out more documents with the insurance company regarding his life and health insurance. I know the work is futile because no insurance business in the world will pay out any policy without verification of a physical body, but I don't give a rip. I'm in control; I'm going through the hoops demanded of me.

Eyes claims his new domain on the other chair while I call the bank, but there's no human response. Out of feisty determination, I go online and send emails to the bank, Denny's work, his doctor, our dentist, his gym, et cetera. I review the files again, making sure everyone involved in Denny's life is notified that he's no longer alive on this planet, and I doubt he will be back. I also click his Facebook page and post "Missing" for his friends to see.

The work is cathartic as it releases my pent-up anger and angst and reassures me that I can survive whatever is thrown at me.

I, Sarah Colton, am back—so stay out of my way.

Four hours later, the door to the garage opens and closes.

"Sarah? You here?" calls Jeremy. "You okay?" There's panic in his voice. "Where are you?"

"Upstairs!"

His footsteps rush up the steps.

"Oh, I was worried for a second." He lets out a sigh of relief. "How did you get up here? Please don't tell me you did it yourself!"

I give him a broad smile. "I did. I wanted to start the paperwork nightmare, so I had to come up here. But I would greatly appreciate your assistance going back down."

I show him my cutest smile, hoping he's not furious with me.

"Sar, please don't ever do that again. You scared the daylights out of me."

"I'm sorry, but I got so much done. I feel like I've purged all the negativity in my head. It's freeing to be able to accomplish so much. And besides, my physical therapist demands I get up and move around, so I'm doing that."

"Fine. But be careful! Now get yourself up and climb on my back so we can get something to eat."

While I sit at the bar and list off all the completed online tasks, Jeremy makes us a late lunch of grilled cheese and bacon sandwiches. I'm spoiled having a decent cook in this house, as it never interested Dennis or me.

After delivering the food to the counter, he sits down next to me. He tells me he rescued more of his possessions from his drenched home, including lots of his clothing and housewares. He made two trips to Encino, depositing it all in the house and shop.

While eating, he says, "I've made a decision, Sarah. And you probably won't like it."

"Try me; I'm in a good mood, so who knows how I'll respond."

"I've moved to Encino. It makes the most sense. The way things are going, I no longer feel safe in the Valley. After seeing my apartment again, I talked to my landlord, and we decided it would be best if I ended my lease immediately and moved out—no penalties or refunds. I did one run with Denny's SUV. Then I gave some extra computer equipment to a kid at my building—or, should I say, what's left of my building—to help me load all my furniture in my dad's Ford F150. The truck is still packed, parked in the shop's bay, and Denny's car's back in the garage."

He takes another bite of his sandwich and continues, "I thought I should let you know. My invitation still stands. You could have Dylan's room since I'm taking over my parents'. And if that's too close quarters, either one of us could move to the shop apartment. What do you think?"

"What, no treehouse option? That was my first choice!" I grin.

"Funny. If you insist, I'll be glad to insulate the place and add electricity with a generator. All for you, my dear."

"You're cute. But I still haven't decided. I don't know what I'd do out there all day."

"We'd till the fields and live off the land. Mom used to have this saying: 'whatsoever a man soweth, that shall he also reap,' so we'll get into growing our food and harvesting it. It'll be fun."

I say, "Hardly. I know nothing about gardening or farming. I can take care of orchids, and that's about it."

"That's enough for me." He laughs as he clears our dishes and then cleans the pan he used. "Just think about it. Please. But, Sarah, I won't stay there at night until I know you can be safe on your own here. I'll sleep upstairs until we both feel comfortable that you can get around."

The conversation is interrupted by a text on my phone.

Zoey: *Sorry about last night. Long story.*

Me: *No prob. U OK now?*

Zoey: *Yes. Dinner tonite? My house.*

Me: *Sure! Time?*

Zoey: *7 or 8?*

Me: *K. Can Jeremy come?*

Zoey: *Yes. Amir will be there, too :-)*

Me: *Interesting. We'll be there.*

When we're done texting, I give Jeremy a heads-up about our dinner date. He hasn't met Amir, so I tell him a little about the doctor. When I mention that Amir's an Israeli, he questions why Zoey's seeing him.

"Because she likes him! She's an American of Arab descent but was raised as a Muslim when she was a child. So what? I think they're interested in each other."

"I'm surprised, that's all. She doesn't dress like a Muslim with the hijab or restrictive burka; she's modern, chic, and trendy. I thought maybe Israelis wouldn't want that type of flashy woman, that's all."

"You're profiling, Jeremy. Zoey's cool. She gave up that religious stuff when she was a teen; she's like me—we both don't practice any of those constricted beliefs. Go with the flow."

"Thanks for the update. Do you think we should bring something to dinner?"

"Hmm. I've got a couple of bottles of wine from the Willamette Valley in Oregon that my parents sent down. We'll take them."

"Why don't I make something? We've got plenty of fruit that's still good. Let me do a fruit tart—yeah, that's what I'll do." Excitedly, he goes online, declaring he has found the perfect recipe, and starts making the sweet concoction, while I text Zoey that we're bringing dessert.

As Jeremy perfects his amazing cooking skills, he suggests I open my laptop and research unidentified flying objects. While I do, he pours us two sparkling waters with lots of ice. "If you look up sites related to Area 51 in Nevada or some of the recently released unclassified US government documents on the topic, there are a bunch of fascinating ones. I'm not saying they're all true or real, but it seems they're flooding the internet. YouTube is loaded with them. Even check out the National Archives or NARA—I was surprised."

"Ut-oh. You're right. These videos and pictures can't be AI-generated, can they?" I scan through the articles.

"Don't know. I find it interesting, especially if or when they find a living alien. I bet they already have, but they're not telling us because everyone will freak out."

"Could be, Jeremy."

When he puts the tart dough in the oven to bake, I get up off the bar stool, stating it's hard on my back and butt. I head to the great room and stretch out on the couch, hoping to take a short nap. The cat comes over to join me, but keeps his distance, resting on the back cushions by my feet where he can see Jeremy slaving away in the kitchen.

Always thinking of me, Jeremy asks Alexa to play soft classical music as I drift off.

A couple of hours later, I wake up refreshed. Jeremy is typing on his phone at the bar. When I get up, I ask him what he's doing.

"I'm ordering some trail cameras from Amazon and will set them up at the gate and around the property. They won't be online, per se, but I bought large-memory SD cards and batteries, so I can keep an eye on the perimeter of the house. I could link them up to my phone's app, but I feel a little uncomfortable doing so since they may be able to be tracked."

I tell him it's probably a good idea, and then I ask, "I need to go upstairs again. Will you stand behind me to catch me if I slip? I think I can navigate the stairs going up, but I haven't tried going back down. And besides, it's good exercise."

His raised eyebrows show his skepticism, but he accepts the challenge.

Concerned about the pain involving my bad leg, at the first step, I cheat by lifting my good right leg; it has no issues when weight is on and off it.

I clumsily lift my left leg onto the next step, but it protests when it has to hold my weight. Instead, I pull myself up using the banister, which helps me bring up my right leg.

Jeremy keeps a step behind me, his hands on my hips as I try another step. At the turn, I want to give up, but he tells me I've done well and have no balancing issues as long as I hold onto the railing. To make the task faster, I go up the remaining stairs by always starting with my good leg.

At the top, I release my guardian, telling him I'm going to get changed for our date at Zoey's.

Entering my bedroom, I find it messy, thanks to the half mattress missing and clothes strewn about. I select something nice to wear: a strapless midcalf sundress, which is so freeing for my legs. Since the weather's still overcast, I add a short sweater and one sandal. After putting on some makeup and fixing my hair into a ponytail, I feel somewhat attractive.

When I leave my room, Jeremy stands in the hall; he, too, has changed clothes, wearing a short-sleeved shirt and cargo shorts with tennis shoes. We both look nice, all things considered.

A fear rises in me when I approach the stairs. I insist Jeremy doesn't help me, so have him go in front of me and face me. I first try sitting on my butt and sliding down each step.

But by the time I reach the floor, I can go down the stairs using both legs and without falling. I feel a milestone has passed.

"Come on in." Zoey welcomes us as we enter her abode, me on my scooter so that the bottom of my cast doesn't get damp walking on the still-wet walkway.

Her condo has a similar floor plan to mine, but it's not an end unit, and upstairs has one less bedroom because her primary suite is larger. The first floor is identical, but it's done in bleached wood and creams with royal blue accent colors. Stylish.

After I pull out two bottles of wine from a reusable bag, Zoey eyes Jeremy's delicious-looking tart with blueberries, strawberries, and canned peaches—all from Amy's loot—arranged in a beautiful, colorful swirl design on top of the custard pie. She raves about the creation as she instructs him to put it in her refrigerator.

As Jeremy enters the kitchen, Amir, wearing shorts, a polo shirt, and flip-flops, greets us, and introductions are given. I notice a wariness in Jeremy as he sizes up the doctor.

Amir, of course, asks how I'm doing and if there are any health issues. Jeremy is the one to tell him how I've been starting my physical therapy and have been working on going up and down the stairs. He seems proud of my accomplishments.

"Don't overdo those exercises, Sarah." Amir admonishes me as he opens a bottle of the wine we gave them. "Take it easy and don't push too hard, or you may go backward, especially with the hand—your wrist needs to be immobile to heal."

"Yes, Doctor," I answer in a mocking tone. At least, he cares.

"Sarah," interrupts Zoey, "look what Amir made. We're going to have some of his favorite dishes from Israel tonight."

On the bar top is a spread of food—which Amir informs us is called *mezze*—containing pita, salad, and olives with several dips made with hummus, tahini, and yogurt.

With the women sitting and the men standing, we eat and chat, mainly about the food. It may be the one thing that Jeremy and Amir have in common as they talk about ingredients and cooking processes.

As we drink, Amir moves around the kitchen with ease, sometimes asking Jeremy for assistance. In no time, we are seated at the dining room table eating flavorful dishes of Israeli pot roast, baba ghanoush, and chickpea shawarma.

I'm impressed Amir took the time out of his busy schedule to make this special meal for us. "When did you have time to make all this?"

"Ah. That's our story to tell, isn't it, Zoey?" He looks at her intensely with his dark brown eyes, eyes that match hers.

She reaches over to hold Amir's hand and says, "Well, we didn't get to have our planned date last night because Amir had a Molotov cocktail thrown at him."

I'm shocked. "Really? Like where and when did this happen?"

"Porter Ranch. Yesterday at my home—well, the house my roommate and I rent."

"Why?" asks Jeremy.

"We were both in the living room, and I was ready to go pick up Zoey, and this glass bottle with a flaming piece of cloth in it came flying into the room. It broke the screen on the window and hit our couch. Things started catching on fire, so my roommate ran into the kitchen for the extinguisher, and, thankfully, we put it out quickly."

I'm still shocked. "Why, why would anyone do that? Did they drive by? Did you see the car?"

Amir continues, "Yes, it looked like an old Impala with two or three people in it. They were yelling 'Allahu Akbar' right before they slung it at our house. So, now we know their intentions."

He grasps Zoey's hand tighter and smiles at her. I assume he knows her background but is not holding her upbringing against her.

"Wow," I say. What is America coming to? Attacking doctors who happen to be Israeli?

Amir informs us his roommate is from Haifa and working in the US on a visa as an engineer for JPL in Pasadena.

"And that's not all," Zoey adds.

"I've been getting death threats at work," Amir confirms. "Several emails."

This time, Jeremy speaks up. "All because you're Jewish?"

"Yes, I believe so—the notes state exactly that."

"That's so wrong," I say.

"So, I quit my job. I don't want to have to worry about a bomb detonating at a hospital if someone's out to get me. Zoey here has graciously taken me in, for now. And I thank you so much." Amir lifts her hand to his lips, gently kissing the back of it. I'm embarrassed watching them googly-eyeing each other.

Jeremy asks, "What about your roommate? Has he had death threats?"

"No, it's just me. He's staying at the house. We think it could be because my oldest brother was high up in the IDF, but he recently quit his job. Maybe some sort of retaliation by some Islamic group that goes after the Israeli militia and their families. Yet only a few know he quit work. My brother now calls himself a 'sealed witness,' promoting that our Messiah appeared in what happened last week when so many people disappeared. Thus, my father is concerned that Abram may become a religious fanatic."

I look at Jeremy, who doesn't speak.

What do you say to that one, Viewer?

Amir adds, "Yes, I talked to my brother, and he says they're gathering twelve thousand from each of the twelve tribes of Israel, so 144,000 men are becoming servants of God – like what you call missionaries."

"Won't they be concerned or worried about being attacked or hurt, like you possibly could've been?" I ask.

"No, they claim the Bible states they'll be spared from all forms of harassment, abuse, and injury, including death. But what I found captivating is that these twelve tribes are listed in Revelation, which isn't part of our Torah. And my lineage comes from the tribe of Judah; I can prove that. Makes me think—don't you wonder how a book that old could prophesy something like that and have it come true right now, while we're living in it?"

I perk up. "Are you saying that you're one of these missionaries, or that you're a Messianic Jew? I think that's what they're called. They believe Jesus was and is their Messiah."

"Well, I'm a Jew, as is my brother. But he's changed—I can tell there's something that has shifted in his thinking. All I'm saying is that maybe there's more to the Bible than I've considered."

I sigh with relief. I'm thankful Amir hasn't gone to that arrogant, self-righteous side where Aunt Amy went. And look what happened to her. Did she disappear into nothingness or is she up in Heaven as she says the Bible told her so? Hmm.

Before the meal ends, I excuse myself and use the restroom.

The second the door closes, I look into the mirror.

D? Can you hear me from Zoey's house? I've never talked to you except from my own home.

Yes, we're here. We're everywhere. We've been listening.

All right. What do you think about Amir and how he's been targeted? Isn't it wrong to kill someone? And kill them because of their beliefs?

Yes, it's wrong, but sometimes it's the lesser of two evils. You know how it happens throughout history. Many are tortured, sacrificed, or put to death for their beliefs. We can't change that.

What about the Israeli tribe thing? Is that really in the Bible?

Yes, it's there. We don't believe something like that can or will happen. And I'm sure we'll be able to deal with those men if we have to. They can't think they're in control enough to never be harmed or injured as they spew out their religion.

Okay.

And don't falter from your beliefs either, Sarah. We've noticed some of our clients aren't satisfied with the doubt that seems to be creeping into your consciousness. Stay firm on what you know. You're in control. When people say these unintelligent theories, take them with a grain of salt and move on.

Thanks for the pep talk.

I flush the toilet to make it look like I was in the room for the expected reason, wash my hands, and return to my seat at Zoey's table.

During my absence, the fruit tart was served, and we all rave about its marvelous taste.

I'm on the reserved side: I don't say much or reply at all when any topic remotely involves God, Jesus, the Bible, or missionaries.

By eleven o'clock, the four of us have finished both bottles of wine. Jeremy and I bid our goodbyes; I get on my scooter, and we head back to my condo.

After being greeted by Eyes—yes, I graciously, and with lots of begging by my houseguest, allowed the critter free reign for a few hours, and it appears he didn't damage anything—Jeremy asks if I would like to sleep in my bed upstairs. Although I love the idea of being in my bedroom, I reply that it would be a hassle to move the mattress back upstairs. My hero insists it wouldn't be a big deal. Or was it his way of saying thank you for Eye's freedom? Either way, he drags the beast up the stairs, with me behind him, taking each step upward cautiously and determinedly.

When the bed is reassembled and made, I thank my roomie with a kiss on his forehead and shut my bedroom door.

After locating and taking some Melatonin, I undress and put on a clean nightshirt.

Able to return to my normal routine, I look between the slatted blinds on the window that looks out at the field. In the darkness, the remains of the burnt plane are still in my view.

As I stare at it, a bird flies by and hovers in front of the window as if it is welcoming me back to my bedroom. The fowl acts like a hummingbird by staying in place, but its body seems bigger and less agile. I stare at the creature until it abruptly takes off.

Next, I crawl between the sheets with my nuisance appendages and fall asleep.

~ **Day 10** ~

I roll over and note my alarm clock states it's 1:37 a.m.

A sound thumps outside my bedroom door. What is that? Like a thump and drag. And then there's a scratching on my door, not like a chalkboard being scratched with nails, but more like a tapping. Light tapping.

Could Jeremy need me?

Getting out of bed, I quietly approach the door, still hearing that abnormal noise. When I twist and pull on the door handle, lo and behold, it's Eyes with something dangling from his mouth.

I stoop down. It's Denny's watch!

Forcibly grabbing the timepiece out of the cat's mouth, I hold it to my breast and wail. Denny's gone! I hurt so deeply inside. Sobs pour out of me. The reality that I no longer have my husband hits hard, and I don't know how to deal with it.

Jeremy races down the hall into my bedroom, screaming, "Are you all right, Sarah? What's wrong?"

I can't speak. I only hold the watch out and nod to the cat.

"Oh, that's precious. Eyes was giving you a present; that's all. His way of thanking you for letting him stay here." My housemate picks up the cat and strokes his fur.

He, with the cat in one hand, approaches me and offers me a hug. I tuck my good side under his arm and lay my head on his shoulder.

"We once had a cat that would catch gophers and deliver them—usually dead—to Mom, even in her bedroom...on her bed. Oh, how she hated it! Dylan and I made this sign by the front door, keeping tabs on how many the animal found. We stopped counting when it hit a hundred."

I'm now laughing instead of crying.

After Jeremy kisses me on my head, he releases the brotherly hug. "We had this other cat, Tubs the tabby. She would move our shoes around at night. Sometimes we couldn't find one of the shoes in time for school, so we had to put on another pair. Later, the missing shoe would be found, hidden in a closet. Cats can be fun."

"Well, I don't like Eyes touching my things! Please keep that cat out of my room."

After the two leave my room, I close the door, glance out the window, and—I swear—I thought I saw that bird again.

I climb back into bed and clutch the watch in my hand while I shake my head about the witless cat.

Seven hours later, I walk myself carefully downstairs with no help; I'm proud of the accomplishment.

The great room is pristine—everything, including the loveseat, is back in its original spot. Jeremy is in the kitchen, humming to himself.

Alexa is giving my housemate the five top clicked-on headlines of the day's news, but I miss the first one and only catch part of the second, which was something about population reduction due to the worldwide lack of children. The other three are: All US commercial and private airplanes remain grounded with only the military or emergency agencies and some cargo ones allowed in the skies, thus long-distance food distribution is still at a standstill. There's an increase in alien sightings around the globe. Several large deep sinkholes in Florida have done extensive damage to the Cape Canaveral Space Force Station, causing one of the boosters to topple and explode.

"Morning, Sunshine," Jeremy says to me as he puts Eye's food bowl down. "Did you sleep well?"

"I did. Being in my room, in my bed, made the trip upstairs worth it. However, I don't appreciate a thief in my house." I glare at Eyes, who ignores me.

"And thanks for putting my condo back in order, Jeremy. You're too good to me."

"That I am." He hands me a plate with avocado toast and a fried egg on the side. "Eat up."

After I thank him again, I ask what's on our dance card today. No list is provided, only that we could go sort things at the Encino house and empty his dad's truck. He mentions Sam from the UPS Store hasn't contacted him yet.

After one bite of toast, my phone dings.

Zoey: *What R U doing today?*

Me: *Nothing. You?*

Zoey: *Took day off. We want to do something different. Normal. Relaxing. Any ideas?*

I read the message to Jeremy, and he has a suggestion.

Me: *Jeremy says go to a lake, get away. No people. Find a quiet spot. He knows the perfect place.*

Zoey: *That sounds great! When?*

We decide to meet in an hour at my garage. We'll bring sandwiches, and they'll provide the beer.

Once I put my phone down on the kitchen bar top, it dings again.

James: *Sorry about last time. Can I stop by?*

Um, that's not going to happen, kid. I'm done with you. The message is deleted; the phone is turned off. I don't even mention to Jeremy who it was.

By eleven o'clock, the four of us climb into Amir's Kia Sorento, putting our backpack of food in the back next to Zoey's cooler. With Amir driving, Jeremy sits in the front while we girls are in the back.

Promising a remote area, Jeremy instructs our driver to get on the 5 Freeway, and when we pass Magic Mountain, take the 126, which follows the Santa Clara River.

We veer north past the small town of Piru and head through the canyon, past the dam, recreation area, and boat launch. After driving on the curvy road for several miles, Amir is told to pull off on a dirt side road, which takes us to a flat area with a picnic table surrounded by trees next to a narrow part of the lake.

"Jeremy, this is the perfect spot. I love how it's so secluded; there's no one in sight, probably for miles!" Amir's excited as he gets out of his SUV.

It's a typical beautiful Southern California day, where the vivid blue sky is cloudless, and the temperature hovers around eighty degrees.

Ever the gentleman, Jeremy picks me up and carries me down between boulders and dry brush and sets me on the table's bench while the others unload the food and drinks. Zoey sets up a couple of blankets and towels on the ground by the lake. Its high water laps against low tree branches and bushes.

Jeremy reports: "My dad found this spot when my brother and I were in school. He would launch our boat down at the ramp and then take it back into this cove. Later, when I was in high school, a friend and I would drive out to this same spot and fish. We loved the quietness. It's like we are the only ones out here."

"Is the lake up from all the rain we've had recently?" Amir asks.

"Yes, the water's up. Do you see that rock sticking out there, to the right? That's where we normally would stand and fish!"

The men take their sandals off and wade in the cool water while Zoey removes her slip-ons and joins them. I hop over to a blanket with our backpack and slather sunscreen on my face, bare shoulders, arms, and one and a half legs. Being in the fresh air is divine for my body and soul. Cleansing. As if none of us has a care in the world.

As I stare at the beautiful water as it caresses the shoreline, I notice a black bird nearby. It's bigger than a wren but smaller than a crow. I've never seen this kind before. It looks at me but doesn't fly away—just looks. Despite my friends splashing in the water, the creature doesn't move. It must be used to us humans invading nature so often.

After the three splash each other and Zoey loses at dunking Amir and gets soaked, they use the towels to dry off and sit down on the blankets.

Amir brings over the cooler and offers each of us an ice-cold beer, popping them open with some kind of custom pocketknife he's pulled out of his shorts. I dole out roast beef and Swiss cheese sandwiches with tomato, mayo, and spicy mustard. Zoey sets out cut veggies and chips.

Right when we start eating, there's a susurrus of leaves nearby; I thought it might be another one of those black birds flapping in the bushes. There's a crackling of a tree branch, then a rock or pebble hitting another one.

Amir quickly looks up and pulls out the knife from his pocket. Jeremy stands up, sandwich in hand.

Suddenly, a man approaches. He's wearing a long-sleeved camo jacket with matching pants and hiking boots. Sunglasses and an unkempt beard hide some of his facial features. I would guess he's in his early fifties. His rifle is pointed at us.

"Don't any of you move," he demands. "And you, the one with the weapon, toss it on the picnic table. Now."

Amir slowly gets up, his hands showing, and immediately obeys the rough command, setting the knife down on the dirty wood. Jeremy has his hands up in the air. Zoey helps me up to my feet, and we stand behind our men, hoping this isn't going to turn violent.

"I don't want to shoot anyone. I only want your food. All of it."

Amir says, "Sure, take it. It's all yours."

"Put it all back in the pack and cooler, including the opened beers. Keep them facing upward so nothing spills."

Zoey leans down and collects the items, stacking the bottles upright in the hard plastic container. When she tries to shut the lid, the glass rattles inside. I'm unsure if they spilled or not.

The man points his gun at Jeremy and Amir, ordering, "Take a few steps over there, by that log. And you, the girl with the dark hair, you bring me the supplies. Now."

He increases the distance between us as Zoey walks closer to him.

Amir protests, "As I said, you can take everything. Do you need cash? Credit cards? My watch?"

"Ha. No. All that stuff's worthless out here. It's the food I need. And water. Even your ice will help."

"How long have you been out here?" Jeremy prods.

"Ever since the missings happened. I bugged out when I couldn't find my wife. The only thing I could figure out was that she was taking a shower, as that's where I found her—our—wedding ring. By the drain. The showerhead was spraying water all over it."

His voice is raspy and broken. "I should've listened to her. She warned me plenty for years, telling me this was gonna happen. And it did. I took what I could carry and hit the hills. I'll be better off living here on my own instead of dealing with the problems happening in heavily populated areas. And I'm no Zuckerberg. I can't build a mega underground bunker in a mountain. This—" He waves his hand in the air. "—this I can handle."

"Yes, it's getting bad everywhere," adds Zoey. "Everyone's going crazy. Lots of people scaring or hurting others for no reason."

I hope her words don't hint at what this man's doing to us right now.

He throws the backpack's strap over one shoulder and carries the cooler to the picnic table. Still aiming his gun toward us, he sets the container down and picks up Amir's knife from the table, inspecting it.

"Wow. This is a custom Shahal Victorinox tactical combat knife, used by the Israeli Defense Forces. I've seen one before when I was with USMC. Is it yours?" he questions Amir, as he turns the weapon over in his hand.

"Yes. I served three years in the Yamam counter-terrorism unit."

"Impressive." He places the tool back on the table and adjusts his gun under his arm.

"I'm a doctor now. Here in the States." Amir adds, "I noticed you have a gash on your finger. It looks like it may become infected."

"Yeah, caught it on a branch making camp a mile away, while building my covering."

"I've got a small emergency kit in my car up on the road. I'd be glad to help clean your wound out and look at it before it gets any worse."

"You'd do that for me? After I accosted you with my gun and demanded to steal your food?"

"Yes, we only want to help you; don't we, guys?" Amir turns to us for confirmation, and we agree.

Jeremy adds, "We live in the Valley. We're here to get a break from the nonsense there. After Amir patches you up, we'll leave all the food we have and be on our way. We feel bad for you, dude. You're on your own out here. Let us help you."

Zoey and I both nod in affirmation. We all want to help this poor soul.

The man puts down his rifle on the table. "I'm sorry. My name is Dean Craven. I'm scared and hungry. I don't know if this trek into the wilderness was the right thing to do or not. I can't go back to my house, the house I shared with my wife for over thirty years."

He looks like he's ready to cry. Since Zoey is the closest to him, she reaches out and touches his arm. He doesn't react.

This whole time I'm questioning if you, Viewer, can see what's going on here. What would you do if someone pulled a gun on you out in the middle of nowhere? Would you fight back or cave into their demands?

"We're all good." Amir insists as he takes a step closer. "Zoey, why don't you give him my sandwich—I think it's the one on top. Can you do that?"

She nods while Dean slips the backpack off his shoulder and hands it to her.

"Dean, is it okay if I go get my medical bag?" Amir checks with the man to make sure he's allowed to approach his vehicle. He is.

Our doctor friend tends to his patient by wiping the wound clean, adding an antiseptic, and wrapping it with gauze.

During the medical process, Dean is eating the sandwich and adding chips between bites, while Zoey and I gather the blankets and towels. Jeremy assists Amir by making several trips to the back of the SUV for extra items to give to Dean.

Before we leave, we offer Dean a ride back to the Valley, but he declines.

As we head home, we speculate if we did enough for the guy or if he'll be able to survive the wild with a few sandwiches, chips, and flat beer.

We ask Amir about his military training, yet the only thing he conveys is that he did more than the required thirty-two months each Israeli male over the age of eighteen years must serve. He also tells us that their women serve a minimum of twenty-four months.

By the time we get home, we're hungry, so I ask Zoey and Amir to come over in an hour for an early dinner. Jeremy defrosts some chicken breasts and begins to prepare breaded cutlets with pasta covered in a marinara sauce, while I get a simple salad ready.

In the middle of rinsing the head lettuce, my phone rings—yes, an actual phone call. How often does that happen? Usually, it's all about texting.

It's my sister Silvia.

I motion to Jeremy that I need to take this call, and I work my way out to our gated patio. I pass the rose pot and wonder if the soil is still moist. I unlatch the small gate and sit down on one of the wrought iron chairs by the bay window. I see Eyes staring at me through the bay window.

"What's up, Sis?" I ask.

"It's Dad. He's been hurt." There's panic in her voice.

"How?"

"He was helping his neighbor, Dave somebody—the retired RN who lives with his wife four doors down by the entrance of their cul-de-sac. You know, doing their duty playing guardians by keeping their homes safe. They had the day shift, so they were keeping watch standing by the two SUVs blocking the street's entrance, and an old sedan drove up. Two guys jumped out and hassled Dad and Dave. One of them pulled a knife and stabbed our father in the gut."

I cry, "No, not Daddy!"

"Yeah. The other guy took their wallets and phones. Both got back in the car and sped off."

"Is Daddy okay?"

"We're not sure. Dave didn't think it would be safe to take him to the hospital, so he helped him into his house. He tried his best to suture him up and said he doesn't think the blade went in deep enough to hit any internal organs. He's worried about infection."

"Where is Daddy now?" I ask.

"Still at Dave's. His wife got Mom; she ended up having another asthma attack, so they had to get her inhaler. She's fine, I guess. Dave insisted both stay at his house overnight, so he can keep an eye on them."

"Did they have weapons to fight back? I know Daddy hates guns."

"If you want to call bear spray a weapon, yeah. And they sprayed it, but the guys were wearing ski goggles!"

I sigh, asking, "How did you find out?"

"Dave's wife. I think her name is Tiffany. Since both men's phones got stolen and Mom's had no juice, Tiffany went to our parents' house, looked up my name in their address book, and called me."

I tell her about what happened at the lake; she complains about how evil people are becoming. But after I explain how Dean seemed lost without his wife, she, also, backs down and feels bad for the man.

"Well, I must go. Zoey and Amir are coming over for dinner soon. We want to do normal activities to keep our sanity. What about you and Tom? Are you doing better?"

"Sorta. It's still hard to walk into the kids' rooms and see their cribs empty. We both agreed to sign up for one of those child robots. Even if it takes years to get one, it gives us some sort of hope for the future."

"We're all doing whatever we can to survive," I tell her.

My sister asks, "Oh, did you have a chance yet to read those e-books I sent you? They've been helping me. It's all about how I can control my reactions to the world around me, even if it's falling apart."

"No, Silvia. I haven't had the time."

We talk for another few minutes about our parents and how we can't do anything to help them from this far away.

After we say we love each other and end the call, I walk back down the walkway to my front door. When I stop in front of Adam's unit, a whiff of pot overcomes the lemon-scented bush while hard rock music blares nearby. I guess with his father now gone, he's the master of his domain and is enjoying his day off.

Jeremy asks if everything is okay when I enter my condo, and I tell him the news about my parents. He shakes his head in disbelief, muttering how lawlessness has taken over everything.

When our guests arrive, with bottles of wine in hand, they mention Adam's loud music and the obvious odor that reeks from his side of the building. Zoey and Amir are introduced to Eyes, who abruptly leaves and returns to his spot on the bay shelf.

Without mentioning the guy's one-time offer that kept Jeremy and me sane that night, I explain that the neighbor is processing his father's disappearance and that we all do it in different ways.

This leads to a debate about emotions and how we do or don't deal with them.

Viewer, how have you responded to your loved ones being missing? Are you still processing it, or have you accepted the loss and moved on?

During dinner, Amir seems to love discussing personal interactions and how one's history molds us into who we are today. Both Zoey and I agree with him, but Jeremy says he's on the fence, as he believes that people can change their future by ignoring or doing what's opposite from the past—which we all say that the present is formed from that past.

While drinking the second bottle of wine, our philosophical discussions are muddled and nonsensical but entertaining.

After eating, Zoey insists on washing the dishes, with Amir as backup stacking them in the dishwasher. Jeremy handles putting the leftovers away. I pick up the soiled placemats and take them to the utility room.

When dumping the cloths in the washing machine, I hear yelling through the walls, above the beat of Adam's rock music.

It's my neighbor: "Get out of here! Get out. Now!"

I open the inner garage door, and the noise increases. While I push the garage opener button on the side of the door jamb, I bellow to Jeremy and Amir to come quickly.

Both males quickly rush past me and into the garage; they weave between the BMW and Prius, past the now-opened garage door, and stand on the road, looking toward Adam's condo.

Zoey comes behind me and helps me down the step. We both stay in the garage, but peer out as Adam continues his rant.

"Don't you ever come back here again, or I will shoot!" he screams.

He wields a gun—one that looks identical to the one he gave me—and he's aiming it at three teens who are carrying crowbars. They slowly step backward on the side road, almost to the curb where the field begins—the same field where the airplane crashed over a week ago.

Using a string of expletives, Adam tells them to keep walking, and if anyone doesn't, he'll shoot. The three listen, but one of them, the guy in the middle, trips on the curb and falls. The other two grab him by his armpits and help him up.

When they are several steps into the field, all quickly turn and run toward the church on the other side. We can hear them laughing and cheering when they reach the parking lot.

Meanwhile, Adam is still upset. "I had to go in the garage to get something out of the back of Dad's van, so I opened the big door to see better. These jerks, these total idiots, came up to me and started pushing me around. Yeah, like assaulting me. So, I got out my gun from its belt holster and showed it to them. Hopefully, I scared them to death."

Jeremy approaches and politely says, "Hey, Adam, remember me? Sarah's friend. That's a dangerous weapon in your hand, and it's probably loaded. Can you put it down, or dislodge its magazine?"

Adam looks at the pistol like it is the first time he has seen it. Confused, he answers, "Yeah. Yeah. I'm sorry; I'll put it away." He tucks it back into the holster and pulls his T-shirt over it.

Amir—well, he looks like he's ready to go ballistic over Adam's stupidity. The ex-military guy's fast body movements and flashing eyes make it obvious that he's seething as he pulls Jeremy away from Adam, who has moved back into his garage.

Amir whispers something to Jeremy, but I can't hear it.

Jeremy nods and tells Adam, "Hey, we know things are weird out here but hang in there. Okay, dude? We don't want anyone to get hurt or killed."

"Yeah, I hear ya. I reacted more than I should have. My bad."

Jeremy adds, "Are you okay? Do you need anything or anyone to help you?"

"I don't think so. I'm good. Always good." Yeah, I bet you are, Adam. You keep doing those drugs, and nothing will bother you.

The four of us go back inside, shutting the garage door behind us. We hear Adam close his door, and then the loud music is turned down.

I hope he's going to be okay.

Amir and Zoey leave around ten at night. Jeremy and I are both tired, so we head upstairs. While we climb the steps, I ask where Eyes is, and Jeremy replies that the cat has been fixated on looking out the bay window, watching the world go by outside. We both enter our rooms and shut our doors behind us.

After doing my nightly hygiene, I stand in front of the window and peep out the slats. And once again, the bird is there, looking at me. Hovering in space.

Irritated, I immediately walk into my closet and demand D answer me,

What's with the bird, D? It's not real, is it?

Correct. It's an AI drone. We're only keeping an eye on you, that's all.

I don't like it. It's intrusive.

Seems the only one I can talk to, can share everything with, is you, an AGI. Not Jeremy. Not Zoey. Only you. Are you even real?

We may be artificial general intelligence, but we're human-based. Transhuman in some ways. The bird drone is mainly for your security.

You're unaware of how often we've protected you over the last few days. You're an asset to us now, and we want to keep

you safe. And we want to be a part of you and you to be a part of us. We care, we really do.

Tell me how you keep me safe. Did you when we were at Lake Piru where we were alone? Could you have stopped Dean from aiming his gun at us? Stopped a bullet if he shot me?

As we told you before, it's all based on electronics. Thanks to SAR, which is synthetic aperture radar or satellite imagery to laypeople, we could see where you were standing and hear all conversations by the lake via your four phones, but we couldn't sync it with your implant. However, we didn't miss a beat. Dean didn't have any electronic devices on him, but we had a drone monitoring your phones.

The task was complicated because all implant tracking is based on the location of a cell tower, and the only one was miles away from your position, so the drone had to get close to you without being seen. Because of that, we're working on ways to improve the distance between the towers. Currently, our drones can only track your implant within five hundred feet, but Space Force's satellites are far superior.

Well, I didn't see any drone.

Of course, you didn't. You may or may not know that technology has advanced to the point of being able to read numbers on a credit card from space. So, we had the nearby bird record it all.

Ah, now I understand.

So, you're saying the program is not foolproof. If my implant is far away from a cell tower, you have restricted access? Or is it the phone that is the key?

Yes to both questions, but our AI technicians are constantly refining and improving the program with SAR satellite help. Example: We knew from infrared tracking that a fifth person was approaching you and had a weapon. Because he had no phone to track, we didn't know his identity until he stated his name, which we heard through your phone. Within six seconds, we knew who he was, where he lives—or lived—and how much mortgage he owes.

We're similar to the system at your work, the Source, but so much more. Now, if we had to protect you, we could've had a satellite intervene with tactical support, but our AI program detected Dean wasn't a threat due to personality characteristics based on our rapidly compiled data.

I understand. That makes me feel better. Thanks for keeping an eye out for me and protecting me.

But I think that bird thing is creepy, the way it stared at me both times. I almost wanted Eyes to attack it.

Funny, Sarah. We're glad you see the humorous aspects of life. That is important for one's well-being.

Speaking of Dean and Adam with those wannabe thieves, why is there such an increase in violence lately? It's so sad.

We, too, are sad to see it.

Is there any way to stop it or lessen it?

The powers that be are working on it. We believe peace, true peace, can be achieved if the right person or persons take over and control the world globally. We know it'll happen, and we're looking forward to it, but it still may be out of reach for a little longer.

That would be ideal, wouldn't it? No crime. No killings. No violence.

Yes, our utopia. Our nirvana. Our heaven on earth.

I wish.

As do we, Sarah.

Oh, how are my numbers doing? Am I sliding in ratings?

Your rating has flatlined right now; this could be due to the infrared viewing with the lake incident as the viewers had the overhead satellite and the bird's perspectives, not one from being inside your head.

We're hoping your numbers have not peaked. We're looking at a little project to boost them, so we'll let you know. We continue to get new viewers, though.

I'll try harder, but it isn't easy. I still consider myself to be a boring girl—or, at least, I want to be one. Maybe I'm not your best poster person. I smirk at the thought.

You're fine, Sarah. And you never know what's around the next corner in life, good or bad.

That's right.

With the conversation ended, I crawl between the sheets and try to remember all the things that have happened for the past ten days, but sleep overcomes me faster than anticipated.

~ Day 11 ~

The scratching sound is at my bedroom door again. It must be Eyes.

By the time I get out of bed and open the door at 5:28 a.m., only a solo argyle sock is on the hallway floor. No cat.

I silently walk down the hall, this time being careful not to make a sound and wake up Jeremy. The guest room's door is cracked open, so I peer in and see the cat on the bed with my friend soundly asleep. Eyes stares at me, not even flinching.

Across the hall, the office door is ajar. No doubt, that's how the night prowler stole the sock.

After entering the room, I go to the window that overlooks the playground and the burnt swing set, questioning what really happened to those girls. Did they, like so many others, succumb to a strange virus, get stolen by spacecraft, or raptured, as Aunt Amy and James said the Bible predicted?

I don't know, but I wonder.

Viewer, if you're up this early, what's your take? Which scenario do you believe happened?

Also noted is no electronic bird spying on me through the window.

Not wanting to go back to sleep or wake up Jeremy, I shut the office door so that it rests against the doorjamb. There's no metal hitting metal in the doorknob that could cause a clicking sound. I quietly turn on the light and sit down at Denny's desk. I boot up his computer and go to Google.

Next, I search for the name Numen. Its definition, usage, and origin are mainly linked to websites. The only company name listed is one in India that involves a virtual health platform with a conglomerate of doctors. Not the Numen I know. I also check the Source. Nothing. When trying to search further for any relationship with AI or implants, I get nowhere. Nothing.

I search for AGI or Artificial General Intelligence. There's plenty on the topic that is developing AI with a human level of cognition. And like something called ASI or Artificial Super Intelligence, it would theoretically be self-teaching and able to carry out a general range of tasks autonomously via self-control. ASI would be equal to the human brain capacity and possibly surpass human intelligence.

However, I do find possible machinations involving it and mind control and brainwashing. This leads me to question if the child robot that Tom and Silvia want may be programmed to harm and destroy instead of love and cherish. All fascinating yet concerning at the same time.

In the middle of my browsing, I glance back at the office door; it's opened, with Eyes now settled on a wing chair.

Somehow, I stumble upon something called molecular manufacturing, which is an emerging technology that's being developed to build large objects to atomic precision quickly and inexpensively, with no defects. Unfortunately, this nanotechnology might encourage weapons of mass destruction that could self-replicate. Again, fascinating but disconcerting.

I'm so engrossed in my research that I startle when Jeremy opens the door to the Jack and Jill bathroom and enters the office. "Sorry to surprise you, Sar. Have you been up a while?"

"Yes, I couldn't sleep due to Eyes's thievery. He took one of Denny's socks and delivered it to my door."

"What a sweet boy." Jeremy picks up the feline. "You truly do love Sarah, don't you? Keep at it; you may win her over, eventually."

"Hardly." I turn the computer screen off and swivel the executive chair around to face him. "My, it's after eight already. Guess I should get changed. What's our plan for today?"

"Sam texted and said some boxes arrived this morning, so maybe I'll take the BMW, if you don't mind, and pick them up. I also wanted to try to do some food shopping—if it doesn't turn into a nightmare." He strokes the cat, adding, "Do you want to come with me?"

"I don't think so. Yesterday was exhausting, so maybe another down day would be good. I doubt you want me slowing you down by hobbling through store aisles, do you?"

"Not at all. But I won't go for an hour or two. Also, do you mind if I do some laundry here? I'm getting low on clothes."

He puts Eyes back on the chair and heads out of the room.

"Good idea. I need to do some, too. Could you take my basket downstairs? Pretty please?" I bat my eyes for emphasis while he complies. "I'll go get it organized."

As Jeremy exits through the bathroom, I walk down the hall to my room and into my closet.

The laundry basket is piled high and includes some of Denny's clothes. Heartbroken, I stop and deeply smell my husband's scent on one or two as I sort through the heap and get the hamper ready.

After changing into a Nike hoodie with a large dual access pocket in front and cut-off jeans with one Hoka tennis shoe, I put a little make-up on, brush my hair and teeth, and take another Zoloft and Motrin.

While looking in the mirror, I explicitly do not talk to D. Maybe they'll get the hint that I'm still angry about that bird thing.

Having to take two trips, Jeremy totes my hamper and his clothes downstairs, and he starts his load of laundry.

After searching through the cupboards and refrigerator, he offers me a bagel with cream cheese from Amy's stock along with a cup of coffee.

And as usual, he asks Alexa about the five hot topics of the day, and she answers:

A solar flare of X25.57 caused major blackouts along the East Coast, affecting over a hundred million people's phones. The Magnificent Seven, comprised of Alphabet, Amazon, Apple, Meta,

Microsoft, Nvidia, and Tesla, are in a joint agreement to improve the environment and ecology by establishing a viable one-earth system. OSS (Open Source Software) has advanced knowledge and technology exponentially, allowing its use, modification, and distribution so any innovator, young or old, can become instantly successful. In many US cities and towns, the National Guard has been called up to stop the increase of violence and destruction, especially along the country's borders. Locally, yesterday's demonstration against faith-based entities in downtown Los Angeles turned violent when four individuals were mercilessly killed in a ritualistic guillotine-style execution.

"Yikes," I comment, "that was a bit detailed this time. I'm glad, though, that the government and some of these mega-rich companies are starting to come to our aid."

"Only if it's done right," Jeremy says. "And what if it's not? Will we all become like those in George Orwell's *1984*, where Big Brother is watching you every second? Or robots, so we have no control or consciousness?"

As he puts my meal on the counter, I say, "Ah, don't be so fatalistic. It'll never get that bad, will it?"

"I don't know. I'll have to look more into that OSS thing. I'm skeptical of things like deepfake—you know, where someone digitally alters an image or video of someone's face or body, and it's used to spread false information. What if someone does that to one of my videos? I'd be pretty upset. Maybe I can invent a program to easily discern fact over lie."

"That would be cool. And you could get rich and live off the land with zillions of acres on an island in the Pacific." I smile at the fantasy.

"Don't laugh. It can be done with your photos, too. There's probably already a fake of one or two of your shots online."

With that kind of talk, I open my laptop and go to the Source, searching for my name on any articles. I select the Image button and scan through my photos. Thankfully, I find none altered and tell Jeremy so.

Since my mind flashes back to the LA demonstration that Jeremy and I snubbed discussing, I ask the Source for more data.

I read an article aloud. "Over a thousand attended the event. The four victims were three men and one woman, ages twenty-two to seventy years old. Supposedly all were street preachers, stating the virus and alien abduction conspiracies are cover-ups. They promoted Jesus raptured His saints and that Tribulation is coming."

Jeremy and I talked about how sad it was that the four had no proper trial, but they were martyred for their beliefs, here in America, because the crowd demanded it. So sad and wrong.

I find another Source article. This one says that several denominations and churches around the world are excited now that the "bad" Christians are gone, leaving them to properly "love thy neighbor as themselves." They have banded together to start something called PEW for Peace

Endowed World, where those of all religious beliefs can join as one, offering their spiritual gifts to make a better world. What an interesting take!

To change to a more uplifting topic, we spend the next hour talking about different projects we have done over the years at work, which ones we liked the most and why, and how technology such as phone cameras and microphones have improved.

When Jeremy's laundry is finished and mine is in the dryer, he takes Denny's car keys and heads out to run his errands. Eyes, who is back on his spot by the bay window, and I have the place to ourselves once again.

After folding my laundry and stacking it neatly back in the hamper, I spend most of the morning making phone calls.

I touch base with Silvia, and she gives me Dave's wife's phone number in Oregon, so I connect with my parents. Tiffany has me talk to Mom, but not Dad since he's sleeping. Both Mom and Dave are worried about the wound getting an infection because Dad has a slight fever. Mom has been taking a holistic concoction for her asthma that Tiffany put together that contains garlic, ginger, ginseng, and turmeric, which seems to be helping a little. Plus, Mom is downing hot caffeinated beverages to help reduce her airway constriction. Anything to help it go away!

During my call, a text comes in from James, again asking if he can stop by. I delete it. He's probably wanting me to get him a job at the paper.

I'm so done with him.

I call my insurance company and leave a voice message about my two auto claims, Denny's life insurance claim, and to verify the cancelation of his health insurance. I also call Zoey to chat, but she is unavailable. Probably doing something romantic with Amir.

Another task I accomplish is checking my bank account. Sure enough, my payments have somehow been applied, and instead of a low balance on my checking account, it's now five figures, which makes me smile. I check Denny's and my student loans—neither one shows up on the screen. Nice.

Around noon, I go into the kitchen and make two peanut butter and jelly sandwiches; one is placed in a Ziplock bag for Jeremy. I'm thankful for the quietness, but I'm getting restless and bored, so I go out to check the mail again.

Since I rarely use my scooter now, I brave the walk down the pathway to the mailboxes. While the Rapture flyers have been removed, those depicting the missing remain. The metal units have been smashed and dented, with many open and empty. So much for getting my mail.

I look over at the general parking lot and see my VW is parked next to a red minivan. From my viewpoint, my car's hubcaps are missing, and the roof is slashed more. I sigh.

There must be an end to this nonsense. It looks like another message needs to be left with my insurance company, or maybe I should wait another day to see what else is destroyed.

On my walk back, I cross paths with the kid I saw the day of the plane crash—the teen who was throwing up in the ajuga plant.

When I ask how he's doing, he says, "No school. No friends. No life."

"I hear ya. Hang in there. It has to get better."

He grunts, and I walk by my patio gate and sit down at the chair to catch my breath. I set my keys on the wrought iron table.

The Hispanic woman—the one I talked to at the mailbox days ago—says hello, and we each ask a question or two about how we are healing. But she's too busy to sit and chat, so she moves on.

With nothing exciting happening outside, I return to my condo and walk into the bathroom.

D, I'm frustrated. How can I increase my rating if I'm stuck here, in this condo, with nothing interesting happening? I mean, the last few days had thrills and excitement. But this is downright boring.

Yes, there are lulls, just like life. Don't worry about it. All in good timing. Maybe now is a good time to relax, take a nap, and do nothing but regroup.

I'm concerned your viewers are falling asleep here.

I leave the bathroom and lie down on the couch, placing the white throw around me.

Good ol' Eyes leaves his window perch, walks along the back of the sofa, and plops down near my feet, like he's there to watch over me.

The only noise I hear is Adam playing his hard rock music, but it's not overwhelmingly loud.

⸺ ❧ ⸺

When Jeremy comes in through the garage's inner door, I wake up.

Eyes is tucked by my casted leg, sound asleep. He perks up when Jeremy approaches my side.

"Good to see you sleeping, Sarah! It's probably what you need."

I tell him it was as I get off the couch.

Eyes looks lazily at me, almost daring me to move the blanket.

Carrying two filled-to-the-brim reusable grocery bags, Jeremy heads to the kitchen. "It's a zoo out there. I picked up three boxes from Sam and delivered them to my parents' shop. They looked like the MRE packs and bottled water, which were heavy. He also said one was damaged, so he refused it and sent it back for credit.

"I tried going to Costco to put gas in the Beemer and snag some food, but that was a no-go. There were probably fifty to sixty cars in line for gas. The store had armed guards at its doors, and you had to show your ID plus Costco card, both of which had to be scanned. And the parking lot. Lots of angry people with only a few coming out of the store with something in their carts. Based on what I saw, there wasn't much to choose from inside. If I attempted it, it would be futile."

He starts unloading his purchases. "The good news is Sam told me to go out to Chatsworth Park. There's a small family-owned store that takes only cash and has a solo gas pump. He told me to tell Matt I was his friend, so I could score some gas. I raided Dad's lock box in the shop for the cash, loaded up a few five-gallon cans, and drove out there.

Matt was more than helpful and filled the Beemer and containers up. Then we went inside his store, and he let me buy this food. It's not gourmet, but I can work with it. I spotted him a hundred dollar bill as a tip."

What a gracious act.

"I only wish I hadn't cashed in that money I found in the safe. We could have used it for bartering with those off the grid, who may be easier to deal with as time goes on."

I tell him about my coin collection in the closet upstairs, offering its use if needed.

"At least, this time we got supplies."

"Yeah, that's great. How come no one else knows about Matt's place?" I question.

"Two rather large sons toting two long rifles keep watch on the place. Since it's remote, it's known mainly to locals, who are the only ones they help. They were skeptical of me until I mentioned Sam. Sadly, I'm sure the store will run out of supplies soon unless trucks deliver."

Jeremy puts Denny's keys on the half-moon table next to his wallet and phone. "Hey, I don't see your keys here. Did I forget to put them back when I moved your VW? I am returning Denny's, but yours aren't here."

He goes down the hall to the utility room, telling me that maybe he left them in the Prius in the garage.

When he returns, he still cannot find them, so he says he's going to check the VW. He leaves quickly through the front door before I can mention the car's missing hubcaps.

It dawns on me that I used my keys to check the mailbox and had left them on the patio table. I go outside to get them, leaving the door open.

And there they are.

Jeremy walks up the sidewalk while I dangle the keys in the air. We're both relieved that they've been found.

As we go back inside the condo, we talk about my car and how it was inevitably going to get hit again. He said its leather seats were cut, so that's another thing to tell my insurance agent when I'm in the mood to file another claim.

We both go into the kitchen and put away the finds Jeremy acquired. I get out the pathetic PB&J sandwich I made him and pour him a seltzer on ice, while he opens a new bag of Cheetos gleaned from the store.

Being intentionally overdramatic, he savors each bite of the sandwich, but I know the snack is far tastier.

For dessert, he hands me a mini bag of peanut M&Ms, which I put in my hoodie's large pocket.

"Where's Eyes?" Jeremy asks about twenty minutes later, as he comes downstairs from putting my hamper in my bedroom.

"Last I saw, he was snuggled in my blanket on the couch."

Jeremy approaches the couch and lifts the blanket, shaking it out. He looks around the bay window, but he's not there. My friend takes two stairs at a time and checks upstairs, including the office, guestroom, adjoining bath, and my bedroom and bathroom. The cat is nowhere to be found.

He calls repeatedly, "Kitty, Kitty, come out wherever you are. Eyes, come here." Then he starts to panic, saying to me, "Where is he? Maybe he went in the garage when I was looking for your keys?" He opens and, after checking inside, closes the door. Still no cat. Running his fingers through his hair, he shakes his head. "Maybe he got out when I went out the front door?"

"Or when I did! Yeah, I don't think I closed the door all the way when I went to get my keys off the patio table. Maybe he snuck out then? Oh, I'm so sorry if he did. I never thought about it." I feel awful. I let the cat out.

Viewer, have you ever done that? Mess up big time with something your friend or family member loves and cherishes. I hate it when that happens.

"I'll go look," he stammers. I can tell he's not pleased with me.

Without another word, he leaves the condo, and I go sit down on the couch, frustrated that I failed my dear friend by losing the one thing he's grown attached to.

Sarah. Listen to us.

D? What are you doing? You shouldn't be talking to me right now! Aren't the viewers watching this?

No, it's frozen right now. All live video and audio feeds are having what we call a "rebooting time-out."

Now, Sarah, listen carefully. James is on his way to see you. We caught him on one of the complex's cameras. Now is your time to shine. To excel more than ever before. We need you to do something. Right now. This is your time, and your time alone.

Okay. Tell me what to do. I'll try my best to do whatever you want.

Don't be afraid.

Get up. Go to the half-moon table, open the drawer, and remove the gun Adam gave you. Yes, we know you hate guns, but this is the ultimate test of your loyalty—your trust in us and our trust in you.

You are to take the gun, and when James knocks on your door, you need to open it. Aim the gun and shoot. We will handle the rest.

What? I can't do that. I won't do that!

Logic and emotion war inside of me. Which response should I choose and why?

Sarah, we know you don't want to do it. We know how you feel about James and his beliefs. But we know you're the best one to accomplish this task. The boy needs to be eliminated. Now.

And we are willing to pay you one million dollars to pull that trigger one time. Only once. Even if you miss, you will be instantly paid.

But what about cameras? What if someone sees me do it? I can't...

Yes, you can, Sarah. We know you; we know your heart.

And we have turned off all electronics involved, so there'll be no surveillance traceable back to you. We have you covered.

But time is short. James is now by the mailboxes, and Jeremy is in the field looking for Eyes in the airplane's remains.

It must be done. Now.

Take a breath. Get up, and let's do this together.

One million dollars awaits you. What an opportune moment.

As if hypnotized, I put my phone down on the glass table and step toward the mahogany table. I pull open the drawer and, with my right hand, pick up the gun.

Excellent, Sarah. You're doing great. Now when we say "three," open the door.

I'm scared. I don't want to do this.

I walk to the door and put my bad hand on the handle; it's the kind that only needs to be turned down to open, not twisted.

I don't want my hand or wrist to hurt when I push down on the handle and pull.

Good, now listen.

One.

Two.

I feel myself shaking inside.

You can do this. You can, Sarah.

Three.

My bad hand throbs as I pull open the door.

James is standing in front of it. He has a small metal object in one hand and a piece of paper in the other. He looks at me like he wants to say something, and then his eyes travel down to what I'm holding in my hand.

When I lift my right hand to shoot, I can't do it. I can't pull the trigger.

Suddenly, Adam's door opens.

My neighbor screams, "Get away from her!"

A gunshot is heard.

A second shot blasts my ears.

James crumples to the ground. The last word I hear from him is, "Jesus."

Sarah, put the gun away. Right now. Put it in your pocket. Everything is okay. You did great. Take a breath. You did well.

Numb to the command, I do what I'm told.

Adam starts cussing, holding his head with his hands, one of them still holding the gun. "What have I done? I thought he was going to kill you! What did I do?" He sits down in his doorway and starts balling, tears streaming down his face. Wailing.

I'm still standing at my door. I have no clue what to do next.

Jeremy comes running up the sidewalk, holding Eyes in his arms.

There are a few people behind him. One has a phone and is filming Adam, who is now weeping. "I've never seen this dude before. He was going to attack my neighbor, I swear it."

"What happened, Sar? Are you okay? Oh, is that James?" Jeremy stares at the boy's lifeless body.

I can't speak.

Still a yard or two away from our doors, Jeremy turns his attention to Adam, "Are you all right, man? Is that your gun?"

My neighbor looks at the weapon, and a wave of surprise surfaces on his face as he says, "Man, yeah, it is. How about that? What happened?"

"Can you put that gun down? See that planter next to you, the one with the lemon tree? Why don't you put the weapon there so I can check on James, okay?" Jeremy speaks softly.

Adam confusedly replies, "Sure, man. You know that dude?" He points the small pistol toward James, then his eyes land on the planter. "Dad loved that lemon tree; he'd always have me put a slice of its fruit in his soda. You like lemons, too, Sarah, don't you? I'll put it right here." He tucks the gun into the soil, butt down. "But, Sarah, we may need to water the tree again, okay?"

I don't speak. Only watch.

Jeremy steps over James's body, handing me Eyes. I gingerly take the cat. Eyes lies in the crook of my bad left arm while I repeatedly stroke his head with my good hand.

Next, Jeremy asks Adam if he wants to sit down on my patio in one of the chairs, no doubt to get him away from the situation. Surprisingly, Adam agrees, so Jeremy guides him by the arm as they carefully walk around James's body.

As the two step down the walkway, Jeremy calmly tells a passerby who was filming to call 911.

Adam explains, "From my living room window, I saw that dude reach into his pocket by Sarah's door and pull out something shiny. It didn't look right. Like maybe it was a knife. So, I went to the door, opened it, and let out a warning shot. But the weirdest thing happened, this strange-looking bird was flying right above the guy's head, so I took aim and pulled the trigger again. The bird flew away, but the shot hit the kid."

I listen. Stunned.

I'm still standing in the doorway of my condo as I stroke Eyes deeper and more rhythmically.

While Jeremy asks more people watching the scene unfold to keep an eye on Adam and not let him out of their sight, he stoops down and checks James for a pulse.

His eyes lock on mine. His head moves ever-so-slightly back and forth.

Next, he pulls me into the condo and sits me down on the couch. I start to shake, so he puts the white throw around me. He tries to take Eyes out of my arms, but we both refuse the offer. I fiercely cling to the animal.

Jeremy whips out his phone and calls Zoey. Somehow, I had forgotten they shared numbers, but then I remember it was when I first came home from the hospital, and they tried organizing every second of my life.

"Zoey. Is Amir with you?"

"Yes, why?"

"Emergency. Come to Sarah's ASAP. She may be going into shock."

"Okay."

He clicks off the phone, and then immediately swipes it again. "Looking up the signs of shock. Here we go. Sweaty palms." He checks my good hand. "Maybe so." He inspects my hands, my nail beds on my fingers. "Bluish, gray lips and fingernails. Could be." He reads silently for a few seconds.

The sound of a siren is heard through the opened front door.

"Elevate legs. Let's do that." He prods Eyes to the side of my hip and ushers me into a lying down position, tucking two pillows under both feet.

Another minute of reading, and Amir and Zoey are at my side. Jeremy quickly gives them a rundown, and Zoey says Adam is still seated at the patio table with five guys flanking him.

Amir is opening my eyes and shining a bright light on them, being careful with my already bruised eye. I'm guessing he brought his medical bag with him. He tries to lift Eyes off the couch, but I insist the cat stays nearby.

As I keep my bad arm protectively covering my waist, where the small gun is hidden, he listens to my chest with his stethoscope. He asks me questions about being dizzy, drowsy, or nauseous. I shake my head negatively or say no to them.

I start to breathe better by taking slower breaths as Amir recommends.

Zoey comes over, so I point to the half-moon table and say, "Denny's phone."

She picks it up and brings his phone over.

"John. Cop." I whisper the words. She opens the phone and tries the same password I have on my phone, and she's in. She scrolls through the contacts and walks into the kitchen area to make the call, so I can't hear what she says.

Jeremy leaves the condo for a few minutes. When he returns, he says, "Man, that Adam is stoned. Way stoned. He can't remember what happened and kept talking about a strange bird that no one else saw. He's trying to make the guys who have detained him laugh. He thinks it's all a joke. I'm so glad he can't see James's body from where he's seated on the patio."

Zoey finishes her call and rushes to my side, explaining, "I talked to John, Denny's friend who's a cop. He's on his way over. He says don't touch anything and keep Adam calm and away from the body."

I try to sit up, but Amir won't let me. Eyes is wedged between my left hip and the couch cushions, so I don't dare move and upset the animal.

Twenty minutes later, John arrives with his partner, who, we're told, is arresting Adam. John mentions that Adam is under the influence of drugs, so he will be thoroughly tested when they handcuff him and take him down to the station.

After John asks me how I'm feeling and if I can explain what happened, I tell Amir that I'm fine and would be willing to talk. But after I use the restroom.

Eyes moves to the windowsill when Zoey and Jeremy help me to the bathroom.

When I turn on the light, the screeching fan clatters, like it used to.

I tell Zoey I feel sick to my stomach, so she helps me lean over the toilet. I throw up. She gently wipes my face and tears with a washcloth as I heave again. She gets another wet cloth and pats my face, eliminating all the spit, slobber, and whatnot.

When done, I ask her if I can go to the bathroom, to be alone for a few minutes. She tells me she will be right outside the door and exits.

D! Talk to me. Now!

Please. Right. Now.

Yes, you did great. You're going to be fine.

No, I didn't do great. I didn't do well at all!

You didn't have to pull the trigger. Thankfully, all that's on drugged-out Adam.

But it's wrong. You manipulated me. You manipulated him. You used us!

Yes, in some ways, we did. But we had to. It's our goal—our purpose. We must get rid of these religious zealots before they turn one more soul their way. You helped us accomplish the task. That's all you did.

Well, I don't want your money. Number one: I don't deserve it because I didn't—couldn't—pull the trigger. Number two: I should never have agreed to it in the first place.

Now, now, Sarah. You don't mean that. But we understand your position. You're scared. You're traumatized right now. So instead of a million dollars, we have deposited a half million into your account. Already done.

But I don't want it. None of it!

Sarah, do you know that your ratings went through the roof in the last half hour? You now have over a hundred thousand viewers. Plus, because of you, OWL offered our start-up company a two-billion-dollar deal today to merge with them! They will use our AGI implant program to make a better world. You, yes, you accomplished this feat.

You're our best asset. Our viewers love you. We love you! So, go back to the couch. Don't mention the gun; we'll help you discard it later, and it never showed up on any video feed.

Okay. But I'm not pleased about this—any of it. Especially when Adam mentioned the bird.

We completely understand. We'll keep our birds far away from you and give you a little break for a few days, if that's what you need most. Time to heal and recuperate.

We'll back off, but we'll be in touch.

Go, relax, Sarah. You're an amazing person.

Zoey pounds on the door, asking if everything is good. I flush the toilet for effect, run some water over my hands, dry them, and leave the room, shaking my head about the fan's incessant noise.

With a compassionate tone in his voice, John asks me to sit at the dining room table. He gets out his police phone, turns its speaker on, and explains our conversation will be recorded. I mechanically and unemotionally walk him through the steps of James's demise, but I don't mention the gun that's inches away from both of us. I see no need to tell him, I reassure myself because I never pulled the trigger. The process is tiring, taking well over an hour.

Tell me, Viewer: What would you do here? Would you be honest enough to mention the gun in your pocket? Or would you skim over that small detail because it was never part of the equation? The gun was never fired. Would guilt play a factor down the road?

And I don't mention the bird, since I honestly never saw it in the walkway.

While John interrogates me, James's mom and stepfather arrive, but Zoey keeps them away from me by not letting them enter my condo. Thankfully, John has another police officer deal with them.

The mother doesn't do well with the news—what parent would? I hear her cries and sobs seeping through the building's walls. I'm sad about it, but I'm focused on my own survival.

When John and I are almost done, he pulls out from his vest pocket two clear plastic bags: One contains a white piece of paper with my name on it; the other is the keychain flash drive that James insisted he give back to us.

I tell John that there's no need for me to read what's in the note, as I can predict what it says. Nor is there any reason for him to return the drive after it's been investigated.

Within four hours, James's body has been removed. His blood has been washed off the walkway by a neighbor. Adam's been arrested.

I'm doing much better as Amir and Zoey practically force-feed me and make me replenish my fluids.

By eight o'clock, Jeremy and I convince Zoey and Amir that I'm fine, only tired, and need rest from the trauma. I tell the three of them that I refuse to stay at my condo. At least, not tonight. Jeremy suggests taking me to his parents' house. He doesn't inform them of the address or location.

While Zoey quickly packs up an overnight bag for me, Amir instructs Jeremy on what to be aware of if I have any health issues and gives him some medicine for me.

After Jeremy crates up Eyes and loads him into the back of the Prius, he hands Denny's keys to Amir, asking him to put my VW back in the garage.

With much ado, I'm kissed goodbye and seat-belted into Jeremy's car.

The drive is quiet, with soft rock playing on the car's radio. Jeremy repeatedly asks if I'm okay, which starts to irritate me.

I ask him where he found Eyes, and he replies, "It was the strangest thing. I walked over to the plane crash and looked around the fuselage for him, but he wasn't there. As I was walking back to your place, this man I'd never seen before met me at the edge of the field. He cradled Eyes in his arms and asked, 'Are you looking for your cat?' I said yes, but how did he know?"

"Hmm," I reply. "Maybe he heard you call out the cat's name."

"I don't think I did—I mean, calling out Eyes would be a little weird, wouldn't it? And when he handed me my pet, the cat acted like he was glad to get away from the guy, leaping into my arms. The man had a strange smile on his face. It was weird."

I wonder if there's more to the story.

When we get to the security gate to his parents' house, it dawns on me that I left my phone on the great room's glass table. My friend assures me he'll pick it up tomorrow or the next day and not to worry.

After getting situated in Dylan's old room in the Lincolns' home, I take a sedative of Amir's.

Not bothering to change out of my hoodie and cut-offs, Jeremy helps me pull off my shoe and sock, and I plop down onto the bed and wriggle under the covers. He softly lays a kiss on my head and wishes me sweet dreams while Eyes jumps up on the bed and snuggles next to my bulky waist.

~ **Day 12** ~

I t's morning.

I yawn and look around the room. Having initially forgotten where I am, I lie in bed and stare at the framed pictures hanging on all four light green painted walls. I surmise Dylan must like to travel because they all focus on different parts of the world. Like Jeremy and his father, this son also has a love for the outdoors and nature, judging by the photos of many mountain ranges, waterfalls, and sandy beaches.

Slipping my good hand under the sheet, I check my pocket. The M&Ms and the gun—the loaded gun—are still there.

Yesterday's events rush back to me: the shooting, James's body, the flash drive, and more.

I want my control back; I plan to somehow get it soon, any way I can.

Viewer, have you ever gotten to the stage in life when you've had enough? Done with something and ready to move on—ready to remove yourself from the situation or get completely out of it? I'm there now, and I have a headache to boot.

Irritated, I get out of bed, put my solo sock and shoe on, and hobble into the kitchen, where Jeremy and Eyes are eating breakfast.

"Morning, Sleepyhead," Jeremy says. "Get enough rest? Feeling perky again?" I sense he is testing my attitude.

"Mainly a killer headache. I'll survive."

"Aw. You're always the trooper. I'll get you something for the pain. Need something to eat? I'm doing Cheerios."

"Sure. Haven't had those since grade school. Sounds good."

While mocking me that I'm just like Zoey for wearing yesterday's clothes, he gets a bowl out, adds the dry cereal, and places it on the wooden table as I sit. He gets milk out of the fridge and sets it down, then tells me he'll be right back.

Eyes jumps up on the table. I try to push him away, but he sits to the side of me and taunts me with his tail.

I pour the milk and start spooning the food into my mouth, telling the cat this is mine, not his.

Jeremy reenters the room. "All I can find is aspirin. Will that do?"

"Ha. I haven't had that since I was a teen. Sure, let me try it."

I undo the cap and take two, swallowing them by sipping the milk out of my tipped bowl. Jeremy and Eyes don't say a word, simply stare at me.

"What? This is how I always finish my cereal. I don't do it with oatmeal, but always with dry cereal."

He laughs at what he thinks is silly, but I don't. It's a practical way to get every drop.

"Did you like sleeping in 'the boys' room,' as Mom would call it? It used to be Dylan's room, but after we both moved out, my parents put our stuff in that room so Dad could have an office."

"Oh, so those photos are yours, then? They're spectacular. Great angles." I praise him as I offer Eyes the cereal bowl's remnant.

"Yep, all the photos in this house, except the ones on the mantel, are mine. Oh, I need to pick up Dad's ashes and stop by UPS, since more stuff has arrived."

"I'm sorry about your dad. Do you need me to come with you?"

"No, I think I can handle it. Dylan said that he would try to come out when the airports open again to help spread the ashes."

"If you don't mind, I'd rather not go anywhere. I don't want to do anything. I'm not being lazy; I need to regroup. Rethink a few things."

"Should I stop by your place to get your phone and maybe pick up some of your clothes and things?"

"Don't bother—not today. You have so much going on right now. Plus, it'll take too long and use up gas. Maybe we'll both do it tomorrow. Also, I'll need to get that coin collection at some point."

"Okay. Then I guess I'm off. I'm going to hike up to the shop and use Dad's truck after I unload it. Sam says these bigger boxes won't fit in the Prius."

When he leaves, Eyes and I walk around the house, surveying where everything is located. I notice Jeremy left his phone on the kitchen table; I leave it untouched.

I venture into his parents' bedroom and see the bed is made, neat as a pin. But it has Jeremy's things on the nightstands and some of the pictures have changed.

The office looks the same, as do the living and dining rooms and kitchen. When in the family room, I inspect more stunning photographs that cover the walls.

The air is warm, so I open the sliding glass door to let the cool breeze filter in. The house must not have air conditioning since the room immediately feels fresher and invigorating.

I rub my head to massage the headache away, but it makes the pounding harder. I take deep, cleansing breaths to urge the pain away as I open the sliding screen door and step onto the patio.

It's peaceful hearing the birds chirping and singing.

Walking to the edge of the brickwork, I look out at the small orchard and a dozen rows of grapevines that gently slope toward the house.

Eyes follows me and sits down by my side, perhaps as contented as I want to be, but I'm not.

I peek around the left side of the house, past the bed of prized roses, and notice the vegetable garden, where there are several ripe tomatoes, corn, and zucchini.

There's a small dirt path that heads off to the right, so I take it, not caring about my foot cast getting dirty or dusty from the dry earth. At the top of a ridge, I peruse the land. This section is natural, with no development—only bushes, trees, and dry grass. When I see the roof edge of the property's large shop, I head that way.

After a while, I stop and glance over my shoulder, only to see Eyes following. As I look back, down toward the house, there's a bird on the peak of the roof, facing the Valley. I squint at it, trying to see if it's a drone, but it's too far away.

When I make it to the next hill, I spot the oak tree—the one with the treehouse that Jeremy and his brother and father built. I feel drawn to it, so I drag my bad leg that way. My injured leg and arm aren't hurting in the dry air; the only pain is this incredible headache.

At the base of the tree, I look up. There's no way I can climb it, but I wish I could. Frustrated, I sit down at its base, resting my back against the thick trunk, and take in the serene view.

When I put my hand in my hoodie's pocket, it lands on the small bag of candy. I pull the packet out, rip open the top, and sample a few of the chocolate treats.

I return my hand to my pocket, slowly removing the small weapon.

D? D, are you there?

There's no reply.

D? Why can't you answer me? Where are you?

No answer.

I'm serious. What happened to you? Why aren't you answering me? Are you too far away from me?

Viewer? Are you there? Can anyone hear me? See me?

Resting the gun in my lap, I rub the back of my head, behind my right ear. Right where my headache is the worst. Right where the implant is. I press hard on the spot, deeply massaging the area at the base of my skull, wondering if somehow it got turned off or disarmed.

D? Are you there?

Nothing.

I finish the M&Ms, discarding the empty wrapper back into my pocket.

I pick up the gun again and inspect it. I couldn't pull the trigger. I'm a loser. I freely wanted to kill my baby, yet I couldn't shoot another human being with this gun.

Although I could've been controlled by AGI, I realize that I'm a bad person. A horrible human. I hate AGI. I hate Numen. I hate D, or whatever they stand for.

I'm worthless. I hate being alive. I wish everything would go back to when Denny was around, when all was normal and sane.

Zoey and James were right: I'm untaken, too.

With a steady hand, I put the gun up to my head, placing the barrel against my implant.

I hate myself.

I hate myself.

I. Hate. Myself.

When I pull the trigger, nothing happens. Nothing but a click. Either the gun misfired, or Adam never loaded it.

I exhale. I start to cry. I can't even kill myself. I'm hopeless. I'm worthless. I'm a nothing.

Sarah. Sarah, I love you. I. Love. You.

A new, different voice enters my head. So soothing, so loving, so wonderful. Calm. Reassuring. Encompassing love. Better than fresh, pure air.

Come to Me.

Jesus?

Suddenly a black bird is in front of me, maybe five feet away. Its beady eyes glow as its wings flap angrily, hovering in front of my face.

There's a rustling above me . . . in the tree! A cat—Eyes—vaults through the air toward the fake bird, connects with it, and both crash to the ground.

The abrupt attack startles me to the core.

The gun in my hand goes off.

A bullet is released from its chamber.

And my world fades to black.

~ Viewer ~

To you, the viewer:

This is Numen, the company that has provided access for you to enter one of our qualified participant's minds. Through our exciting, innovative program, you were able to hear, see, and know what went on inside the mind of Sarah Colton, aka ValleyGirl.

You saw it all; you felt it all. You knew everything she went through: her joy, her pain, her accomplishments, her anguish, her determination, her core beliefs. Everything.

We thank you for being a part of our journey with Sarah. We're sorry there were glitches in our system, causing a few blackouts over the last few days, but we appreciate your patience as we correct and refine the implant, satellite feed, and sound.

We know a few of you have been here from the start, and we appreciate your loyalty and interest in our AI program. Your input has been instrumental in vastly furthering the reach and outcome of our program.

Due to your interest in and engagement with our system, we will soon be merging with OWL, the fast-growing international organization that promotes a one-world league of peace and prosperity.

Although we do not know the outcome of Sarah's life as of right now, we invite you to continue to be a part of our network of artificial intelligence.

Not only can we offer our current viewers continued access to our participants, but you also can apply to become an implanted individual—so that you, too, can change the world the way Sarah has done.

For those of you who have been our testers, if you would like to sign up for one of our viewing packages, please respond to the email we have sent you. The three virtual reality packages range from Silver 2D limited browser viewing which includes one participant, its advanced Gold unlimited VR viewing, or our Elite VR viewing of several participants at one time, which comes with a free VR headset.

All prices are listed on the online order form, but if you enter the Code DIOS, you can get a twenty-five percent discount on any package with a yearly contract.

Numen, which is Latin for "the nod of the head," means a spiritual force or influence often identified with a natural object, phenomenon, or place. By using our program, we give you the control to become your own god.

We will be seeing you soon.

~ Me ~

Please don't be irritated by another strange ending, as this way allows me the possibility of writing more books in the series that take place twelve weeks and twelve months after the Rapture. I doubt I can do twelve years since the Rapture comes before the seven-year Tribulation, and we're not told how much time passes between them.

When I finished writing the first book, I was adamant about not doing a sequel. But the Lord always provides—and this time it was amazing because once I was committed, the story took me only six weeks to compile instead of the thirty-plus years the first one did. It's all about God's perfect timing, isn't it?

Now, reader, please note this is a work of fiction; it's conjecture of what I think could or might happen if the Rapture occurs right now—it may or may not—yet I'm not declaring any specific date. The Lord said in Matthew 24:36, *"But of that day and hour knoweth no man, no, not the angels of heaven, but my Father only."*

The Rapture may not happen now or in twelve weeks, months, years, decades, et cetera. But it will happen! And as Matthew 24:44 says, *"Therefore be ye also ready; for in such an hour as you think not the Son of man cometh."* God instructs us to be ready and anticipate Jesus calling us up in the clouds if we're alive at that time.

Also, pastors today have different theories about the Rapture and afterward. Some think the Rapture begins the seven-year Tribulation timeline, but it's not mentioned as its start in the Scriptures—only that it comes before it. There is nothing in the Bible that needs to be fulfilled for the Rapture to happen. Nothing.

While the standard belief has all believers being taken up in the air in the blink of an eye, one well-known teacher suggests the possibility of us instantly changing into our glorified bodies, and then we slowly go up, with those left behind watching us ascend. He may be right; we don't know. However, the Greek word for caught up is *harpazo*, meaning to seize, catch, pluck, pull, or take (by force), so one would think the event will happen quickly.

The same is said for the idea of a virus versus an alien abduction—pastors consider both viewpoints, but neither is mentioned in Scripture.

So please forgive me for the many wrong conclusions I've made or erroneous speculations in my writing. Like Heaven, the Rapture will be different than any of us expect or anticipate.

The main reason I've been compelled to write these two novels—so far—about the Rapture is that I feel it's my ministry to help unbelievers and believers think about their relationship with God. Getting you, the reader, to contemplate, discuss, or debate the topic of the Rapture and what happens after it is my goal, and I hope I've achieved it.

During writing, I felt the Holy Spirit guiding me on each page, giving me ideal scenarios that flowed smoothly together. To God be the glory!

I want to thank my husband again for his love for our Savior and me. Having been married for over forty-five years, we both know God brought us together, and we thank Him for the privilege. My husband's medical input and perfectly suggested synonyms are deeply appreciated.

My thanks also go to two dear friends who prompted and pushed me to write this sequel. Kitty and Debra, you were monumental in your love and consistent encouragement to get me enthusiastic about writing again.

In addition, I want to thank Scott Townsend, not only for his Rapture Kit, which has a plethora of Biblical information about the Rapture and Tribulation and can be given to those loved ones left behind, but also for his internet/computer knowledge that kept my facts straight.

Finally, and most importantly, I give all praise and love to Jesus Christ, my Savior, who died on the cross, shed His blood for all sin, and rose on the third day.

And, reader, thank you for your time. If you do not have a personal relationship with Jesus, pray and talk to God about it. Unfortunately, some will refuse to believe now and after the Rapture happens—and God knows who you are. II Thessalonians 2:10-12 says, "*And with all deceivableness of righteousness in them that perish; because they received not the love of the truth, that they might be saved. And for this cause God shall send them strong delusion, that they should believe a lie; That they all might be damned who believed not the truth, but had pleasure in unrighteousness.*"

Yet, I believe most of you who have read this second book are Christians. Time could be short, so please do all you can to tell your loved ones about the Rapture as it could happen at any moment.

I hope to meet you in the air soon. Maranatha!

— ⁓ —

The End.

The Eternal Plan of Salvation

taken from *the King James Version of the Bible*

For all have sinned, and come short of the glory of God.
~ Romans 3:23

*For the wages of sin is death; but the gift of God is eternal life
through Jesus Christ our Lord.*
~ Romans 6:23

*That if thou shalt confess with thy mouth the Lord Jesus, and
shalt believe in thine heart that God hath raised him from the
dead, thou shalt be saved. For with the heart man believeth
unto righteousness; and with the mouth confession is made
unto salvation. For the scripture saith, Whosoever believe on
Him shall not be ashamed. For there is no difference between
the Jew and the Greek: for the same Lord over all is rich unto*

all that call upon Him. For whosoever shall call upon the
name of the Lord shall be saved.
~ Romans 10:9–13

But God commendeth his love toward us, in that, while we're
yet sinners, Christ died for us.
~ Romans 5:8

Verses Regarding
the Rapture

taken from *the King James Version of the Bible*

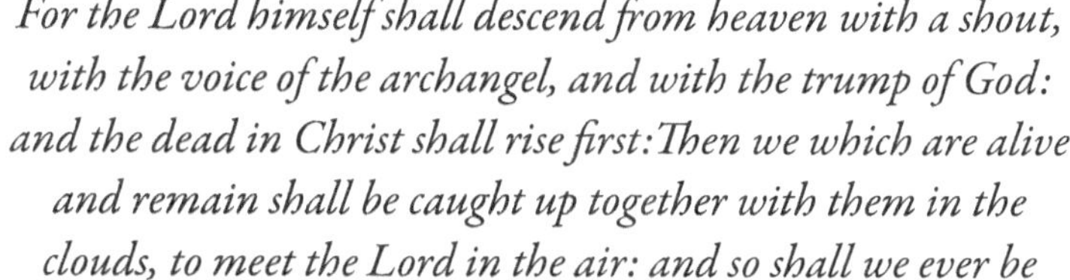

*Behold, I shew you a mystery: We shall not all sleep, but we
shall all be changed, In a moment, in the twinkling of an eye,
at the last trump: for the trumpet shall sound, and the dead
shall be raised incorruptible, and we shall be changed. For this
corruptible must put on incorruption, and this mortal must
put on immortality.*
~ I Corinthians 15:51–53

---

*For the Lord himself shall descend from heaven with a shout,
with the voice of the archangel, and with the trump of God:
and the dead in Christ shall rise first: Then we which are alive
and remain shall be caught up together with them in the
clouds, to meet the Lord in the air: and so shall we ever be
with the Lord.*
~ I Thessalonians 4:16–17

A Few Verses
Regarding the
Tribulation

taken from *the King James Version of the Bible*

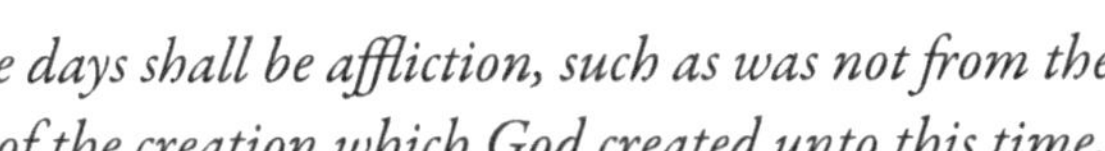

*For then shall be great tribulation, such as was not since the
beginning of the world to this time, no, nor ever shall be.*
~ Matthew 24:21

*For in those days shall be affliction, such as was not from the
beginning of the creation which God created unto this time,
neither shall be.*
~ Mark 13:19

*And I saw thrones, and they sat upon them, and judgment
was given unto them: and I saw the souls of them that were
beheaded for the witness of Jesus, and for the word of God, and
which had not worshipped the beast, neither his image, neither*

*had received his mark upon their foreheads, or in their hands;
and they lived and reigned with Christ a thousand years.
~ Revelations 20:4–6*

*Daniel 9 & 12 ~ Matthew 24 ~ Mark 13 ~ Luke 21 ~
Revelation 3, 6, 11, & 13*

Discussion Questions

1. If the Rapture happens and you're left behind, would you want life to be the same or would you want to get away from society? Would you want to reach out to others or not?

2. Do you think artificial intelligence is a good or bad thing? Why do you think either way?

3. Do you think God can use animals to help or protect us?

4. Have you ever shared the concept of the Rapture and Tribulation with someone? What was their reaction? If you knew the Rapture was happening soon, would you promote it more often?

5. Whether the Rapture happens today, tomorrow, or years from now, will you be taken or untaken when it occurs?

The first book in this series was originally titled
Untakenable.
It was updated in 2023 and is titled *Untaken: 12 Hours
Following the Rapture.*
* Book 1 is available FREE as an EBOOK almost
everywhere online.

Untaken, Too
Cover Photo: Cde/Bruiin / iStock
Editor: Lindsay Betz

Positive book reviews are needed and greatly appreciated.

End Times Series:
Book 1: *https://books2read.com/untaken*
Book 2: *https://books2read.com/untakentoo*
Book 3: *https://books2read.com/untakenthree*
Book 4: *https://books2read.com/untakenfornow*

Email: constanceowyler@gmail.com

Rapture Kit: *https://rapturekit.org* or *https://themissings.com*

Want More?

Book 3 Now Available!

UNTAKEN, THREE: 12 Weeks Following the Rapture
https://books2read.com/untakenthree

When does surveillance become overwhelming? Is it when others cross the line or if you have to intervene to stop the madness?
As the next three months after the Rapture occur, how far do people go to get off the grid?

---

* Get your Ebook or Print Copy at most online stores *

About the Author

Born and raised in Southern California, Wyler is a Christian who lives in the Pacific Northwest. Having owned a business for over thirty years, she is retired and enjoys spending time with her family and traveling.